Who Knew?

A Novel

Marianne Clyde

Published by Freiling Agency, LLC.

P.O. Box 1264
Warrenton, VA 20188

www.FreilingAgency.com

PB ISBN: 978-1-963701-94-4
E-book ISBN: 978-1-963701-95-1

Acknowledgments

Writing my very first novel has been a joy, though I'll admit, it began with a fair amount of fear. Stepping into the world of fiction after years of nonfiction felt like standing on the edge of a cliff. Yet, so many supportive and generous people paved the way for me, making this journey not only possible but profoundly rewarding.

First, my gratitude goes to my publisher, **Tom Freiling**, for taking a chance on me as an unknown fiction author. Believing in my story before it was fully formed was no small act, and it gave me the courage to step forward with confidence.

When my idea was still rough and uncertain, my first instinct was to reach out to someone I knew to be a true expert in his field. **Bill Woolf**, founder of The Woolf Group, with his extensive experience in law enforcement and his tireless work with missing and exploited children and anti-trafficking, gave so generously of his time. He patiently walked me through how things really work, answered endless questions, and helped me bring authenticity and depth to this story. His contributions shaped the novel in ways that I will always be grateful for.

I also want to thank **Nara Ekhsigian**, a talented young adult fantasy author, whose words freed me to write fiction in the first place. When I asked her how she imagined such vivid worlds, she told me: "I just enter the world of my characters, and they point the way." That simple wisdom inspired me to take the risk of stepping into my own characters' lives and following where they led.

To my husband, Bob, for his support and wisdom, as this book became a reality, I'm truly grateful.

And to all of you who walked alongside me in this process—whether by giving your time, wisdom, encouragement, or inspiration—I am deeply thankful.

Chapter 1

Danny woke with a gasp, hands clawing at the damp sheets as if fabric alone could keep him from the drop. Heat pressed on his chest; the room was thick with late-summer humidity, yet his skin ran cold, slick with sweat. Breath ragged. Heart sprinting. The dream clung like wet cloth.

Wind screaming past his ears.

Pebbles rattling loose and skittering toward the void.

And his brother's scream.

God help him—that scream.

He pressed his palms into his eyes until sparks pulsed behind his lids, but the images only burned brighter: the knife-edge of cliff against a too-white sky; the river below, a hard silver ribbon; Rick's face—eyes flaring wide, mouth twisted, not just fear there but fury, and something that felt like betrayal.

It had started with words. It always did with the two of them. Twenty-five years, and he could still hear his own voice—sharp, taunting, every sentence tipped like a blade. Rick was quicker with comebacks; Danny was better at finding soft spots. That day, he'd aimed for all of them. A shove. A shove back. Boys jostling on a high ridge until the earth itself decided the joke was over.

The moment lived inside him, a bead of time that never rolled forward: Rick teetering, arms flailing for purchase; Danny frozen, feet fused to stone. He didn't move. Couldn't. By the time he lurched, Rick was already gone from the frame.

The fall.

The cut-off cry.

The river's roar swallowing the world.

Then silence—so vast it carved itself into Danny's marrow and stayed there.

He'd woken into that silence a hundred times, a thousand. But tonight the dream had shifted by a hair's breadth. Tonight, at the edge, Rick's face carried something else. Not only fear. A knowing. A secret folded into the final glance, carried with him into the depths.

He swung his legs over the side of the bed. The floorboards were warm, the air heavier than his breath. The red digits on the travel clock glowed like embers on the nightstand.

3:14 a.m.

Too late for sleep. Too early for confession.

He crossed the apartment by feel, hip brushing the back of a rattan chair, shoulder grazing the cool wall. A gecko clicked from somewhere near the ceiling fan. He turned the tap; the pipes shivered awake, coughed, then spilled water warm as the night into a tin cup. He let it run until it cooled against his fingers and drank.

Outside, through the wide window, Phnom Penh lay in a hush that was never quite silence. Motorbikes whispered through the alleys beyond the courtyard. A dog barked twice and gave up. Even now, humidity shouldered its way into the room, carrying the faint metallic scent that comes before rain whether or not rain intends to fall. The city's patchwork of tin roofs and temple spires held a dull silver under the moon, deceptively serene—as if this place had never known sorrow.

But Danny knew better.

Two streets over, a string of prayer flags lifted and fell like sleeping breath along the roofline of the healing center, the one he had built with donations and stubbornness and a ledger of mistakes he'd never learned to balance. The sign over the gate—hand-painted once and replaced twice—named it in Khmer first and English second. People had begun to call it famous, though the word sat wrong in his mouth. Famous wasn't the point. The center belonged to the women and girls who pushed its doors open at dawn and dusk with hollow eyes and unbroken bones, or sometimes the reverse. Counselors came early. The cook came earlier. Monks in saffron robes would pass with their alms bowls just after sunrise; staff kept a pot of rice ready.

He told himself the work was for them, and it was. It was also a covenant he kept with a dead boy and the part of himself he still despised. Penance is a long road. He'd paved his with schedules and staff meetings, with trainings and court affidavits, with midnight phone calls and a calm voice that didn't belong to the boy who'd frozen on a cliff.

A tuk-tuk rattled past, its canvas flapping softly; somewhere a lone vendor sang a few notes to no one. The fan ticked with its lazy wobble. He set the tin cup on the counter and braced his hands on either side of the sink, head bowed, breath evening out because that was what he had learned to do: make the body quiet so the mind did not shatter.

He could pretend the dream was only a dream. He could file it beside the others, where it would sit and throb until the next time. Instead, he let the afterimage run: the ridge; the sky; Rick's eyes not just wide but aware; the sense that something—some final shard of fact—had always been missing.

On the far wall, his conference badge from Kenya still hung from a nail by the door, the lanyard a bright strip in the dim. He'd meant to tuck it away and never had. The women there had asked hard, necessary questions. He had given measured answers, the way you do when you have seen too much and not enough. Afterward he'd stood alone under a big African sky and thought of a much smaller one over Westridge, a sky edged by trees and cliff, and the single, ruinous choice that had rerouted his life. And took him around the world.

Westridge had a way of burying the past in plain sight—Sunday smiles, fresh paint, a casserole when something couldn't be fixed. It was a town skilled in silence, and somewhere along the line he had learned that art better than most. He'd left, and then he'd left again, and then he'd built a life halfway around the world in a city that understood both suffering and survival. A place where the work never ran out, where his competence could be of service, where nobody knew the boy he had been.

He pushed off the counter and went to the window. From here he could see the center's courtyard: the worn stone path, the lush spray of bougainvillea that one of the residents tended with near-religious focus, the bench where girls sometimes sat shoulder to shoulder and did not speak. He watched and waited, for what he wasn't sure—dawn, maybe. Or a sign that the night would turn him loose.

It didn't. Nights like this rarely did.

He thought of Rick's hands, always nicked from whatever he'd been tinkering with. He thought of the summer they both learned how to change a tire in under five minutes and the way their mother had leaned on the porch rail, laughing, pretending to be impressed. He thought of the last thing Rick had said before Danny weaponized it into something cruel. The line blurred there; it always did. What had he missed? What had he chosen not to see?

The gecko clicked again. In the street, a rooster misunderstood the moon for morning and crowed, indignant. Somewhere, a bell sounded from a temple—one soft note, then another.

He checked the clock again out of habit. *3:26.* The numbers shifted with that slow, unbothered certainty clocks have when they're not the ones awake at night.

"Too late for sleep," he said to the empty room, voice rough. "Too early for confession."

The window glass held his reflection—older now, angles softened into a man's, eyes hollowed by a grief no time had washed clean. And behind that reflection, like a second ghost in the window, was Robin. Not her face exactly, but the ache of her. The girl he'd left without a word, without an explanation, without the decency of goodbye.

There had been a life there once, waiting for him, a life that could have been—maybe should have been. He'd walked away from it with the same reckless silence he'd carried off that ridge. What right had he ever had to return?

Outside, the city breathed its humid breath. The healing center sat steady two streets away, a testament to the man he'd tried to become. But sometimes—nights like this—he still wondered if all of it, the work, the reputation, the fragile scaffolding of redemption, was only another way of running from her, from the boy he'd been, from the truth of what was lost.

Beyond the roofs and palms and the soft flare of a distant neon sign of Phnom Penh, the dream still stood where he'd left it: a strip of rock, a knife-edge of sky, a boy he loved and could not save. The cliffs that weren't here rose anyway in his mind, dark and patient, unmoved by time.

They waited. They always had.

And tonight, for the first time in twenty-five years, Danny wondered if they were waiting for him.

Chapter Two

The wood beneath Robin's legs was rough, splintered from years of weather and neglect. She pulled her knees tight against her chest, arms wrapped around them as if the pressure might keep her from unraveling. Morning hung over Westridge like a damp cloth—gray, heavy, unwilling to give her the light she needed.

From the back steps, she could see the jagged ridge cutting its dark silhouette against the pale sky. The place still looked untouched, serene even, as though yesterday had never happened. But she knew better. The rocks up there had tasted blood. The trees had swallowed a scream.

The last of the police cars had wound their way down Westridge Road before dawn, red-and-blue strobes flickering through the branches like ghosts retreating to their graves. Now the road was empty, but Robin still saw the afterimage every time she closed her eyes—sharp lights burning holes in the dark. Sheriff Stone's voice, low and careful, replayed itself in her ears.

A tragic accident, he'd said. Case closed.

The words sat in her chest like stones. Accident. As if something that hollow and simple could explain the silence in this house, or the way her skin prickled whenever the wind shifted. An accident was a dropped glass, a tire skidding on gravel. This—whatever it was—had hollowed out her world.

Danny was gone.

Not just from the cliffs. Gone from Westridge entirely. No note. No goodbye. Just absence, sharp as a blade.

She rocked forward, hugging her knees tighter. The chair beneath her groaned, its rhythm matching the shallow tremor of her breath. For a moment she let her eyes fall shut, as though the darkness behind her lids could steady her.

It didn't.

Instead, the quiet ushered in memory.

She was thirteen again, walking the corridors of Westridge High with the giddy awkwardness of a birthday crown no one else could see. Rick had come up behind her, all lean limbs and sharp confidence, and slung an arm across her shoulders.

"Happy birthday, big girl," he'd said, grinning down at her in a way that both thrilled and unsettled. He was eighteen, practically a man.

She had stammered a "Thanks, Rick," already edging away, but he'd leaned in just enough to make her heart kick. *You're a beautiful girl, Robin. Any guy here would be lucky to have you.*

Flattered. Suspicious. Excited. Terrified. She had carried all of it at once, a tangle of emotions too heavy for her small frame. Rick had walked off then, so sure of himself, while she stood blinking, trying to decide whether to blush or run.

And then—Danny.

Danny with his lopsided grin and sun-warmed eyes, bounding toward her like a lifeline she hadn't realized she'd been clinging to. He hadn't seen Rick leave; he hadn't cared. "What are you doing after school? Let's stop at the ice cream shop—milkshakes on me, birthday honor."

The safety of him had been like cool water over a burn. With Danny, she felt seen but not devoured, wanted but not consumed. Being beside him was as natural as breathing.

It was that boy—his grin, his kindness—that she mourned now. Not only the man he might have become, but the steady, grounding presence he had always been.

The chair creaked again, dragging her back into the fog-heavy morning. She dug in her pocket for another cigarette, lit it with a hand that wasn't as steady as she wanted it to be. The smoke burned her throat in a way that was almost welcome. She drew in hard, then exhaled, watching the tendril drift up into the gray.

Rick.

Good riddance.

If the ridge had only taken him, she would've lit candles in gratitude, whispered prayers of thanks to any god who was listening. But it hadn't. It had taken Danny, too—or at least, taken him away from her.

And now the silence in his absence yawned wide and endless, like a sinkhole.

From the road, voices carried thin on the breeze. Neighbors. Already gathering. Westridge had a way of showing up, casserole dishes in hand, murmured condolences half-whispered in doorways. She could hear Mrs. Porter's voice, pitched low but not low enough, telling someone it was "a blessing, in a way—better Rick than . . . "

Robin stopped listening. The words buzzed in her ears, cruel in their carelessness.

Children were hushed more sternly than usual that morning, their questions silenced before they reached the air. Dogs were kept inside. Even the birds seemed subdued, as if the whole town had agreed to bow its head in mourning.

Robin closed her eyes, pressed her forehead to her knees. She told herself she'd stop this—stop thinking about him, stop replaying every half-smile, every quiet kindness. She told herself she'd get on with life.

But the truth hung there, undeniable, in the morning air that smelled faintly of woodsmoke and wet leaves.

She needed him.

And he was gone.

Chapter Three

Ingrid always arrived first. She liked the quiet before the day fully opened, the clatter of mugs behind the counter, the low hiss of the espresso machine, the smell of cinnamon rolls fresh from the oven. Thursdays had been a ritual for nearly four decades now—anchoring her life in ways few other things had managed to do.

She traced the rim of her mug with one finger and let her mind wander, as it always did, to Wilson. She missed him most in these small, ordinary moments. Not the holidays or the birthdays—those came with noise and distraction—but the quiet, unremarkable Thursdays where he should have been across from her, chuckling at something Winsome said or winking when Anna pretended not to eavesdrop.

She remembered how they used to scout houses together under the guise of "real estate work," when the truth was they loved dreaming aloud about the lives those walls might hold. They had been partners in everything: in business, in joy, in spotting the same odd detail—an etched windowpane, a lopsided porch swing—and grinning like conspirators who had discovered a secret.

Cancer had stolen him piece by piece, until letting go had been an act of mercy. Still, the ache remained—steady, quiet, folded neatly into her days. She pressed her palm against her chest, the way she sometimes did, as though she could steady the hollow space that lingered there.

The bell over the café door jingled, pulling her back. Winsome breezed in first, trailing laughter like a ribbon, her smile big enough to light the whole café. Anna followed, calm and grounded, her presence like the weight of an anchor dropped into shifting water.

"Morning," Anna said warmly, slipping into the chair across from her. Winsome darted toward the counter to fetch their drinks, calling over her shoulder that she'd order the usual.

Anna leaned in, lowering her voice. "Did you see the *Gazette*? That high school principal—the one they jailed twenty years ago for molesting a student. He's up for parole."

Ingrid arched her brows but said nothing.

Anna shook her head slowly. "I swear, that sort of thing doesn't happen here."

"Oh, it happens here," Ingrid said evenly. "It happens everywhere. The difference is, people here cover it with a nice glossy finish. Happy Valley style. Keep the church directory smiling. Sweep the shadows under someone else's rug."

Anna's mouth tilted in a half-smile, though her eyes stayed troubled. "Like that story I heard when we first moved here. Something about a boy whose brother died on the ridge? Danny . . . something? No one says much, just that he left and never came back."

Ingrid's lips pressed into a knowing line. "Around here, silence is usually louder than words. And where there's silence, there's always more story."

Before Anna could respond, Winsome returned with steaming cups—black coffee for Ingrid, chamomile for Anna, frothy cappuccino for herself. "All right," she said, sliding into her chair. "What gloom are we wallowing in today?"

Anna explained, and Winsome gave a low chuckle. "Typical. Westridge paints itself as heaven and then gossips like hens when the cracks show."

The heaviness lingered for a moment, until Ingrid shifted the air. "Speaking of heaven, my garden has turned into hell with an abundance of weeds! Every weed in the county has taken up residence."

Anna grinned. "Then let's fix it. Winsome and I will come this weekend. We'll clear the weeds, get your bulbs planted. You can take us to lunch after."

Winsome raised her cup. "Done. But really, Ingrid—you're the only person I know who could call weeds 'abundance.'"

Ingrid gave a small, wry smile. "Point taken."

Their laughter rippled through the café, drowning the earlier shadows. Still, Ingrid noticed the undercurrents: a boy in the corner booth hiding bruises beneath his sweatshirt hood, the pastor's wife whispering fiercely into her phone, old Mr. Hensley nodding over his crossword. Westridge always looked ordinary, but if you sat still long enough, the shadows bled through the cracks.

Anna leaned forward again, softer this time. "So—your new Mastermind group. How's it really going?"

A warmth spread through Ingrid's chest. "Better than I hoped. They look polished, every one of them. But underneath? Insecurities, heartbreaks, secrets they've never told. Watching them carry each other, watching them heal—it's a privilege. We meet above the old bookstore now. It feels more . . . sacred than Zoom ever did."

Winsome reached across the table, squeezing her hand. "They're lucky to have you."

Ingrid smiled, but her thoughts wandered, unbidden, back to Wilson's easy grin. Back to the ridge. Back to the way Westridge had always preferred silence over truth.

Chapter 4

It was seven sharp, as always. A cool mist hung low over the fields, softening the edges of fences and trees, and at the stop sign where their two streets met, Ingrid and Sophia fell into step without a word. Their morning ritual was as much about silence as it was about conversation. Fifteen minutes passed, gravel crunching under their sneakers, before either spoke.

"I've got that Mastermind coming up Wednesday night," Ingrid said at last.

Sophia glanced over, a smile tugging at her mouth. "How's it shaping up?"

"Better than I could have dreamed," Ingrid answered. "These women are treasures—deeply spiritual, each in their own way, ambitious, but carrying their own unspoken pains. Strong women so rarely have a safe place to set it all down. That's the honor of it for me: to hold that space. That's why I'm so careful about who belongs in each group. The diversity is what amazes me—different faces, different goals, different heartbreaks—but together they enrich each other. And me." She exhaled, a quiet laugh. "Every time we meet, I come away fuller."

Sophia nodded, her expression warm.

"I'm grateful you called me here," Ingrid went on. "For all its loveliness, this town doesn't always make room for women to be themselves. It matters, having a place that does."

They passed a pasture where cows lifted their heads to stare at them, chewing slowly, unbothered. The women laughed, as they always did at that solemn bovine scrutiny.

"It does make you wonder," Sophia said lightly, "what they think of us."

Ingrid chuckled, shaking her head. The sound of their laughter melted into birdsong—the quick, sweet chatter of finches, the sharper song of the bluebirds.

"I had friends," Ingrid said suddenly, "who would sing at parties, just for fun. *The Bluebird of Happiness.*" And before she could stop herself, she sang a few lines, her voice clear in the morning air.

So be like I, hold your head up high

Till you find a bluebird of happiness . . .

Sophia joined in on the last line, and the two of them dissolved into giggles like schoolgirls, breathless and bright.

"Every time I see a bluebird, I think of it," Ingrid said, wiping her eyes. "And it lifts me."

As they reached the stop sign again, mist lifting off the fields and the cows still watching with their slow curiosity, Ingrid gave Sophia a sideways smile.

"You know," she said, brushing a bit of gravel dust from her sleeve, "Winsome and Anna are planning to meet me at the Fall Festival later in October. Pumpkin pies, fiddlers, hayrides—the whole small-town circus. You should come."

Sophia raised an eyebrow. "Me? At a pie contest?"

"Yes, you." Ingrid laughed. "Not as Dr. Sophia, therapist extraordinaire. Just as Sophia, my friend who needs a good apple cider and a night of laughter."

Sophia hesitated, then chuckled, shaking her head. "All right. But only if you promise not to make me bob for apples."

"Deal." Ingrid squeezed her hand before they parted ways. "It'll be good for you. And for me, too."

Chapter 5

The smell of fresh-brewed coffee drifted up the stairwell, meeting Rebecca halfway to the landing. She paused, one hand on the rail, letting it wash over her. Just the scent made her shoulders ease a fraction. Step-by-step, she climbed, thinking—*not for the first time—I've got to get this extra weight off.* Then she smirked to herself. "Who's on dessert duty tonight? Oh, right . . . Melody."

Melody's brownies had become a fixture at these meetings. Rich, gooey, suspiciously good—Rebecca sometimes wondered if there was something extra in them to account for Melody's boundless, wiry energy. Probably not, but the woman could singlehandedly fuel a party.

Rebecca loved these evenings. She looked forward to them every other week—her safe place, her little slice of heaven above the everyday noise of Westridge. Climbing to that big room above the old bookstore always felt symbolic, like she was stepping to a higher level—away from errands and dishes, into a space that made room for her bigger self.

At the top step, the room welcomed her with unpretentious warmth. Cushy brown leather chairs, worn to a gentle shine, invited you to sink and stay. Along the far wall, a brick fireplace waited for colder nights. Tonight, the old building's lack of air-conditioning meant the tall windows stood wide open, curtains breathing in the late-summer breeze. Ingrid always got there first to start the coffee and "let the fresh air—and the Spirit of God—flow in," as she liked to say.

"Rebecca!" Ingrid's voice, warm and bright, carried across the room. "So good to see your face. Haven't spotted you around lately. Been busy?"

"Pete and I took a trip out west—Yellowstone," Rebecca said, setting her bag on a chair. "We just drove, wandered, hiked a little. It soothes my soul."

"Sounds wonderful," Ingrid said, smiling. She tipped her head toward the stairs. "Is that . . . yes, that's Melody I hear bounding up."

Rebecca laughed. "Bet you a hundred bucks she's carrying brownies."

Seconds later, Melody burst in, grinning, a plate heaped with them. "You guessed it! And thank goodness you've got the coffee going, Ingrid."

"You never know when we might run out of energy," Rebecca deadpanned, and they laughed as more footsteps echoed on the stairs.

One by one, the women arrived—each greeted with hugs or clasped hands. They'd only been meeting for a month, but already this felt like a haven, a place where no one judged and no dream was too outrageous. They came here to stretch, to explore, to share visions big enough to shake their own corners of the world.

Ingrid chose her members carefully—six other women besides herself, matched for variety in strengths but a shared drive. Powerhouses, each with her own goals. Women who wanted expansion—of mind, spirit, influence, purpose.

The door opened again and Patsy King entered, carrying a bright bowl of fruit. "I know Melody always brings brownies," she said with a wink, "but I thought some of us might want something a little less . . . chocolate-dripping."

"You girls need to learn to live a little," Melody shot back, rolling her eyes.

Ingrid clapped her hands together. "All right, ladies, find a seat—but not the one you sat in last time. I want you to see the room differently tonight. New perspective, new energy."

Bags were dropped, coffee poured, plates filled—some with brownies, some with fruit, a few with both—until everyone settled in. Floorboards creaked. Night air slid through the open windows carrying the faint scent of cut grass and distant rain.

At exactly 7:00, Ingrid spoke. "Okay. Let's start with three deep breaths. In . . . hold . . . out—let the stress of the day go. Again—in, hold, and breathe out every scrap of self-doubt. One more—in, hold, and as you exhale, release the outside world. Know you are safe here tonight, gathered with women who share the Master's mind."

Stillness settled. The quiet here always felt different—thicker, almost golden—like something you could rest inside.

Ingrid waited until a few eyes opened. Then she smiled. "What a beautiful group you are. I'm thankful for each and every one of you. Let's go around and share one or two things you're grateful for today."

Rebecca went first. "I'm thankful Patsy brought fruit; We needed some balance."

Laughter circled the room. The tone softened.

Then Rebecca continued, "and grateful for the recent trip that Pete and I took to Yellowstone a couple of weeks ago. It shook loose some things for me, that I desperately needed to let go of."

Patsy went next. "We won our tennis match today—our team's in second place now. I'm grateful to be surrounded by winners."

Tanya Burberry, internationally known speaker and frequent flyer, leaned forward. "I'm just grateful to be home this week. No airports, no hotels. Just here, with you all, in a safe space."

Melody bounced in her seat. "My screenplay is finally coming together. The plot makes sense, and I'm excited to share pieces of it with you."

Sandra McKee, the group's functional medicine doctor, spoke more quietly. "Last week's talk brought in three new clients. It's always fulfilling to see people commit to real food, real change."

Robin smiled at her. "Sandra, I really think I need to book with you. At forty-one I shouldn't be feeling this creaky."

Ingrid's eyes softened. "Sounds like a great idea, Robin. And what are *you* grateful for?"

Robin's smile widened. "That old office building at the edge of town? It closed today." Huge relief!

Ingrid beamed. "That's exciting, both of you. Thank you for sharing." She turned to Melody. "Since you brought dessert, you get the hot seat tonight. Take the next twenty minutes to remind us of your vision—and tell us the main obstacle you're wrestling with right now."

Melody grinned. "You got it."

Melody's Hot Seat Moment

"Well, as most of you know, Bruce and I spent a month in the Galápagos Islands, wandering among sea lions, giant tortoises, blue-footed boobies—creatures so ancient and unafraid they make you feel like you've stepped out of time. We didn't just see them; we studied them, and we listened to the people who live alongside them. The locals spoke about the animals almost as if they were neighbors—family members—to be respected, guarded, protected.

"This screenplay started as a way to capture all of that—the species, the ecosystems, the cultural heartbeat that keeps them alive. On paper, it's becoming something like a documentary: a sweeping look at wildlife, conservation, and the raw beauty of the islands. And it *is* beautiful. Life-changing beautiful.

"But . . . there's a restlessness in me. A whisper that there's something deeper under the surface, something I haven't touched yet. It's like staring at a horizon and knowing there's land beyond it, even if you can't see the shape.

"We could wrap this up quickly, release it early in the new year, and call it done. But I don't want to just tell the story everyone expects. I want to tell the story that keeps me awake at night. I don't know exactly what it is yet, but I feel it—like a thread I'm meant to follow.

"Maybe tonight you can help me figure out what I'm really chasing here . . . because I think it might be bigger than animals, and bigger than me."

Tanya leaned forward, bracelets catching the lamplight. "Oh, Melody, it truly does sound incredible. But I get that deeper question. Traveling the world is such a privilege—the beauty, the stories, the learning—but no matter how far we go, we always carry ourselves with us. The questions, the longings, the unfinished pieces . . . they come along, too. Lately I've felt that same tug—like there's a thread I'm supposed to follow, but I'm not sure yet where it leads."

All six heads nodded; understanding moved through the circle like a quiet tide. Melody smiled, relieved.

What followed for the next ten minutes was a generous brain-storm—no judgment, no choosing, no labeling right or wrong—just a bright, swirling cloud of possibilities. Then the room rested. Ingrid never rushed to break silence; she trusted it. Wisdom liked the stillness.

It was Melody who spoke first, voice lower. "I think I've always been afraid of trusting anyone. Even myself. Sometimes I block out the deeper thoughts because . . . maybe I couldn't handle the answer."

Ingrid let that land. Her gaze moved slowly around the circle, giving each woman permission to add her truth—or not.

Tanya again, thoughtful. "My work takes me around the world, and it's incredible—the people, the places—but lately I wonder if I'm pouring so much into everyone else I'm leaving nothing for myself. And there's this relationship I'm trying to grow . . . I'm not sure if it's what I want, or if I'm afraid to admit I still don't know what lasting love looks like."

Rebecca cleared her throat, firm but reflective. "For me, it's my work. I've been a lawyer a long time, and I'm good at it. But lately I'm asking if fighting cases in court is the best way I can make a difference. I know I have more to give. I just don't know what shape it takes."

Patsy shifted, tennis-strong arms folding loosely. "I watched a documentary this week about women rescued from trafficking in Cambodia. It . . . broke something open in me. I've lived a comfortable life, and suddenly I keep thinking—*is that all I'm here for?* I want to do something that actually matters. I don't even know where to start."

A small current moved through the room. Tanya's eyes flickered, thoughtful, as if a distant door had opened in her mind. She said nothing yet.

Dr. Sandra smiled faintly, though her eyes were far away. "I came here for marketing—how to attract more clients. But the truth is . . . I think I'm also here to figure out if I still matter. My work helps people, I know that. But at home, sometimes I feel invisible. And if you feel invisible long enough, you start to wonder if the world sees you at all."

No one rushed to respond. The air felt charged—not heavy, but alive. This was the magic of the circle: when one woman dared to speak her truth, it gave the others permission to find theirs.

The group murmured—agreement, curiosity. Ingrid caught the glint in Robin's eye and tucked it away. Useful, later.

Tanya, meanwhile, finally placed the itch in her thoughts. "Patsy—your documentary. Was it the one with the man who runs a healing center in Cambodia? I heard him speak when I was in Kenya for the *Empower You* conference. Quiet speaker. Powerful. I can't remember his name." She frowned slightly, then let it go. "Anyway—your reaction makes sense. Once you hear those stories, you can't unhear them."

Patsy nodded, eyes bright. "That's the one."

For a fraction of a second, Robin's fingers stilled on the rim of her cup. The tiniest catch in motion—then she brought it smoothly to her lips, face unreadable. If anyone noticed, they said nothing.

Ingrid let the room breathe again, then gathered the threads. "You've laid beautiful work on the table tonight—vision, restlessness, truth. Between now and next session, one *tiny* step toward any of it. Doesn't matter which. Motion matters."

Around them, the windows lifted a cooler breeze. The lamp hummed. The brownies were mostly crumbs; the fruit bowl was half-empty and bright.

And the circle held—women hand-picked by Ingrid for their strength and their ache, different as fingerprints, bound by the quiet courage to tell the truth out loud. Somewhere in those truths, a new story was already assembling itself, bone by bone.

Chapter 6

Sophia could still remember the exact date. Twelve years ago, almost to the day, she had first driven into Westridge with her car packed full of books, framed diplomas, and the quiet certainty that she was stepping into her purpose.

The decision had come quickly, almost too easily. She'd read the article in the *Westridge Gazette* announcing that the town's only counseling center was closing its doors. She had shaken her head in disbelief—how did a place like that fail? In her mind, there would *always* be need for healing. Surely people in small towns wrestled with grief, family struggles, broken hearts, eating disorders, and all the other tangled strands of human living.

Sophia had called her friend Ingrid that night. "They're shutting it down," she said. "But that means there's an opening. I'm going to Westridge. It's only a couple of hours from you, so we can still meet up. And I feel—I don't know—it feels meant to be."

The *Gazette* editor had been eager. Local businesses were cherished here, and when Sophia stopped by the office to introduce herself, he'd nearly leapt at the chance to run a feature. Within a week, she was on the front page, smiling beneath the headline: "A New Beginning: Westridge Welcomes Private Counseling Practice."

Sophia had carried that folded clipping in her purse for months, a talisman of sorts.

But the charm had begun to crack one morning at The Bean, where she'd gone for a macchiato. At the table beside her, two townsfolk were talking.

"Of course that old counseling center closed," the woman said. "Things like that don't happen here."

The man nodded. "Not enough business for it. People around here don't go blabbing about their problems. They just get a grip."

Sophia had sipped her coffee slowly, hiding her frown. That offhand remark had told her more about Westridge than the *Gazette* ever had. This was a town where wounds stayed covered, where silence was stitched into the fabric of respectability. And she was walking straight into it.

Still, she pressed forward. That was her way.

The first week after the feature, she had her answer. A man made an appointment, presenting himself as a potential client. He was polite enough at first, but halfway through the session his tone shifted. His words weren't overtly threatening, but the meaning beneath them was clear: *be careful.* Sophia had felt the hairs rise at the back of her neck. When he left, she stood in her office doorway a long moment, steadying her breath.

"All right, Lord," she whispered into the silence. "I hear You. If this is the work You've called me to, then fill me with Your Spirit. Give me wisdom, because apparently, there's something deeper here than I imagined."

Oddly, the encounter only strengthened her resolve. She had walked through storms before. She would walk through this one, too.

The very next day, her phone rang. The voice on the line was hesitant, almost apologetic.

"Hi . . . my name's Robin. I don't really think I need therapy. But—well, there are a few things running around in my mind. I saw your picture in the paper, and I thought . . . maybe I could just come talk."

Robin had become the first thread in a tapestry Sophia hadn't yet glimpsed. Others followed—some seeking help, others arriving with shadows in their eyes and stories that hinted at why the old counseling center had *really* closed. Little by little, Sophia pieced it together: not everyone in Westridge wanted light shone on certain corners.

Still, she stayed. She built her practice, one person at a time. She found her footing, and in the quiet hours she'd call Ingrid.

A couple years later, she had laughed down the line, teasing her old friend. "You know that fellow Stanley? The needy one who keeps pressing you into a relationship? Maybe he's the reason you should pack up and come here instead. I've got a cabin waiting just outside town. And I'll start looking for properties for you, because I already know you'll say yes."

Ingrid had chuckled, evasive but warm. "You've always been the wise one, Sophia. Let's talk more later. And yes—I miss you."

Sophia had hung up smiling, knowing she had planted a seed. Westridge might not have welcomed her openly, but she was certain of one thing: she had been led here. And when Spirit led, she followed.

Chapter 7

Ingrid ended the call with Stanley and let the phone drop onto the arm of her chair. A deep, aggravated sigh escaped her lips—rare for her, because it took a great deal to rattle her. But the man simply would not give up.

That first date, years ago, had been the mistake. She should have known better, but compassion had always been her default. Stanley was newly widowed then, raw with loneliness, and she had seen in his eyes the hollow hunger of someone trying to outrun grief. He had been decent company at first—witty, well-read, able to converse on books and travel and even Thai cuisine. And because her heart could not bear the thought of another human suffering in silence, she had agreed to the occasional outing: a concert under the stars, a play in the community hall, a shared dinner where conversation, not romance, had been the order of the night.

But Stanley had been weaving a different story.

The evening it all came to a head was still sharp in her memory. Ruby Thai, their familiar haunt, fragrant with curry and lemongrass. They had been sipping wine when he pulled a velvet box from his pocket and opened it, his hands trembling slightly. Inside was a ring that caught the light like fire. Ingrid had nearly choked on her food.

"Stanley," she'd said carefully, her voice steady despite her racing pulse. "It's beautiful. Truly. But I've told you before—I have no wish for marriage. I've had the love of my life. He's gone on to his next adventure, and though I miss him dearly, I have no need to replace him."

His face had fallen. Then the anger came, hot and wounded. He accused her of double messages, of leading him on. A scene followed—one that drew sidelong glances from nearby tables. But beneath his bluster, Ingrid had seen only a man laid bare with loneliness.

23

Still, she had principles. Communication must be clear. Boundaries must be honored. Without them, her coaching practice, her very calling, would be a sham. So she had spoken calmly, with the same voice she used to steady her clients when they faltered.

"Stanley, I treasure your friendship. But I will not marry again. You deserve a woman who longs for what you long for. I cannot be that woman."

She had been grateful, that night, for having driven herself. It gave her the freedom to walk away with her dignity intact, while Stanley gathered what remained of his.

But he had not stayed away. For a time, his calls came once a month. Then, every week. Lately, there was an edge to them—neediness, pushiness, even flashes of anger. Each time she held the line, refusing to yield an inch, knowing that any softness would be read as consent.

It was wearing her down.

So when Sophia had phoned, her timing had been uncanny, as it so often was. "I think you're needed here in Westridge," Sophia had said, her voice steady with conviction. "Come. Start fresh. I have a cabin for you. You'll see."

The seed had lodged itself deep in Ingrid's mind. For the past two weeks, in nearly every free hour, she had imagined disentangling herself from this place—from Stanley, from the community obligations that tethered her—and beginning again. She still had a thriving coaching practice, full Mastermind groups, commitments to honor. But the idea of Westridge shimmered before her like a horizon.

She missed Sophia, more than she had admitted aloud. Their morning walks, their long talks—the easy companionship that had always steadied her. And though starting over at her age was no small thing, Ingrid felt a flicker of excitement each time she allowed herself to picture it.

God had a way of sending her challenges at just the right moment—tests to sharpen her clarity, to call her into deeper strength. Perhaps Stanley was just that: the push she needed to step into her next chapter.

Chapter 8

Tanya Burberry carried the kind of beauty that drew eyes without asking. Light-skinned, auburn-haired, elegant in the way of a woman who had learned the art of presence. Her clothing was never off the rack—bright silks from Mumbai, hand-stitched cottons from Malawi, tailored skirts from Rio—pieces chosen not just for their style, but for the stories they carried. Every seam whispered of the hands that made it, of women she had promised to support, of dignity stitched into fabric.

A year ago, her life had shifted like a tide. *My Money, My Life* had catapulted her onto the international stage, an overnight best seller after years of groundwork, quiet hustling, and book signings in small towns where she'd wondered if anyone at all would show up. Now she stood in boardrooms of multinational corporations, spoke in village huts with dirt floors, sat on panels with ministers and nonprofit leaders, her voice steady as she told women: *You have value. You have power. You are the architect of your future.*

She'd seen it in their eyes—women who had walked miles for water, who had never once considered that their lives could be different, suddenly daring to imagine. She'd seen it, too, in high-level executives, women already running empires but still questioning their worth. Her message had cut through both worlds like a bell.

Kenya had been the turning point. The Empower You Conference had gathered voices from across the globe—scientists, entrepreneurs, activists. Tanya had delivered her keynote on financial wellness and watched the faces in the crowd shift as she spoke about microenterprise, about trust, about the near-perfect repayment rates of women-run lending circles. *Give women a chance,* she told them, *and they will change not only their families, but their nations.*

And then—Danny Kessler. Quiet, steady, with eyes that seemed to carry centuries. She hadn't planned to attend the trafficking seminar, too heavy, too dark. But something pulled her into that room. She sat in the back and listened as he spoke of children sold, girls vanished, families deceived. His words were measured, almost gentle, but they carried a gravity that silenced the room. He didn't dramatize. He didn't need to. His sadness was its own authority.

She had spoken with him later, two speakers comparing notes, both exhausted and lit by the fire of the work. There had been something in him that unsettled her, as though his wounds could see hers. She had thought of him more than she meant to on the flight home.

Now she lived in Westridge, a town she never expected to call home, drawn here by a man with a pilot's license and a Brazilian lilt in his voice. Love, or something like it, had tugged her closer. They both traveled constantly, ships that passed but at least in the same harbor now and then. She told herself it was enough. She told herself she was lucky. And yet, in quiet moments, she wondered if she was too old to want the ceremony of marriage—or if she only feared repeating the pattern that had carved itself into her heart when she was five years old.

Her father's back, the door closing, the angry silence that followed. She had carried the blame like a secret badge ever since. *Men leave. I drive them away.*

And still, paradoxically, she had become the one in the group who knew the right words when relationships cracked. Who could see where love was tangled and name the knot with gentleness. Her gift, her irony.

Now she sat in the nail salon, auburn hair catching the afternoon light, the scent of acetone and lavender hanging in the air. She let herself lean back as the chatter of women rose and fell around her, thinking again of the conference, of Danny's quiet voice, of her own restless heart. She loved these women—strangers and sisters alike. She longed to see each of them lifted, empowered, laughing in their strength. That was her calling, her joy.

Yet beneath it all, she knew her own vulnerability. The child who lost her father still lived inside her, whispering. And so she kept her practices: morning meditation, her gratitude journal, the daily run that steadied her spirit. She filled herself with joy because she knew the world would try to drain it away.

When the technician finally called her name, Tanya rose with that effortless grace, a woman who carried both wounds and wisdom. Her pedicure was a ritual, not vanity. Self-care was not indulgence; it was armor. She moved to the chair, smiling, ready to receive, ready to give again tomorrow.

Chapter 9

The rain came down in sheets, hammering the roof with such force it felt like the sky itself was emptying over Westridge. Lightning cracked open the evening, thunder rolling behind it, and still the women came. They climbed the narrow stairs to the upper room of the old building, shaking out umbrellas and stamping wet shoes, laughing at their own determination.

They came because this mattered. They came because every time they left, they knew themselves a little better. Stronger. Sharper. And tonight, as the storm raged, they found their haven in the glow of a small fire, the scent of strong coffee, and the promise of strawberry cheesecake—their comfort food, always waiting.

Ingrid, as always, carried the calm authority of a woman who knew how to hold space. She let them chatter while coffee was poured and plates were passed. Sandra leaned toward Melody, her voice carrying over the clatter of forks.

"I was watching Bruce's news show the other night," Sandra said, "and that old high school principal from twenty years ago—he finally got parole."

Melody shook her head. "Hard to understand sometimes. But the law's the law. If he was up for it . . . " she let the thought trail off, "life goes on."

Across the circle, Robin stiffened. Tanya noticed the almost imperceptible cringe, the way Robin's eyes flickered down to her plate as though she wanted to disappear. Before Tanya could dwell on it, she turned toward Patsy.

"By the way," Tanya said lightly, "I wanted to give you the name of that speaker I mentioned last month. You were interested in the trafficking documentary, remember? His name's Danny Kessler. Ever heard of him?"

From the other side of the room came a sharp clatter. Everyone looked up to see Robin fumbling to rescue her plate before it slid to the floor. Flustered, she laughed it off. "Guess I'm all thumbs tonight." She brushed the crumbs aside, forcing a smile, but her cheeks were still flushed.

Tanya made a quiet note to herself.

By seven sharp, everyone had found their seats. At Ingrid's urging, they shuffled around, swapping places. "Shake it up," she always said. "Change your seat, change your perspective." Sandra laughed as she moved, acknowledging how even small changes could shift the way she saw things.

Ingrid lifted her hands. "All right, ladies. Let's begin. Inhale deeply—"

The group followed, eyes closing as thunder rumbled overhead.

"Breathe in the wisdom in this room. Exhale self-doubt, worry, and the weight of the world. Again, breathe in the wisdom of the Creator. Exhale all that does not serve you. One more time—breathe in solutions, breathe out fear. Open your eyes. Welcome."

The women opened their eyes, their shoulders visibly lighter.

"As always," Ingrid said, "we'll begin with gratitude."

Tanya smiled, auburn hair glinting in the firelight. "I got my nails done this week. Simple, maybe, but it's my reminder that I matter. That feeling good matters."

Rebecca followed, her tone steady. "I'm grateful for a case that finally found a win-win resolution. It's a relief when things work out for everyone."

Robin grinned, a little self-satisfaction in her voice. "I've had a win-win too. That CrossFit gym I joined? Turns out I'm actually getting stronger—and I've even dropped two pounds."

Laughter and congratulations circled the room.

Sandra drew a deeper breath before her turn. "I'm thankful for clarity. My husband and I . . . we've had some hard conversations. They hurt. But knowing the truth feels better than living in the fog.

And yes," she added with a small smile, "I brought the cheesecake, so I'm on the hot seat tonight."

The women's eyes softened toward her, a shared warmth that spoke volumes.

Melody leaned forward, excitement sparking. "Bruce and I are planning a trip. We're heading to Phnom Penh. After last month's conversation, I can't stop thinking about the trafficking issue there. We're exploring whether it could be the next subject for our documentary."

The room stilled. The word *trafficking* carried its own weight.

Patsy nodded slowly. "That struck me too. I've reached out to a couple nonprofits. Planning to attend some events, see what I can learn. It feels . . . important."

A murmur of agreement circled the group, each woman sensing the thread weaving quietly through their individual lives.

Ingrid, steady as always, drew them back. "Gratitude reminds us who we are. And who we are is women of solutions. Life brings problems; we will always have them. But our work here," she gestured around the circle, "is to stay anchored in love, joy, peace, creativity, wisdom. That is the frequency where solutions are born."

She turned to Sandra. "Now, let's hear your story."

Sandra hesitated, then nodded. "One of the reasons I joined this group was clarity. I've suspected for a while my husband's been . . . distracted. And not just by work. This week, I finally confronted him." Her voice wavered, but she pressed on, describing the "new" soap scent, the rehearsed confrontation, and his shaken admission.

"Yes, it hurt. But I was more relieved than anything. At least now, we can talk."

The room went silent, heavy but not oppressive. Silence had become their teacher.

Finally, Patsy leaned in, her voice soft. "If you ever need to talk, Sandra, my door's open. There's always coffee on."

One by one, the others nodded. *We're here. You're not alone.*

Ingrid's eyes glistened as she met Sandra's gaze. "Bold truth-telling. That takes strength. And it creates space for trust to rebuild. Thank you."

She looked around the circle. "Who else is taking bold action this week?"

The discussion flowed, weaving through triumphs, small risks, and quiet victories. By the time the fire had burned down to embers, the women were already scribbling their "one small action" for the week ahead.

As they cleaned up, the rain finally eased. The air outside smelled fresh, washed, alive. Streetlights glowed against the wet pavement as they hugged goodbye, each one carrying away the comfort of the group and the strength of their shared trust.

None of them knew how much they would need it in the days to come.

Chapter 10

The café was nearly empty, the kind of small-town spot where the clink of a spoon against a porcelain cup echoed. Tanya slid into a booth by the window, auburn hair catching the weak afternoon light. She had suggested coffee casually at the end of the Mastermind meeting, but in truth she'd been deliberate. Robin's dropped plate, her too-quick laugh, the flash of something unguarded in her eyes—Tanya wanted to understand.

Robin arrived late, as if reluctant. She swept in with a gust of damp air, her leather tote slung over one shoulder, phone still in hand. "Sorry," she said briskly, sliding into the opposite seat. "Client call. Never ends."

Tanya smiled. "I figured as much. Thank you for coming."

A server appeared, and Robin ordered black coffee without glancing at the menu. Tanya added a chai latte and waited until the woman left before speaking again. "I realized, during group, I don't know much about you. You fascinate me."

Robin barked out a laugh, quick and sharp. "Fascinate? That's a new one. Most people just think I'm bossy."

"Maybe," Tanya said gently, "but bossy usually means a woman knows what she's doing. I admire that."

Robin waved the compliment away, but not unkindly. "I work hard. That's all. Real estate's not forgiving—you hustle or you drown." She leaned forward, warming now to the subject, describing a recent closing, a tricky negotiation, the relief of finally selling a dilapidated office building she'd carried on her books for months. "Ugly as sin, needed a fortune in renovations. But someone finally bit. I'm glad it's off my hands."

Tanya listened, letting the energy of Robin's voice fill the space. Beneath the bravado, she heard something else—a drive that sounded less like ambition and more like survival.

"You must love it," Tanya said.

Robin hesitated, just long enough for Tanya to notice. "It pays the bills," she said at last. Then, softer, "And it keeps me . . . busy."

The coffees arrived. Robin wrapped her hands around her mug as though it anchored her. Tanya took a sip of her chai, studying the other woman.

"You seemed startled the other night," Tanya said carefully, "when I mentioned that trafficking speaker. Danny Kessler."

The spoon Robin had been stirring with clinked hard against her cup. She forced a laugh, too bright. "Did I? Probably just clumsy. Happens."

Tanya tilted her head, but didn't push. Silence, she knew, could be more powerful than a question. She let it stretch, sipping her chai until Robin filled it.

"You know," Robin said, voice brisk again, "I don't really do personal talk. Never saw the point. But you—" She gestured vaguely toward Tanya. "You have this way of making people spill their guts. Dangerous."

Tanya smiled. "Only if you need to."

Robin gave a half-smile, half-grimace. "Trust me. Some stories are better left where they are."

And with that, she changed the subject—asking Tanya about her book tour, her time in Kenya, her keynote on microenterprise. Robin listened more than she spoke, but her eyes carried the weight of someone holding back an ocean.

When they finally stood to leave, the sky outside was bruised purple, rain beginning to spit against the pavement. Tanya touched Robin's arm lightly. "Coffee again sometime?"

Robin shrugged, but there was the faintest softening in her expression. "Maybe. If I'm not buried under contracts." She tugged her tote higher on her shoulder. "Thanks for the coffee. And . . . for not prying."

Tanya watched her walk away, brusque and self-contained, the echo of that dropped plate still sharp in her memory. There was a story there—one tied to Danny, whether Robin admitted it or not. Tanya could feel it in her bones.

Robin pushed through the café door into the damp evening air, the rain quickening as if to chase her to the car. She exhaled hard, relief and unease tangled in her chest. Tanya's warmth had unsettled her more than the questions.

For the briefest moment, Robin heard Sophia's voice in her mind, calm and steady as it had been a hundred times before: *You don't have to tell everything, Robin. But you do need people who can see you. Healing isn't just about surviving the past—it's about risking the present.*

It was Sophia who had nudged her toward Ingrid's group in the first place, telling her she'd done enough work in the safety of a therapy office. *Now you need peers, a tribe, women who won't just analyze you but stand beside you.*

Robin unlocked her car, shaking her head at the irony. She had resisted, resisted, resisted—and yet here she was. Coffee with Tanya. A group she actually showed up for. And still, the mention of Danny Kessler had nearly unraveled her.

She slipped behind the wheel, gripping it tight. "One step at a time," she whispered, echoing Sophia's old refrain. But tonight, that step felt heavier than ever.

Chapter 11

The ridge was smaller than he remembered.

Or maybe he was simply larger now, no longer the wiry seventeen-year-old who had stood here last. A man's shoulders filled his jacket now, a man's hands braced against the weathered guardrail. But the outline hadn't changed—the same jagged edge of rock cutting into sky, the same sheer drop that could make a stomach heave even from a safe distance. The same waiting stillness, as if the ridge had been holding its breath all these years for him to come back.

The wind pressed up from the gorge, cool and metallic, laced with the tang of stone and river water. A falcon circled somewhere below, its cry thin and fleeting. Danny leaned into the rail and closed his eyes. For a moment he could hear it—the faint scatter of pebbles rolling loose, tumbling into the void. Memory supplying the sound when silence would not.

He had told himself this trip was about duty: about his parents, about the old house they could no longer keep up, about paperwork and repairs and the tedious sorting of what to keep and what to throw away. That was the reason he gave when anyone asked, and he nearly believed it himself. Nearly. Because beneath all that, he had known: sooner or later, he would have to stand here.

The road up had been crueler than he'd expected. Every curve unfurled a ghost. The long hill where he had once raced his bike, flying down with the reckless conviction of youth. The turnout where the valley spread wide, fields and rooftops arranged like a painted backdrop. And then that bend—the one where the trees pulled back and the ridge revealed itself, stark and sudden. His chest had clenched there, a fist of breath and memory, the old panic squeezing.

He hadn't planned to stop. He'd meant to drive on, straight into town, head down, teeth gritted, get it over with. But here he was.

And there it was—the air itself, the same stretch of space that had swallowed Rick whole.

The image rushed up too easily: Rick's arms pinwheeling, boots scrabbling for hold, his face lit with a raw, impossible terror. And behind it all, the sound—that scream torn out of him, ripped from marrow. It had never really stopped falling. It lived still in Danny's bones, deep in the hollow places no laughter could reach.

He had been carrying it for twenty-five years. A second's worth of sound, stretched across a lifetime.

Behind him, a car door slammed. A woman's voice, sharp and ordinary, calling for a child to hold her hand. Life going on, blind to the ghosts it walked past.

Danny pushed away from the rail. Straightened. Shoved his hands into his jacket pockets as if to hide the tremor that wanted to betray him. The ridge remained behind him, unmoved, eternal, keeping its silence.

Ahead lay Westridge. A few miles down the road. A town that had not forgotten, even if it pretended to.

So was everything he had been avoiding for half his life.

Chapter 12

Robin spotted him before he saw her.

She was leaning against the counter at The Westridge Bean, one hand braced on the scarred wood, the other curled around her phone though she wasn't looking at it. The air was thick with the hiss of steaming milk and the roasted bite of coffee beans, the comfortable morning hum of a small-town café. And then the bell over the door gave its cheerful chime.

She looked up.

And there he was.

Danny Kessler.

For a split second, her brain scrambled to fit the man in the doorway with the boy she remembered. The bones of him were the same—the line of his jaw, the tilt of his head as if the world weighed heavier on one side. But time had carved him deeper: broader in the shoulders, narrower in the face, his skin weathered in a way that spoke of years under foreign suns. It startled her, the jolt of recognition that punched through her chest before her mind caught up.

Twenty-five years was a long time to pretend someone didn't exist.

He scanned the café the way people do when they're bracing for recognition, as though every familiar face might demand something he didn't have to give. His gaze swept past her at first, indifferent. But then it stopped, locked, and in that heartbeat his jaw tightened—just slightly, but enough. She knew the look. A man holding something back.

"Robin." His voice wrapped her name carefully, like a word he wasn't sure he was allowed to use.

Her grip tightened on her phone. "Danny." She was proud of the steadiness in her voice, though inside her pulse was leaping, reckless as a teenager's.

The barista set her cappuccino on the counter with a solid ceramic thud. Grateful for the anchor, she picked it up, let the heat bite her palms. Something to hold. Something to do.

"Back in town?" she asked, casual as she could manage.

"Yeah." He cleared his throat, the sound rough. "For a while."

A pause opened between them—thin but strong, like wire stretched taut. Neither of them spoke the words that hovered unsaid: the ridge. Rick. The night everything cracked. The way he'd disappeared without goodbye.

"You look . . . " He started, stopped, the unfinished sentence hanging between them like an untied thread.

"So do you," she answered automatically. But it wasn't true in the same way. He looked older. Worn. There was something in his eyes—a distance, the kind that came from carrying things too heavy, too long. She'd seen it before, once, that summer at camp, after he'd come pounding back down from the hike alone, silent, eyes hollow. She hadn't asked then. She didn't ask now.

Behind them, the bell jingled again and a man in a work jacket stepped inside, calling out Danny's name with the ease of someone who'd known him once and was glad to see him again. Danny turned, nodded back, relief flickering over his face like a man spotting an escape route.

He looked back at her just long enough to offer the smallest of nods—half apology, half retreat. "Good to see you, Robin."

And then he was gone, carried off in the rhythm of another conversation, another orbit.

She stood with her cappuccino warming her hands, her heart thudding in her ribs like it hadn't in years. The old questions surged, raw and familiar, as if no time had passed at all.

What happened up there, Danny?

And why, after all these years, do I still care?

Chapter 13

Danny pushed open the coffee shop door, and the bell gave its last cheerful ring before the cold met him head-on. The autumn air wrapped itself around his shoulders, crisp and insistent, and for a moment he let it bite, let it remind him he was no longer inside with Robin's eyes fixed on him. He kept his hands in his jacket pockets—not from chill, but because it was the only way to stop them from betraying the restless twitch that came whenever his mind raced faster than his body could keep up.

Robin.

He hadn't prepared for that. Not really. In all the vague rehearsals of this trip—the imagined faces, the old storefronts, the drive up the ridge—she had existed only as a shadow, an inevitability. Like the hardware store clerk or the high school coach who still whistled at games. Someone he might bump into, exchange a polite nod, and move past.

But she hadn't been a shadow. She'd been carved into the morning like she belonged there, leaning against the counter with that same tilt of her head, the same dark eyes sharp and soft all at once. Time had added something steadier to her—an edge of steel, maybe, or armor polished so bright it could blind you if you stared too long. Yet beneath it, he thought he'd seen a flicker of what had once undone him: a compassion so deep it frightened him, wrapped now in confidence and brusque certainty.

His throat had caught when he said her name. He knew it; he'd felt it. Her voice, steady as a stone in a stream, hadn't faltered at all. That was Robin. Always meeting the moment head-on, even when it rattled the walls.

He told himself it didn't matter—that this was just two people colliding after decades, an awkward hello between survivors of the same long-ago fracture. Yet as he walked away, he could still feel the heat of her gaze between his shoulders, like static clinging to his coat. The air itself seemed to hum with the questions she hadn't asked.

What would she say if she knew how many times he'd thought of her over the years? Not just in the quiet moments, but in the loud ones too—the clamor of Phnom Penh streets, the low chanting at dawn in temple courtyards, even in the laughter of the women at the healing center when joy finally broke through their scars. She'd been there, a ghost pressed into his mind, tethered to the one day he could never untangle.

And not only the fall. No—before. Hours before, the way she'd looked at him when she thought no one noticed. A glance that had said she saw more than he wanted to show. A glance that stayed.

He crossed the street now, not daring to glance back at the window of The Bean. His steps fell too fast, too loud on the pavement, as though he could outwalk memory. But memory kept pace, relentless.

Westridge was thick with ghosts—he'd known that before he ever pulled into town. His brother's. His own. The unspoken ones that lived in the silences of its people. And now Robin's, alive and unyielding, as present as if twenty-five years had been a breath.

She wasn't the only ghost here. But she was the only one who made him wonder if facing them—facing her—might be worth it.

Meanwhile, Robin waited a beat, then hurried to her car. She sat behind the wheel, hands tight on the steering wheel, her cappuccino untouched. The old ache returned. She dialed Sophia almost instinctively—like muscle memory.

"Sophia . . . it's Robin. I know it's been a while, but . . . could you fit me in? Something's come up."

Sophia was warm and perceptive as always, didn't ask. "Of course. Come in tomorrow at three?"

Robin exhaled. Relief mixed with dread. "Thanks. I'd like that."

Chapter 14

On her way home, still shaky from the unexpected collision of past and present at the café, Robin pulled into the grocery store. She told herself it was only to pick up coffee for the morning, maybe a few basics. But once inside, she found herself circling the aisles with Sandra's voice in her head.

For weeks now, Sandra had been nudging her—gently, insistently—toward better choices: *real* food, not potato chips and the emergency stash of chocolate that had too often stood in for dinner. Living alone had dulled her appetite for cooking, and for years she'd simply . . . stopped caring. But Sandra was right. If she wanted strength—energy—hell, if she wanted her life back, she had to nourish it.

So she filled her basket with spinach and kale, berries for smoothies, a package of grass-fed beef. *I'm doing it this time,* she told herself. *I'm building the body, the vitality, the life I choose.* Ingrid's voice joined Sandra's in her mind, a chorus of strong women reminding her: vision first, reality follows.

Robin glanced down at the basket, surprisingly proud of the color there—green, red, deep purple. She thought of the Mastermind group, Sophia's gentle push that finally persuaded her to join. The women had begun to feel like something she'd never let herself want: a tribe. A safe circle. She wasn't sure she was ready to be vulnerable, but maybe safety came not from silence, but from being seen.

Distracted by the thought, she steered her cart too close to the endcap of the aisle—and bumped directly into another cart.

"Oh!" She looked up, startled.

Danny.

He stood across from her, his hand braced lightly on his cart, his expression caught between surprise and something heavier—something she couldn't name.

For a heartbeat too long, neither spoke.

Then he gave a low chuckle. "Seems like fate's working overtime today."

Her pulse quickened, as if her heart had been waiting for his voice all along.

Danny tilted his head, studying her with a steadiness that unsettled her. "I meant what I said at the coffee shop. We're due for a catch-up. A real one, not just polite hellos."

Robin's throat tightened. *Twenty-five years I've both dreaded and dreamed of this,* she thought. And now here he was, the boy who had left and the man who had returned, asking her to step directly into the storm she'd avoided for decades.

Sophia's words whispered in her ear, unbidden: *Sometimes the only way through is straight ahead, one step at a time. Do what you can, with what you've got, in the moment.*

She managed a half-smile. "You're probably right."

His eyes warmed, just a flicker, and then he pressed gently: "Do you have room in your schedule Saturday night? Dinner?"

The question lodged like a stone in her chest. She hesitated, fumbling for composure. "Wow. You caught me off guard. I don't have my calendar on me . . . but I'll check."

"Good." He reached into his wallet, pulled out a business card, and scribbled a number on the back before handing it to her. "I'm at my parents' place for now. Call me."

She slid the card into her purse, still too aware of the steady drum of her heartbeat. "I haven't seen them in ages. How are they?"

"They're hanging in," Danny said, a wry smile pulling at his mouth. "Getting older. The house feels too big for them. Might be time to think about downsizing." He paused, then added lightly, "Maybe that's something we can talk about too."

Robin let out a small laugh, her voice thinner than she intended. "You remember my parents? They've always been into themselves more than anything else. Retired a few years ago. Now they're living it up in Sun City."

"See?" Danny said softly. "We've got a whole lot of catching up to do." His tone wasn't casual; it held a weight that left her both longing and terrified.

"Maybe Saturday," she said, retreat already in her step.

"Seven o'clock," he offered, almost as though he believed she'd say yes.

She nodded but turned quickly toward the checkout, pretending sudden urgency. Halfway there, she stopped short—*damn, the coffee*. She swung around, retracing her steps, aware of his eyes on her as she passed back down the aisle.

Danny stood where she'd left him, his cart half-full, his gaze following her with a look she couldn't quite decipher. He thought of the girl she'd been, of what he hadn't said back then, of the weight they both carried from a past neither had escaped unscathed. She hadn't changed much—and yet he knew, with a certainty that knifed him, that everything about her world had changed.

He drew a breath, finished gathering the groceries his parents had asked for, and headed to the car. He hoped she'd say yes. God help him, he was nervous that she just might.

Danny's Drive Home

Danny watched her go, grabbing coffee in her haste, and only when the automatic doors closed behind him did he let the air out of his chest, realizing he'd been holding it the whole time.

The bags rustled on the seat beside him, his mother's list fulfilled with military precision. Milk, bread, apples, the brand of tea she liked. He drove without really seeing the road at first, the hum of the tires a counterpoint to the hammering in his chest.

Robin.

The name itself still had the power to drag him backward in time. Her eyes—unchanged and yet different—had looked at him across the narrow space of the grocery aisle, and he'd felt that same tug, like gravity insisting on itself.

She hadn't forgiven him. How could she? He hadn't saved her. He'd seen enough back then to know something ugly was happening, but not enough—or maybe not brave enough—to stop it. And when Rick fell, the truth had been buried along with him. Danny had left town with blood on his hands and guilt in his bones, certain that Robin's silence meant blame.

But today . . . she hadn't turned away. Hesitant, yes, caught off guard—but she hadn't shut him out.

He gripped the steering wheel tighter, his knuckles whitening. Maybe he was a fool for asking her to dinner. Maybe it was selfish. But when she stood there in front of him, basket full of greens and berries, trying—he could see it in her, the effort, the determination to claw her way toward life again—he couldn't not ask.

He remembered the girl she'd been. Quick to laugh, quicker still to retreat into herself when shadows fell across her. He remembered her braids, the way she'd sit on the ridge with a sketchbook balanced on her knees, pretending she wasn't watching the world.

And he remembered the day it all cracked apart.

Danny slowed at a stop sign, his chest tightening. He'd replayed that fight with Rick a thousand times—every word, every shove, the look in his brother's eyes when his foot slipped. It had been an accident, but it had also been the culmination of something twisted, something Danny had only half understood. *Stay away from her,* he'd shouted. But Rick hadn't listened, and then he'd never have the chance to again.

Danny exhaled, forcing air into his lungs. He hadn't come back to this town to stir up ghosts, but the ghosts were stirring anyway. And now Robin stood at the center of it all, just as she had back then.

He wanted to protect her. He wanted to make it right. And—God help him—he wanted more than that.

Turning down the long, familiar road to his parents' place, Danny loosened his grip on the wheel. He'd asked. The rest was up to her. Maybe she'd call. Maybe she wouldn't.

But for the first time in twenty-five years, the possibility existed. And that was enough to keep him both terrified and alive.

Chapter 15

Robin sat in her car for ten minutes before she finally went inside. She'd driven the familiar route almost without thinking, turning onto the quiet street where Sophia's office stood tucked between a bakery and a consignment shop. The air smelled of cinnamon and old books the second she pushed the door open.

Sophia looked up from her desk, her face breaking into that steady, calm smile Robin remembered. "You're right on time," she said, as though twelve years of history had folded neatly into this one moment.

Robin shrugged, pretending it was no big deal. "Guess I haven't forgotten the drill."

Sophia gestured toward the same chair Robin had always chosen. It was faded now, but comfortable, familiar in a way that made Robin's chest ache. She sank into it, crossing her legs, arms tight against her sides.

They sat in silence long enough for Robin to fidget. Finally, she blew out a breath. "I saw him today. Danny."

Sophia didn't move, didn't flinch. "How did that feel?"

Robin let out a sharp laugh. "Like getting hit with a brick I didn't see coming. He said my name, Sophia, and it was like . . . like time collapsed. I was fifteen again. Stupid, vulnerable. Wanting him to see me."

Sophia leaned forward slightly. "You've worked through a lot of grief—Rick, the betrayal, the way he shaped so many of your choices. But Danny . . ."

Robin's throat tightened. She shook her head. "I never worked through Danny. He left. Just left. And I hated him for it, but part of me—" She broke off, pressing her palms against her knees. "Part of me missed him every damn day."

Sophia let the words hang. Robin hated that she could still feel tears pressing at the edges of her eyes.

"You know," Sophia said softly, "grief doesn't only belong to death. Sometimes the hardest grief is for what could have been."

Robin bit her lip hard. "I don't want this to undo me. I've worked too hard."

Sophia nodded. "Then maybe don't see it as undoing. Maybe it's unfolding. A chance to look at what's still locked away. You don't have to rush. But you don't have to hide either."

Robin stared at her hands. "He asked me to dinner."

"And how do you feel about that?"

Robin laughed again, but it cracked in the middle. "Terrified. Curious. Furious. Hopeful. All of it. Which probably means I'll say yes."

Sophia smiled, warm but firm. "Then say yes. But walk in with your eyes open. Not the fifteen-year-old's eyes. The woman you are now."

Robin closed her eyes, inhaling deeply, holding that truth like a fragile thing.

"Sophia, what things do you still think are locked away?"

"What makes you ask?"

Robin rubbed her temples, voice low. "Well, the last few weeks, since the principal was granted parole and then Danny just showing up at The Bean out of the blue, I'm shaky all the time. I can't seem to keep my mind focused, even at work—where I'm usually at my best. I can't sleep, and when I finally do drift off, I wake up within minutes. I can't even imagine that the two things are connected, but it feels like any semblance of control I thought I had is slipping away quickly. I'm not sure what to do."

Sophia tilted her head, thoughtful. "Robin, it makes sense you're unsettled. Danny was your safe place back then. Even if you couldn't name it, your heart knew it. And now that he's back, that sense of safety is colliding with the memories you tried to bury. Safety can stir what danger forced you to lock away."

The words hit Robin with the force of recognition. Safe place. She hadn't wanted to admit it, but it was true. When Rick's shadow had been suffocating, it had been Danny's presence—his grin, his steady walk beside her—that had kept her breathing. And when he left, that safety left with him.

Sophia's voice cut gently through the silence. "Sometimes, when the body feels safe again, the memories it's been holding down rise to the surface. Not to break you. To be healed."

Robin's breath caught, sharp in her chest. "Then why does it feel like I'm coming apart?"

"Because healing often feels like unraveling at first," Sophia said softly. "But unraveling is not the same as breaking. It's the beginning of weaving something new."

Robin sat very still, pressing those words into her bones. Somewhere beneath her fear, beneath her anger, a small, dangerous spark of hope flickered.

Chapter 16

The restaurant was warm, golden light spilling from candles on each table, soft jazz curling in the background. Robin paused just inside the doorway, tugging her coat tighter around her shoulders as if she could still turn back.

Then she saw him.

Danny rose immediately, just as he always had—awkwardly polite—pulling out her chair before she even reached the table. Some habits never died.

"Robin," he said softly.

Her name in his voice made something low in her chest tighten. She forced her chin higher. "Danny."

They sat. Menus became shields, their eyes darting everywhere but across the table. Finally, she ordered wine. He followed suit. The waiter left, and silence pressed in, heavy and expectant.

Robin broke it first. "So . . . small-town dining hasn't changed. Same specials as ten years ago."

Danny chuckled, the sound both familiar and foreign. "True. Though I guess I've changed a bit."

She arched a brow. "Still the faithful, loving son, back to help your folks decide whether or not to downsize? Is that why you came back?"

"Well, it's part of it," he admitted. "I haven't exactly been the attentive son. When Rick died, my parents sank into grief—and I just . . . left. Told myself it was for college, for work, but really? I couldn't face them. I couldn't explain what was happening inside me because I barely understood it myself."

Robin's expression softened for a moment. "Sometimes just being present can be healing." She shook her head quickly, not letting herself go down that road. "At least you're here now. I'm sure they appreciate it."

"I wrote letters. Told them how school was going. But I could never bring myself home. I thought I'd screwed up too badly to explain. And not saying goodbye to you . . . " He broke off, his throat tight. "I convinced myself I was doing you a favor."

The food came—plates of pasta and salad they barely touched. Their conversation stumbled from weather to business to the fall festival on the square. Harmless things. Safe things. Until Danny set his fork down and looked at her with eyes that hadn't aged out of honesty.

"I've thought about this," he said quietly. "For years. About you."

Robin's fork froze halfway to her mouth. She set it down slowly. Her voice was steady, though her pulse thrummed in her throat. "Then why did you leave?"

His jaw tightened. He exhaled, leaning back. "Because staying would've meant dragging you into something darker than you could have imagined. And I . . . I couldn't bear for you to get hurt."

Anger flashed, sharp and hot. "You don't get to decide what I could or couldn't handle. You disappeared, Danny. No explanation. No goodbye." Her voice caught before she could stop it. "Do you have any idea what that did to me?"

The rawness in her words silenced the table beside them. Danny's gaze dropped to his hands. "I know. I've replayed it a thousand times. It was cowardly. But if I told you everything back then . . . " He shook his head. "I'm sorry. There's so much to say. And I'm not even sure how to begin."

Robin swallowed hard. Part of her wanted to leave. Part of her wanted to throw her glass at him. And part of her—traitorous, aching—wanted to reach across the table and take his hand.

Instead, she sat very still, the weight of twenty-five years pressing between them. She forced a small smile. "My therapist always says the best way is straight through—one baby step at a time."

Danny flinched before he could stop himself. Therapy. Of course she'd needed it. And where had he been? Running. Always running.

He cleared his throat. "One thing I knew, even back then, was that everything was screwed up all around me. I felt caught in the middle of a tangled web and needed to get free before I could think straight. Leaving seemed like the only option. Stupid, selfish, naïve, maybe even cruel—but I couldn't breathe under the grief and guilt."

Robin's voice dropped, gentler now. "Danny . . . you were my safe place. The one who cared, who made me feel seen. You were my best friend."

His eyes darkened. "I tried. God knows I tried. But the more I saw, the more I realized you were in danger—and Rick was in deeper than either of us knew. I only caught pieces of it, fragments. Never enough to protect you the way I wanted."

Her throat closed. Hearing it out loud made her chest ache in places she hadn't let herself feel in years.

Silence stretched. Only the clatter of dishes and the closing chatter of staff remained. They looked around and realized they were the last ones in the restaurant.

Robin cleared her throat softly. There was so much left unsaid, and yet both of them needed time to process.

Danny's voice dropped, low and earnest. "I'm not asking for forgiveness. Just . . . a chance to explain. A chance to be here now. With you."

Robin searched his face—the lines around his eyes, the silver at his temples, the familiar earnestness that had always undone her. Her heart whispered yes. Her pride whispered no.

Finally, she nodded once. "There's so much to say. But maybe . . . tomorrow. Fresh. In the light of day. You're just a few houses away—why don't you come by for coffee in the morning?"

Danny's smile was small, almost cautious, but in his eyes there was relief—and the faintest flicker of hope. "I'd like that."

He stood and offered to walk her to her car.

Outside, a light sprinkle misted the air, cool and refreshing. They lingered, standing close, the warmth of their bodies mingling with rain and unspoken words. For the first time in years, tomorrow didn't feel impossible.

At her car, he opened the door for her, the consummate gentleman. "Shall I come by around ten?"

"That works. Thanks for dinner."

Their eyes held, the air thick with longing and hesitation. After one last searching look, Danny whispered, "Till then."

Reluctantly, he turned away and walked slowly to his own car.

Chapter 17

Even though she'd been expecting it at ten o'clock on the dot, the knock on the door startled her. Robin smoothed her sweater with both palms, breathed once, and opened it.

Danny stood there, the faintest smile on his lips, and for an instant the years between them collapsed. The rich scent of coffee and freshly baked quiche drifted past her, and he inhaled. "Smells amazing," he said. "You always did know how to make a place feel . . . alive."

She stepped aside, gesturing him in. The little table was already set, quiche cooling beside a bowl of fruit, flowers from her garden tucked into a jar. A picture of control, though inside she felt anything but.

"I'm glad you're here, Danny," she admitted, her voice low. "But God, I feel so vulnerable. Shaky. And I'd never tell that to anyone but you."

He met her eyes, steady, gentle. "You amaze me, Robin. Always have. That mix of gentleness and strength—you've been holding the world together for as long as I've known you."

She blinked back the sudden sting in her eyes. "Coffee?"

"Only if you share."

They chuckled, breaking the tension. Robin carried two steaming mugs onto the porch, Danny trailing behind. The rocking chairs waited, familiar as old friends. They sat, the motion grounding them, the morning alive with the rustle of leaves and the bright chatter of birds.

For a few minutes, they said nothing, letting the air between them settle. Robin could feel her heartbeat slowing with the rhythm of the chairs. It felt like both an ending and a beginning.

Danny spoke first. "Last night was . . . good. Hard, but good. I can't expect you to forgive me, not yet, maybe not ever. But I hope—" His voice caught. "I hope you'll let me try. We've both carried different stories through these last twenty-five years, both half-blind, both heavy. Maybe it's time we start weaving them together."

Robin's fingers tightened on her mug. She stared into the coffee, watching the ripples settle. "Danny, you said last night that you left because you knew things . . . things you couldn't tell me. What were you afraid of?"

He drew in a slow breath, rocking once, twice. "That if I said it out loud, it would crush you. That you'd look at me and see failure—for not stopping it, for not protecting you, for not protecting Rick either. I saw enough to know something was wrong. The bruises you tried to hide. The way you went quiet when he was around. And Rick . . . " Danny's voice dropped, heavy with memory. "There was something in his eyes I couldn't unsee. Like he was carrying someone else's darkness. I only had pieces. Not enough to put the puzzle together, but enough to know it was poison."

Robin's breath snagged, her throat tight. Images flickered at the edges of her mind—Rick's temper, his control, the secrets she had buried so deep she had convinced herself they weren't there.

"Danny . . . " Her voice was almost a whisper. "I don't remember everything. Not clearly. But I know something happened. I feel it more than I see it. And with you back . . . it's like the lock is breaking open."

He turned toward her, his gaze unwavering. "Then let it come as it will. You don't have to force it. And you don't have to face it alone. Not this time."

The porch went still, save for the creak of rocking wood. Robin gripped her coffee tighter, the warmth seeping into her hands. For the first time in decades, she felt like maybe—just maybe—her safe place had returned.

Robin studied him, the rocking chair creaking under her weight. "Danny . . . what *have* you been doing all this time? You vanish, and now you just . . . show up. I don't know who you are anymore."

He leaned forward, elbows braced on his knees, coffee cradled in his hands. For a moment he looked younger, like the boy she remembered, searching for words. Then he exhaled, steady.

"After I left, I thought I'd go to college, keep my head down, just . . . disappear into normal. But normal didn't stick. I studied psychology because I wanted to understand people like Rick—like me, even. Why we make the choices we do. Why some survive what others don't." His mouth twisted faintly. "That degree didn't fix anything, but it gave me language for what I'd seen."

Robin felt her chest tighten. *What I'd lived,* she thought, though she didn't say it.

Danny went on. "I worked as a cop in my college town after that. At first, it was just routine—DUIs, bar fights, petty theft. But every now and then, something darker slipped through. A runaway girl. A house raid where the kids were living like prisoners. And I started seeing patterns—things that reminded me of . . . back here." He paused, his gaze catching hers, though neither of them said Rick's name.

"And the more I saw, the less I could ignore it. So I dug deeper. Took training. Found mentors. One job led to another. By the time I realized it, I wasn't just policing—I was tracking trafficking cases. Working with nonprofits, then federal task forces. Somewhere along the way it stopped being just about . . . penance." He swallowed. "It became the only thing that made sense of what happened to us."

Robin's grip tightened around her mug. The word *us* rang in her ears, a reminder that he'd seen more than she ever wanted anyone to see.

"I heard . . . " she began, then hesitated. *Confidential,* she remembered. The group was a circle of trust. But Tanya's voice lingered in her memory—*Danny Kessler, speaker in Kenya.* Robin's breath caught. "I heard somewhere that you've spoken. At conferences. About trafficking."

His eyes flickered—surprise, maybe even guilt. But he nodded. "I have. Sometimes I wish I didn't have to. Every time I stand up there, it's like I'm back on the ridge, trying to shout down what I couldn't stop. But if my voice helps wake people up—if it saves one kid from living what you . . . " He stopped himself, jaw tight. "What others have lived through—then maybe it's worth carrying."

The morning hung quiet between them. Birds still sang, leaves rustled, but Robin felt the porch tilt beneath her, like truth was pushing up from the ground.

She swallowed. "Danny, I don't remember all of it. Not clearly. But I know enough to know it wasn't just Rick being cruel. There was more. And maybe . . . maybe you saw pieces I've buried."

His gaze softened. "I did. And I should have said something. Should have done more. But Robin—" He reached out, stopping short of her hand. "I'm here now. And if you ever want to unlock those memories, if you ever need to put the pieces together . . . I'll be here."

Robin rocked once, slowly, her chair creaking in rhythm with his. Vulnerability felt dangerous on her tongue, but the porch, the coffee, and Danny's steady eyes made it almost possible.

Almost.

The porch held them in a cocoon of autumn quiet, rocking chairs creaking, coffee cooling between their palms. The silence between them wasn't only absence—it was presence, thick with what they'd begun to name.

Robin drew in a breath, steadying herself. "Danny, I don't know how to do this."

He gave a half-smile, tired but warm. "Neither do I. But I think we've got time."

The rocking slowed, then stopped. She stood, gathering herself. "Come inside. I made breakfast."

In the kitchen, the air was rich with the scent of baked eggs and herbs, the quiche she'd pulled together in a moment of restless nerves. A small vase of marigolds sat in the middle of the table, bright against the soft morning light.

Danny's brow lifted as he took it in. "You've gone domestic on me."

Robin rolled her eyes, but there was a flicker of humor. "Don't get used to it. I live on takeout and coffee most days. This is . . . Sandra's influence. My functional medicine doctor. She's been nudging me toward actual food."

He chuckled, settling into a chair. "Remind me to thank Sandra. This smells amazing."

They served themselves in companionable quiet. Robin set out berries and poured more coffee, her hands steadier now with the ritual of it. For a while, the talk was easy—travel stories, old classmates, how the town had both changed and stayed the same. She found herself laughing once, startled at the sound in her own mouth.

Danny watched her, not intrusively, but with the kind of attention that had always made her feel seen. Between bites, he said softly, "You know, Robin . . . you don't have to carry all of it alone anymore. Not with me back here."

Her fork paused, then lowered to the plate. She held his gaze. Vulnerability still felt like a cliff edge—but maybe, just maybe, she wasn't standing at it alone this time.

"Don't make promises you can't keep, Danny," she said, her voice quiet but steady.

He leaned back, a hand wrapped around his mug. "Then let's start with the ones I can."

The morning light stretched wider across the kitchen table, touching the marigolds, the coffee steam, the space between them. The years between them no longer felt insurmountable. They felt like a bridge waiting to be crossed—slowly, one step at a time.

After breakfast, the day opened wide with crisp sunlight and a sky so blue it seemed almost too much. Robin slipped on her jacket and, almost against her own instincts, said, "Want to walk a bit? The town looks pretty in the fall."

Danny smiled—gentle, relieved. "I'd like that."

They strolled down Main Street, leaves crunching underfoot, the air tinged with chimney smoke and the faint sweetness from the bakery. The shop windows were dressed with cornstalks and pumpkins, banners for the upcoming Fall Festival fluttering in the breeze.

Robin pointed toward the corner by the old hardware store. "Do you remember when you and Rick tried to ride your bikes off that loading dock?"

Danny groaned, shaking his head. "Don't remind me. Rick broke his handlebars, and I skinned half my face."

"You lied to your mom and said you ran into a fence," Robin said, grinning. "I think she believed you, but your dad didn't."

They both laughed—an easy, surprised sound that lightened something heavy between them.

A little further down, they paused outside the bookstore with its peeling green paint. Danny glanced at the display in the window. "Still the same sign, still the same creaky door."

Robin smirked. "And still the same Mrs. Callahan, glaring if you touch a book without washing your hands."

"God, she terrified me," Danny admitted. "But you . . . you marched in there like you owned the place."

"That was the only place in town I felt brave," Robin said softly, almost to herself. Then, more briskly: "She had the best Nancy Drew collection."

Danny glanced at her, catching the flicker of vulnerability before it was tucked away again. He let it be. Instead, he pointed toward the park across the street, where kids scrambled over a jungle gym that had long ago replaced the old rusted swings.

"Want to loop through the park?"

Robin nodded, and they crossed at the light. For a while, they walked in companionable silence, the sound of children's laughter carrying on the breeze.

Finally, Danny said, "You know, this—walking here with you—it almost feels normal. Like we could just be two old friends catching up."

Robin's voice was quiet, thoughtful. "Maybe that's exactly what we are. Maybe that's where we start."

Their steps fell into rhythm, leaves crunching, the town moving gently around them. For the first time in years, Westridge didn't feel like only a place of shadows. It felt like somewhere a new story might actually begin.

He admitted, almost reluctantly, that he'd need to help his parents begin clearing out the house. "They've never even touched Rick's room, Robin. Twenty-five years . . . it's like time just froze there. You can imagine the clutter we'll have to face before we can even think about putting it on the market."

Her voice softened. "I'll be here if you need me."

He looked at her, steady for once. "Me too."

They walked back to her house together, where he helped her tidy the dishes, both moving through the easy rhythm of shared silence. Then, with a quiet nod, he left to return to his parents'—the weight of the past still between them, but the faintest outline of something new taking shape.

Chapter 18

Danny pushed open the front door, bracing himself against the familiar sag of the hinges. The air inside smelled faintly of mildew and mothballs, undercut with the sharp tang of old paper. Stacks of magazines and unopened mail narrowed the hallway so much he had to turn sideways to pass. It was as though time itself had clogged the arteries of the house.

His parents sat in the living room, the television flickering before them, though their eyes seemed glazed past it. Watching—or simply marking the hours—he couldn't tell. The sight pierced him like an arrow. Twenty-five years of silence. Twenty-five years of grief calcified into routine. And he had left them to it.

He drew a breath through his teeth, let it out hard. "I think I'll get started in Rick's room."

Both parents turned sharply, his mother's face blanching as if he'd struck her. His father's gaze stayed locked on the screen.

"Oh, Danny," his mother whispered, "I've never touched a thing in there. Or in your room either. Some part of me always hoped you'd both come back."

Danny swallowed, throat raw. "Then maybe it's time. Things can't stand still forever."

His mother's lips trembled, but then she surprised him—squaring her shoulders. "You're right. It's time. We need to clean out the closets of our lives and start living again, even if it's only what's left of our living."

Danny placed a hand briefly on hers. "Why don't you and Dad step outside for a while? Take in some fresh air. I walked through town with Robin earlier—the air was crisp, full of fall. Might do you good." He hesitated, realizing the words applied just as much to himself. "Might do us all good."

Half an hour later he returned from Home Depot, arms laden with boxes, tape, and markers. The sound of the cardboard snapping into shape felt almost satisfying—something orderly, something he could control.

Rick's room hit him like a wall. The stale scent of mildew and dust. Posters curling at the edges, clothes spilling from drawers. Shoes lined up like soldiers gone AWOL. He forced himself to begin methodically: jackets in one box, jeans in another, shirts folded with hands steadier than he felt.

For a moment, he let the rhythm soothe him. But as he worked, the memories surged: Rick's possessiveness of Robin, the bruises Danny had glimpsed once on her upper arms, the way Rick had grown withdrawn and mean those last two years. Danny's chest tightened. What had he been thinking, leaving her then? What had Rick been thinking, pulling her so far into his darkness?

He shook his head hard, returning to the task. Shoes into a box, shoeboxes stacked. And then—something different. A small cardboard file box, tucked under the bed, nearly lost in the dust. He dragged it out, expecting old homework or comics.

Inside: a jumble of receipts, scraps of paper, and . . . a ledger.

Danny flipped it open. His stomach clenched. Columns. Names. Amounts. Dates. The handwriting jagged but deliberate. He read a line, then another—his breath catching.

And suddenly bile surged hot in his throat. He stumbled into the bathroom, clutching the porcelain as his stomach emptied violently.

When he finally raised his head, sweat beading at his temple, the reflection in the mirror stared back hollow-eyed.

"What the hell," he whispered hoarsely. "What the living hell . . . "

Danny sat on the edge of the bed, the ledger open in his lap. His hands shook as he turned the pages again and again, the neat columns searing into his mind like neon signs: dates, amounts, initials—each one undeniable, each one pointing to a truth he had refused to name.

It was proof. Cold. Meticulous. The kind of proof he had dreaded and long suspected.

His eyes blurred, but he couldn't stop scanning, couldn't stop tracing the handwriting as though a new detail might change the meaning. Round and round his thoughts went, the wheel spinning faster until he thought his skull might split from the pressure. He had wanted so badly to believe that Rick's darkness was only anger, only rebellion. But this—this was commerce. Exploitation. Organized.

He pressed the ledger shut, only to open it again seconds later, trapped in the cycle. Memories rose unbidden: Robin's bruised arms, Rick's haunted eyes, the tight way he'd snapped at anyone who came near her. Danny had wanted to protect her, to save him, and he had failed both.

For a long time he simply sat there, the stench of dust and old sweat thick around him, the nausea still burning the back of his throat. Twenty-five years gone—flushed away with the contents of his stomach.

Finally, he dragged his hands down his face and whispered the question he'd avoided since he left town: *What do I do?*

And then, as though Sophia herself had whispered it into the air, he remembered what Robin had told him the night before—her therapist's words: *Sometimes the only way out is through. One step at a time.*

Danny closed the ledger with finality, this time not reopening it. His pulse steadied, a strange calm threading through the horror. The hamster wheel slowed, then stopped.

This couldn't sit buried in a box another twenty-five years. It had to end.

He stood, tucking the ledger under his arm. For the first time since Rick's death, he felt something like clarity.

"It stops now," he said into the empty room. His voice was quiet, but it carried the weight of resolve.

Three Doors

Danny sat on the edge of Rick's bed, the ledger open across his knees like some cursed relic. He'd read the same page five times now, but the numbers didn't blur the way he wanted them to. They burned. A litany of names, initials, payments, scrawled in his brother's uneven hand. Denial wasn't possible anymore.

The house was still, save for the muted drone of the TV down the hall where his parents sat half-watching, half-sinking into their own silence. The air smelled of dust and old grief. He ran a hand down his face and exhaled, long and hard, the sound almost a growl.

What now, Danny?

He stared at the ceiling, as if it might give him an answer, then dropped his gaze back to the pages.

Door number one: Robin.

Tell her. Lay it bare. She deserved to know—hell, she lived it. She was the one who'd paid the highest price. She'd hidden her scars under the armor of confidence and bravado, but he'd seen the tremor in her hand at The Bean, the way her plate crashed when his name was spoken. He could be honest with her now, respect her strength, and maybe—finally—make her feel less alone.

But then the image rose: Robin pale, shaking, her control slipping. Sophia's words echoing through her. *I can't sleep . . . my mind won't stay still . . .* He could crush her with this too soon. He could lose her all over again.

Door number two: a colleague.

Practical. Call one of the guys he'd worked with back in his cop days, someone who knew procedure. Evidence. Chain of custody. Protect the victim, protect the case. That route meant safety, order, maybe even justice.

But it also meant exposure. Once the system had it, the story would spiral, names pulled in, questions asked. Robin's life laid bare without her choosing it. He'd sworn never again to take choice away from her. Could he risk that? Could he betray her like that, even in the name of protecting her?

Door number three: his mother.

She'd kept Rick's room frozen for twenty-five years, as though grief could be preserved like a shrine. Maybe she knew more than she ever said. Maybe she'd seen things, heard things, pieced together things in the silence. If anyone held a missing piece of the puzzle, it might be her.

But her eyes earlier—horror at the suggestion of opening this door. She'd survived only by *not* looking too closely. If he forced her to, it could shatter her. And what kind of son does that?

Danny pressed the heels of his hands into his eyes, the ledger slipping closed on his lap.

Robin. Colleague. Mother. Heart, head, history.

He rocked forward, elbows braced on his knees, breath coming shallow. For years he'd avoided this moment, pretended time would dull it, distance would dissolve it. But now the truth sat in cardboard and ink, undeniable.

Sophia's voice—though he'd never met her—came back to him through Robin's words. *Sometimes the only way out is through. One step at a time.*

Danny swallowed hard. One step. But which?

His pulse hammered, the room spinning with memory and dread. Then, with a sharp inhale, he straightened. Whatever the first step was, it had to happen *now*. Not tomorrow. Not another twenty-five years.

He slid the ledger into a box and taped it shut, his hands shaking but firm. "Enough," he whispered to the empty room. "It ends here. One step at a time."

Chapter 19

Danny poked his head into the living room, where the glow of the television flickered against his parents' still faces. The sound was on, but he doubted either of them was watching. They were just . . . sitting. As they had, it seemed, for twenty-five years.

"Hey, Mom," he said softly. "I made us some tea. Will you join me in the kitchen?"

His mother blinked, startled, but then nodded, pushing herself up with the slow grace of someone long accustomed to moving carefully. His father didn't stir.

The kitchen smelled faintly of lemon cleaner, the linoleum floor worn smooth in front of the sink. Danny had already set two mugs on the table, steam curling upward. He gestured for her to sit. She wrapped her hands around the cup as though she were cold, though the room was warm.

He waited a beat before speaking. "Mom . . . as I've been going through Rick's things, boxing up the clothes, folding the pieces that should've been cleared out years ago—I can't shake a feeling. I need to ask you something."

Her eyes flicked to his, then away, wary. "Ask."

"Do you remember anything in those last months—anything about Rick—that disturbed you? Something that made you wonder if he was caught up in something?"

She went very still, the mug trembling slightly in her hands. For a long moment, Danny thought she might not answer. Then she sighed, the sound deep and frayed at the edges.

"He changed," she said finally. "It wasn't gradual. One day he just . . . came home different. His eyes looked dark, older, like they'd seen something I couldn't reach. I asked, once, twice, but he brushed me off. After that, he kept to himself. Started staying out late. Avoided me. And then he began dating Robin . . . " She shook her head, a faint crease between her brows. "That never made sense. Robin was your friend. Your girl, I thought. It felt wrong, all of it. But I told myself it was just rebellion, teenage moodiness. Something he'd outgrow."

Her gaze drifted to the window, but her voice had dropped lower. "Deep down, I think I knew better. I just couldn't bear to name it."

Danny's throat tightened. "I meant to ask him. That's why we went hiking that day. I thought if I got him alone, he'd finally talk. But I never got the chance." He pressed his palms flat against the table. "And now—" He faltered, then forced the words out. "I found a box under his bed. Notes. Receipts. A ledger. Mom, it's dark. Too dark. I can't unsee it."

Her fingers whitened around the cup. "What kind of dark?"

"The kind that makes me sick just reading it." His voice cracked, raw. "The kind that explains the anger in his eyes. The weight he carried."

She closed her eyes, shoulders sagging under invisible years. "Oh, Danny. I was afraid of that. I prayed I was wrong. But something had happened to him—I could see it, even if I didn't understand." She opened her eyes again, brimming with tears she refused to let fall. "And then we lost him before we could ever find out what it was."

Danny leaned back, the ledger's memory burning behind his eyes. For the first time in decades, he and his mother sat together in their shared grief, both of them knowing now that silence had been its own kind of prison.

Danny let the words hang, watching his mother's hands tremble around her mug. Finally, he reached into his jacket and pulled out the ledger. "Mom . . . do you want to see it? What I found?"

Her eyes widened, then shuttered. She shook her head, slow and firm. "Not yet. I've lived twenty-five years with ghosts in this house, Danny. If I look at that now, I'm afraid I'll drown in them. You tell me—what do you think you should do?"

Danny swallowed, the weight of her trust pressing on him. He turned the ledger over in his hands, then set it gently on the table between them. "I think . . . I need to talk to Robin. She was closest to him in those last months. She deserves to know. Maybe . . . maybe Sophia could be there, too. A safe place. Someone who can help us navigate it."

His mother's shoulders sagged in relief, though her eyes remained haunted. "Sophia. Yes. She's strong. That woman carries wisdom. If you and Robin must dig this up, better to do it with someone steady beside you."

Danny nodded. He rubbed a hand over his jaw, the decision crystallizing as he said it out loud. "And after that, I'll call an old colleague. A cop I trusted, back when I was on the force. Just . . . hypothetically, at first. See how he thinks I should move forward with this kind of evidence."

His mother reached across the table, laying her hand over his. Her skin was thin, papery, but her grip still carried strength. "It's been too long, Danny. Too many years of silence. If you believe it must stop now—then don't waste another day."

Danny squeezed her hand, feeling the truth of it sink into his bones. Twenty-five years of buried pain was about to break open. For Robin. For Rick. For all of them.

Chapter 20

Robin poured herself a glass of wine, the dark swirl catching lamplight in the quiet of her living room. She told herself it would help settle the nerves, but each sip seemed to deepen the swirl inside her—nervous, excited, scared. Underneath it all pulsed one undeniable truth: Danny. The familiarity of him. The comfort of him, even after twenty-five years.

She was tempted—dangerously tempted—to feel safe again.

Instead, exhaustion won. She rinsed the glass, set it in the sink, and dragged her weary body to the bathroom. The light over the mirror buzzed faintly when she flipped the switch. Robin splashed water across her face, bracing for relief, but when she looked up, her breath caught.

It wasn't her forty-one-year-old face staring back. It was fifteen-year-old Robin: hollow-eyed, too thin, mascara clumped where it had been laid thick to hide the bruises. Her reflection blurred, then sharpened into something worse—the pungent tang of sex, the cheap overlay of lilac perfume, rumpled sheets in a strange bed. For the briefest moment, she saw a shadow in the doorway. Not Rick. An older man. Faceless, but undeniable.

Her whole body shook. She gripped the sink as though it might steady her.

"Oh God," she whispered aloud. "It's happening. It's happening. What am I going to do?"

The mirror returned her own face—present-day Robin, trembling, but no less shaken. The foggy vision clung, visceral, real.

Her instinct was immediate: Sophia.

Hands unsteady, she dialed the number. Predictably, the office line rolled to voicemail. "Sophia," she said, her voice breaking. "It's happening. Can I come in? Call me as soon as you can." She hung up, pressing the phone tight to her chest as though it could absorb her panic.

She forced herself to breathe. Once. Twice. Three times. "I am safe," she whispered with each exhale. "I am grounded. Danny is back."

She clung to ritual then—washing her face again, brushing her teeth, combing her hair slow and steady. Movements that tethered her to the present, pulling her back from the fog.

When she finally crawled beneath the covers, darkness pressing close, Robin clasped her hands together like a child at prayer. "God, please," she whispered. "I need to sleep."

Chapter 21

They had agreed—without needing many words—that if anything more was to be said, it had to be here. Neutral ground. Safe ground.

Sophia's office smelled faintly of lavender and chamomile tea, the same as it had twelve years ago when Robin first walked in desperate for air. Books lined the walls, spines worn, titles about grief, resilience, trauma. A single quilt draped across the back of the couch, stitched in deep blues and soft creams. The lamp beside Sophia's chair cast a steady, unblinking light.

Robin sat first, perching on the edge of the same chair she always claimed, arms folded tightly across her chest. Danny lowered himself onto the couch opposite her, broad shoulders slightly hunched, hands clasped between his knees like he was bracing for impact. He looked out of place—like a man carrying the weight of the world into a room designed for laying burdens down.

Sophia entered quietly, her presence soft yet commanding. She settled into her chair and took them both in with those steady eyes that had a way of making silence feel less like a void and more like a vessel.

"It seems," she said gently, "there are threads between you— threads that never quite frayed, even when you both walked away."

Robin's laugh was brittle. "Walked away? He disappeared."

Danny didn't flinch at the bite. He drew in a long breath. "I left. Because I thought staying would break you worse than leaving."

Sophia glanced at Robin. "How does it feel to hear that?"

Robin's eyes filled before she could stop them. She blinked hard, jaw tight. "Like a lie. Like an excuse. He was my safe place, Sophia.

The one person who made me feel like I wasn't drowning. And then—gone. No explanation. Just gone."

Danny's voice cracked. "You don't know what I saw. What I suspected. With Rick. With . . . " He faltered, his hands flexing against each other. "I didn't have the words back then. I barely have them now. But I knew you were in danger, Robin. And I couldn't fix it. Not at seventeen."

The silence that followed was heavy, electric. Robin's breath shuddered out. Images flashed—her gaunt reflection in the mirror, bruises beneath too much makeup, that faceless man in the shadows.

Sophia leaned forward, her tone even, grounding. "Robin, you said last time that something inside you feels shaky. That the past is pushing forward. Can you let some of it speak now?"

Robin's hands gripped the armrests until her knuckles whitened. For a moment she thought she'd suffocate on the words. Then, slowly, they came. "It wasn't just Rick. There were . . . others. I didn't remember clearly, not until this week. Just flashes—hotel sheets, perfume that made me sick, a man's voice I didn't know. I thought I'd buried it all. But now it's clawing back."

Danny's head dropped into his hands. A sound broke from him—half groan, half prayer. "God, Robin. I didn't know how far it had gone. I suspected . . . but I didn't know."

Sophia let the silence hold them. Not to avoid the truth, but to make room for it.

Finally, she said, "The fact that both of you are here, now, means there's still courage in the story. Robin—you survived. Danny—you're choosing not to run anymore. That's where we begin. One step, then another."

Robin wiped at her face with the back of her hand. Danny lifted his head, eyes raw.

And for the first time in twenty-five years, they sat together with the truth between them—not all of it, not yet, but enough to know the rest could no longer stay buried.

Sophia let Robin's words settle into the quiet, her gaze steady but gentle. Then she turned slightly toward Danny. "And you," she said, "have carried your own silence all these years. Would you like to put any of that into the room now?"

Danny's jaw worked, as if the words had to break through stone before they could emerge. He clasped his hands tighter, then finally looked up. "I left because I thought it was the only way to make sense of what I was seeing. I didn't have language for it then—but I knew enough to know it was wrong. What Rick was doing. What others might have been doing." His voice cracked. "And I hated myself for not stopping it."

Robin flinched, tears threatening again, but Sophia lifted a hand slightly, holding space for him to continue.

"So I ran. But I didn't run away—not really. I studied. I became a cop in my college town. Thought I could make up for what I'd failed to do. Thought if I could put away enough bad men, I'd balance the scales. Later, I worked with units focused on trafficking—first in the States, then overseas. Cambodia, Kenya, Malawi. Places where the patterns were the same, just more visible. I've spent twenty-five years trying to understand the machine that chewed up Rick . . . and tried to chew up you, Robin."

Robin's hands tightened in her lap, trembling. He saw it, but pressed on.

"I don't have all the answers. But I know enough now to recognize the signs I missed back then. And I know this—secrets left in the dark only grow teeth. They have to be dragged into the light."

Sophia's voice was calm, grounding them both. "That's part of what therapy is. Confidentiality gives you a container, a place to examine what feels unbearable without fear of it spilling everywhere."

Danny nodded, his expression raw. "That's why I want us—" he glanced at Robin, careful, searching—"to keep working here. Under your guidance. Because this isn't just Robin's story, or Rick's, or mine. It's tangled. And if we're going to make any sense of it, it has to start with truth in a safe place."

He leaned back, breathing hard, then added almost reluctantly, "I've also been thinking about reaching out to an old colleague from my police days. Just . . . hypothetically. To ask what steps might need to be taken if what I found in Rick's things points to something bigger, something still alive. But before I do that, I needed this. To say it out loud here. To let someone else hold part of it."

Sophia folded her hands in her lap. "That sounds like wisdom. First step: name it. Second step: decide together what to do with it."

Robin pressed her palms against her knees, grounding herself. Her voice was rough, but steady. "Then maybe this is the first step."

For the first time since sitting down, Danny allowed himself to lean back, not in relief, but in readiness. He had carried this weight alone long enough.

Chapter 22

The narrow stairwell creaked under their boots as the women climbed to the "upper room," the laughter already spilling upward ahead of them. Robin carried a white bakery box in one arm, shaking it at the others like a confession.

"Don't even start," she said. "It's my turn for dessert, and no, I didn't bake. I keep the bakery in business. Frankly, it's why I sell so many houses—I don't waste my time with pie crust."

Sandra chuckled, her scarf slipping off one shoulder. "Busy is one thing, but you are doing great at CrossFit, Robin. I can see it. How's your energy outside the gym?"

Robin gave a theatrical sigh. "Let me grab my coffee before I admit anything. You'll hear it all in the hot seat."

The familiar space welcomed them. Ingrid had already prepared the room, as she always did—candles flickering in mason jars along the windowsills, a bouquet of fading dahlias from her garden brightening the table, chairs drawn into a circle. The windows were cracked open just enough for the crisp October air to slip in, carrying the smell of woodsmoke and damp leaves. Coffee percolated in the corner, the rich aroma mingling with the pastries Robin laid out.

At seven on the dot, they each found a seat. Then, like children caught breaking a rule, they grinned at one another and stood again—reshuffling chairs, scraping across the floor. Ingrid lifted her brows in mock severity. "Change your place, change your perspective." The ritual always broke the ice. By the time they sat again, they were smiling like conspirators.

Ingrid held her hands palms-up, her voice low and steady. "Breathe with me. Inhale—take in the love and humor in this room." A collective breath. "Exhale what drags you down: anger, guilt, unforgiveness." Another. "Breathe in the crispness of the night air,

God's Spirit moving through us. Exhale isolation, fear, loneliness. One more—breathe in well-being, trusting all things are working together for good. Exhale doubt."

The silence afterward held a weight all its own—holy, grounding.

"Gratitude," Ingrid said, her eyes sweeping the circle. "Who will start us off?"

Patsy lifted a hand. "I will." Her voice was warm but tentative. "I walked in restless tonight. Tired of tennis games and mahjong and wondering what on earth my life amounts to. But this week I started volunteer work. And it felt like a piece of me woke up that I'd buried. It's messy, it's real, and it makes me feel useful again."

Sandra's face softened. "That's beautiful, Patsy. And me? I'm grateful for something harder. My marriage—it's unraveling. But we're managing mediation with respect, even care, and that's no small thing. It still hurts like hell, but it isn't destroying me."

Tanya nodded, her auburn hair catching the lamplight. "Good for you, Sandra. And me—well, my gratitude's for work too. My book. *My Money, My Life*, has been the ride of my life, and this week I signed a second contract. I can't say more yet, but just knowing it's coming—" she pressed her hand to her heart, eyes shining. "It feels like fresh wind in my sails."

Melody clapped her hands together. "Tanya, that's amazing. And I've got news too—Bruce's network is funding our Cambodia trip. Finally, a documentary I don't have to scrape to fund myself. We leave in a few days. I even hope to interview Danny Kessler while he's here. Did you know he's back in town?"

Robin's spine went rigid, her hands tightening on her mug. Tanya, sitting close enough to notice, shot her a quick glance—steady, protective. Robin forced a smile. "That's . . . wonderful for you, Melody. Congratulations."

Rebecca shifted in her seat, speaking next. "My gratitude is clarity. At work, I've been sorting which cases line up with my values and which don't. My husband and I have had late-night talks about it, and for once, it feels like we're steering together. It's a gift."

Ingrid let the moment linger, weaving the threads together in her usual way. "Do you see it? Gratitude lifts the frequency in this room, so the truth can breathe here. Every share adds light."

Her gaze rested on Robin. "Your turn. Hot seat."

Robin inhaled sharply, her eyes darting toward the pastries she'd brought. Her armor. Her distraction. Then she set her coffee down, folding her hands. "Most of you know I keep things close. Too close. Success has been my way of staying safe. But . . . " She hesitated, searching the faces around her. "I want to share this much. My therapist, Sophia—she's been a lifeline for me. Recently we've cracked open memories I didn't even know were there. I'm not ready to share the details, not yet. But I need something from you."

The women leaned closer. Robin's voice lowered, trembling but steady enough. "Hold me in your prayers. In your thoughts. The ground feels shaky, and I don't know where it's leading, but I believe—God help me, I believe—it's toward healing. And maybe toward something bigger than me."

The silence was absolute. Then Patsy reached across, brushing Robin's hand. "You're not alone. Coffee, my place. Any time."

Others murmured the same. "Wine," Tanya offered softly. "Or chai. Your choice."

Ingrid's eyes glistened as she looked at each woman, one by one. "This is why we gather. A burden shared is lighter. A light joined to others becomes brighter. Remember: journal this week. One action, no matter how small, that carries you forward. Even in the darkness, this—" she swept her hand around the circle—"is what healing feels like."

"Oh, before I forget—the Fall Festival's this weekend. I'll be there with Sophia, Winsome, and Anna. Why don't you all stop by? It might be nice to meet outside these four walls, in the fresh air, surrounded by music and kettle corn."

"Thanks for the reminder, Ingrid." A ripple of nods moved around the circle, a few smiles breaking out as someone added, "It might actually be fun." The women murmured in agreement, the thought of cider and fiddles lingering in the air like a promise.

The group rose slowly, almost reluctantly, still carrying the quiet weight of Robin's words. Outside, the night smelled of woodsmoke and falling leaves, the crisp air bracing their cheeks. Though the season pressed heavy with endings, their steps felt lighter—threads of courage stitched tighter between them.

Chapter 23

The air carried that unmistakable October sweetness—the mingling of woodsmoke, cinnamon, and the sharp tang of fresh apples. Lanterns strung between the old oaks flickered in the dusky light as the Westridge Fall Festival spun itself alive on the town green. Children darted past in face paint and knitted scarves, while fiddlers on the bandstand set an old-time rhythm that kept feet tapping.

Ingrid spotted Winsome and Anna by the cider stand, laughing at something the vendor had said. She raised a hand, then turned to Sophia beside her. "See? Not so scary."

Sophia adjusted her scarf, taking in the bustle. "I'm still not convinced. But . . . it smells better than my office."

"High praise," Ingrid teased.

When they joined the others, Winsome immediately pressed a cup of hot cider into Sophia's hands. "Drink this. It's the cure for everything. Heartache, bad clients, even cold toes."

Anna looped her arm through Sophia's. "And if that fails, we'll bribe you with pie."

Sophia laughed, surprised at how easy it felt. They wandered past pumpkin-carving tables, stopping to admire a lopsided jack-o'-lantern grinning like it knew all the town's secrets. Ingrid bought a bag of kettle corn to share, and the four women found themselves perched on hay bales near the bandstand, boots brushing straw, shoulders pressed close in the crowd.

As the fiddler slid into a reel, Winsome clapped in time, Anna's laughter ringing out beside her. Ingrid leaned back, watching the golden light fall across Sophia's face. She saw the shift—the therapist who carried so many stories was, just for tonight, simply a woman among friends.

Sophia sipped her cider, cheeks pink from the firelight. "All right," she admitted. "You win. This was worth it."

Ingrid squeezed her hand. "Told you. Sometimes healing is cider and fiddles."

Just then, Rebecca's voice called from nearby. She and her husband were weaving through the crowd, a banjo slung casually over his shoulder. He was grinning ear to ear, freshly finished with a set alongside the bluegrass band that had just vacated the stage.

"Caught you all in the best spot," Rebecca said warmly, slipping into their circle. "Pete insisted on playing, of course. Can't keep him away from a banjo or a festival."

Pete gave a mock bow, then kissed his wife on the cheek. "You ladies are in for a treat—this town has the best fiddlers east of the mountains." With that, he was drawn back toward the stage as another set kicked off.

Rebecca settled in with them, her face glowing from the firelight and the pride she carried for her husband's music. "We chase bluegrass festivals like some folks chase baseball games. But it feels good to play here, close to home."

The circle expanded easily, Sophia shifting closer, Winsome offering kettle corn, Anna laughing as if they had all been doing this together for years.

The tractor rattled as the wagon rolled forward, hay bales scratchy beneath their coats. Children shrieked with delight when the driver lurched them over a rut, lanterns swaying. Ingrid laughed, steadying Sophia with a hand to her arm.

"Not sure I've done this since I was ten," Sophia admitted, her voice softer than usual. "Back then I thought hayrides were silly. Too simple. Now . . . " She trailed off, eyes lifted to the October stars, breath visible in the chill air. "Now it feels like medicine."

Ingrid gave her a knowing smile. "Sometimes joy is the best therapy."

Sophia chuckled, a little self-conscious, but she didn't move away. Instead she let the sound of fiddles drifting across the fairground wash over her, the warmth of friendship settling in deeper than she'd expected. For once, she wasn't the one listening, holding, advising— she was just another woman on a hayride, bumping along in the dark, and it was enough.

And yet, as she watched the others laughing, Sophia felt a quiet certainty press against her ribs: bonds like these weren't only for nights of kettle corn and carved pumpkins. They were being forged for something deeper, something the town didn't yet know it needed.

Chapter 24

The laughter and music from the Fall Festival drifted faintly through the open window, carried on the crisp October air. Danny paced Rick's room like a man walking a cell, every creak of the floorboards another reminder of the twenty-five years that had been left to rot in here. Boxes half-filled with clothes and books leaned against the wall, but the ledger—Rick's ledger—sat on the desk, its presence too loud to ignore.

He rubbed his palms against his jeans. Everyone else was at the square, sipping cider, clapping along to fiddles, maybe even forgetting their troubles for one night. But Danny's mind spun like a wheel he couldn't slow. The question he'd been avoiding pressed harder: what now?

One name surfaced, steady as a buoy in rough water. Marcus.

He pulled out his phone, scrolling until the old number lit the screen. His thumb hovered for only a second before pressing call.

The line clicked once. "Daniel Kessler," a familiar voice barked. "Lord, I haven't heard from you in years. What's wrong—you need money?"

Danny huffed a humorless laugh. "No, Marcus. I need your wisdom."

That sobered the voice on the other end. "Go on."

Danny hesitated, framing it the only way he knew how. "Hypothetically . . . say I found something. A box hidden under a bed. Ledgers, receipts. They look like records—payments, names, dates. Trafficking. From way back." His throat tightened. "And say the girl involved—she's just now remembering pieces of it, decades later. What would you tell me to do?"

Silence. Then Marcus's voice dropped, the clipped tone of a man still on the job. "First? You don't burn it, don't scatter it. You preserve it. Evidence is oxygen—without it, nothing breathes. Second, you corroborate. One ledger is paper. A pattern is proof. If there's one box, there might be more. Check every closet, attic, garage. People hide things in plain sight."

Danny sat on the edge of Rick's bed, pressing a hand to his forehead. "I was afraid you'd say that."

"And third—listen to me—if she's remembering now, she's fragile. You push too hard, you can shatter her. Protect her first. Case comes after."

Danny swallowed, his chest heavy. "That's what I'm trying to do."

"Good. Because if your timing's right and that principal who went down twenty years ago is walking free, then someone else is still out there. Ledger like that?" Marcus let out a low whistle. "People would kill to keep it buried. Literally."

The words hung between them, stark and cold.

Danny's fingers tightened around the phone. "So . . . what do I do?"

Marcus's answer came firm, measured. "One step at a time. You've always had that savior streak, Danny, but you're not twenty anymore. Don't go charging in like you can fix it all with your fists. If you're going through with this, go smart. And don't go alone."

Danny exhaled, long and hard, his pulse steadying for the first time all day.

"You'll back me up if I need you?"

"You call, I'm there," Marcus said without hesitation. "But start where you are. Protect her. Gather. And Daniel—watch your back."

When the call ended, Danny sat for a long moment in the dim room, the ledger still open on the desk, its ink a map of sins he could no longer ignore. He thought of Robin's trembling voice, Sophia's steady presence, his mother's haunted eyes.

Sometimes the only way out is through, Sophia had told Robin.

He squared his shoulders, closing the ledger carefully, as if it were both weapon and wound. There was no going back now.

Chapter 25

The faint rise and fall of music from the fall festival drifted on the evening breeze, carried over the rooftops like a reminder that the world could still be bright and carefree. Robin, however, stood in her kitchen pouring a glass of wine with hands that weren't entirely steady. The day had left her dizzy, as though her world were spinning beyond her control, and she prayed the wine might blunt the edges.

She stepped outside into the cool night air, settling into the old rocker on her porch. The motion soothed her, slow and steady, as though she were rocking that small, frightened girl who still lived inside her—the girl who needed someone to whisper, *It's going to be all right. You're going to be all right.*

Silence had never been Robin's companion, not comfortably. Tonight, the faint hum of fiddles and laughter from the festival was a lifeline, proof she wasn't completely alone. She took a long swallow of wine, felt its burn trail down her throat, and sent up a quiet, desperate prayer.

Lord . . . You know what went on then. You know what's happening now. You know the blank spaces in my mind. Danny's back. I'm shaking apart, and I don't know why. But if it's time, if You think I'm strong enough . . . help me open up. Help me remember.

Her eyes closed, the rocker's rhythm lulling her. She hadn't realized she'd drifted until a jolt of terror snapped her awake. The images came sharp and merciless: grotesque faces, older men—some heavy, some handsome, all ravenous. Not Rick. Not anyone she knew. Just shadows of hunger and power. But one face rose from the blur, distinct and undeniable—Dr. Denver Pyle, the high school principal, recently granted parole.

Her breath caught hard. She gripped her glass, swallowing fast to push the nausea back, the wine's bitter comfort no match for the wave of disgust that left her trembling.

She set the glass down with shaking hands, whispering into the darkness, "Oh God . . . oh God, what's happening to me?"

Her phone was in her palm before she realized she'd reached for it. She dialed Sophia's number, voice breaking as soon as the voice-mail picked up.

"Sophia, it's happening. The memories . . . they're starting to come. I need to come in, as soon as you can see me. Just me first—I need to get this out before it swallows me whole. And then . . . then we'll bring Danny."

She ended the call, laid the phone in her lap, and pressed her hands against her face. Three deep breaths, the mantra Sophia had taught her: *I am safe. I am grounded.* But tonight, the words felt fragile.

Finally, she dragged herself back inside, clinging to ritual—washing her face, brushing her teeth, combing her hair. Each small act anchored her. Slipping beneath the covers, she whispered one last prayer into the dark.

God, please. Let me sleep. Just for tonight. Please give me rest.

Chapter 26

"Sophia," Robin breathed her name with relief and exasperation all at once. "Thank you so much for letting me come in on your day off. This is . . . it feels like such a privilege."

Sophia's expression softened, steady as always. "Robin, it's no inconvenience. I hold this as a sacred trust. Tell me what's going on."

Robin twisted the tissue in her lap, her throat tight. "Last night, when everybody else was at the fall festival, I stayed home. Sat on the porch with a glass of wine, just rocking. Thought it would help me calm down, maybe help me feel less . . . dizzy. I must've drifted off, because then the flashes started. Faces. Men's faces I didn't recognize but felt familiar. The smell of them. The suffocating air of cheap motels. That same wave of fear and anger rolling inside me like it could split me open. And then—" she drew a shuddering breath— "the principal's face. The one who was just paroled. It was like he was right there in front of me."

Her voice cracked. "After that, the whole night was chaos. Dreams. Confusion. Forgetting who I was for a moment, where I was. I'd wake up shaking, fall back asleep, then start all over again. I wouldn't call it sleep at all." She pressed her palms against her knees. "Sophia, my head is spinning. Spinning. What do I do with this?"

Sophia leaned forward gently, her tone even. "First, let's ground you. Feel your feet on the floor, the weight of your body in this chair. You're safe here, with me. Take a breath in . . . and out. Notice the smell of cinnamon rolls from the bakery next door. Taste the chamomile tea you brought to your lips earlier. This is what our healing journey feels like. Safe. Supported. Strong. You can be here."

Robin closed her eyes, inhaling shakily, then nodded. "Safe. Supported. Strong."

"Good," Sophia said. "Now tell me—what stands out most from those flashes?"

"The feeling," Robin whispered. "Not even the faces, though they were horrible enough. The feeling that I was . . . used. Passed around. Disposable." She swallowed hard. "I always told myself it was just Rick. That it ended when he—" Her voice broke off, and she shook her head violently. "But this? These other men? I don't know what's real and what isn't. And that terrifies me."

Sophia let the silence sit for a moment before speaking. "Robin, what's happening now isn't a betrayal of your healing. It's the next layer of it. Your mind protected you before by shutting things away. Now, with the safety you've built, those memories may be surfacing because you're strong enough to face them."

Tears welled in Robin's eyes, though she fought them back. "Strong? I feel like I'm breaking."

"Breaking open," Sophia corrected softly. "Not down. And you're not alone in this. We'll walk it one step at a time. Just like you told me Danny said last night—you don't have to run. You can go through."

Robin's lips trembled at his name. "Danny . . . I don't know if he's part of the problem or the solution. But when he looks at me, I don't feel invisible anymore. And that scares me too."

Sophia nodded, her voice steady. "That's worth exploring. For now, your job is to notice. Breathe. Name what comes without needing to solve it all today. And remember—you're safe here. And you'll be safe again when you step outside."

Robin nodded slowly, her breathing evening out. For the first time in a long time, the spinning in her chest began to ease.

Chapter 27

Danny woke up Sunday morning feeling like he hadn't slept at all. His call with Marcus the night before replayed in his head in jagged loops—Marcus's steady voice urging patience, caution, *one step at a time*. But patience was the one thing he didn't have. The evidence was here, in this house. Maybe in this very room. And every hour it sat hidden, it felt like a danger waiting to resurface.

He splashed cold water on his face, poured himself a mug of coffee, and stepped outside onto the porch. The crisp air bit at his skin, sharp with the tang of wet leaves and woodsmoke drifting from neighboring chimneys. He inhaled deeply, letting the clean autumn air scrape some of the fog from his head. *Slow down, cowboy,* Marcus would have said. *You'll see straighter when your mind is steady.*

Back inside, Danny walked into Rick's room—the shrine his parents had left untouched for twenty-five years. The air was heavy, carrying the stale mix of life gone by. Posters still curled on the walls, trophies lined neatly on the shelves, frozen in time as if Rick might come back from practice any moment. Danny's chest tightened. This had once been his brother's sanctuary. Now it felt like a mausoleum.

He sat on the bed for a moment, studying the photograph on the desk: him and Rick, arms slung around each other's shoulders, grinning wide, both of them so young, so certain that the world was theirs. A stab of grief and guilt punched through him. He set the photo down gently. "That was then. This is now," he muttered, forcing himself to stand.

He started methodically—bookshelves first, running his hand along the spines, opening notebooks that had gone untouched since high school. Nothing. He pulled open the desk drawers, sifting through loose pencils, ticket stubs, old homework. Then, under the pencil case in the middle drawer, his fingers brushed a worn photograph.

It was Rick and Robin. She couldn't have been more than thirteen, maybe fourteen—too young, far too young. Her makeup was heavy, her smile stretched, but Danny's stomach twisted at her eyes: hollow, bruised shadows beneath them, the sparkle he remembered from childhood gone. Rick looked older, cocky, possessive, his arm clamped around her shoulders. Danny's throat constricted. *Why her, Rick? Why Robin?*

He whispered a prayer, "Show me. Show me what I need to know."

He kept digging. In a folder shoved to the back of the drawer, yellowed with age, his breath caught. A photo of Rick and Dr. Pyle—the principal, grinning like best friends. Pyle's hand rested on Rick's shoulder in a way that now made Danny's skin crawl. He remembered that man hovering at games, clapping Rick a little too hard on the back. At the time, it had seemed like mentorship. Now it reeked of grooming.

Danny turned the page. More photos. Rick and Robin again, but later—their smiles brittle, the tension visible even in the frozen images.

And then the notes. His hands trembled as he unfolded the scraps of paper. "DP" scrawled at the top of some. Neat handwriting, addresses, times. One read: *Meet RB at the Wayside Inn, Sat, 10 am.* Another: *MG at noon. ST at 2. Be prompt.*

Danny's mouth went dry. The initials weren't random. They were people—kids. His classmates, maybe. Or worse.

The words blurred as his eyes burned with rage. His body lurched before he could stop it—he staggered to the bathroom and vomited, retching until there was nothing left but bile and the terrible knowledge that his brother hadn't just been troubled. He had been used. And in turn, he had been made into something Danny could barely allow himself to name.

When he returned to the room, he sat heavily on the bed, folder in his lap, Robin's face staring up from the photo. Her forced smile, her frightened eyes. "I'm so sorry," he whispered, voice breaking. "I should have protected you. I should have seen."

For a long time he just sat there, the weight of twenty-five years pressing down, the hamster wheel of his mind spinning faster with every damning detail. The urge to run, to torch the folder and pretend it had never been found, clawed at him. But Marcus's voice echoed: *Be careful. Be smart. One step at a time.*

Danny drew a ragged breath. Slowly, deliberately, he slid the folder into a cardboard moving box and taped it shut. His hands shook, but the act steadied him. For the first time in decades, he wasn't running from Rick's shadow. He was turning to face it.

And he knew there was no turning back.

"I need to talk with Robin, and then we need to meet with Sophia," he whispered to nobody in particular, as a plan percolated in his brain.

Chapter 28

"Danny," Robin said softly into the phone, her voice trembling but sure. "Can you come over? I need to chat."

"Good timing," he replied. "I need to talk too. I'll be right there."

Not fifteen minutes later, he knocked. By instinct, Robin opened the door and gave him a quick, almost desperate hug, resting her head against his chest for a heartbeat before stepping back. "Come in."

Danny felt both the comfort of her embrace and the sharp edges of terror scratching at his own heart. They sat together in her living room, silent at first, listening to the steady tick of her grandfather clock. Finally, he turned toward her. "What's up?"

Robin swallowed, her voice halting. "I've . . . I've started having flashbacks. Not full stories yet, no clear narrative—but faces, smells, feelings. Like my mind is pounding at the door, trying to get in." Her eyes flicked toward the clock, its tick-tick-tick sounding louder with every word. "I went to see Sophia yesterday morning. On her day off. She made time for me—she always does. She's a lifesaver. And we both agreed . . . it's time for the three of us to meet."

Danny's chest tightened, but he forced himself to breathe. "Make time?" His voice steadied. "Robin, you are my priority. I will make time." He hesitated, then added, "I've made some discoveries while cleaning out Rick's room. Things that confirmed what I feared. Things I wish I could unsee. I even called an old friend—a cop I worked with years ago—for advice. He told me the same thing: it's time. We need Sophia. All of us."

Robin tilted her head, squinting, as though weighing his words. She didn't press him for details, though her silence said she wanted to. Finally, she nodded. "I'll call Sophia. I'm pretty sure she'll find time in the next couple of days."

Danny leaned forward, his gaze steady. "That's good. Safe. Confidential. The right place."

For a moment, neither spoke. The clock ticked on, steady and relentless. Then Robin whispered, almost to herself, "Yes. Sophia's office is where it belongs."

And Danny let out a slow breath, relief and dread knotted together. At last, they had a direction.

When he finally rose to go, Robin walked him to the door, her hand still trembling faintly on the knob. As the latch clicked behind him, she reached for her phone with new resolve. Sophia would hear from her tonight.

Danny, stepping out into the crisp evening air, tightened his coat against the chill. His steps were heavy but certain. Whatever the past had buried, it was time to bring it into the light.

Chapter 29

Sophia's office was quiet except for the faint hum of the heater, the bright afternoon sun slanting across her desk. Robin sat forward on the couch, her hands clenched in her lap. Danny, at first perched stiffly on the edge of the chair beside her, now leaned back as though bracing himself.

Robin's voice cracked the silence. "Sophia, I think it's time. Some things are coming back. Not all of it, not clearly—but enough to terrify me."

Sophia nodded slowly. "Take your time, Robin. What's surfacing?"

Robin swallowed, her throat tight. "Faces. Men's faces—older, different, all blurred, but the feelings . . . those I remember. The smell of cheap hotel rooms, the sick weight of being trapped. And last night, when I closed my eyes, I saw him—Dr. Pyle. Just a flash, but enough. He was there." Her voice faltered. "And I don't know what's memory and what's nightmare anymore."

Danny sat up straighter, his hands gripping his knees. "Robin . . ." He stopped himself, forcing his voice steady. "I've been finding things in Rick's room. Notes, receipts, photographs. Proof that Pyle was tied to him. Proof you weren't imagining this."

Robin turned toward him, eyes wide, filling with both relief and dread. "So it's real."

"It's real," Danny said softly. "Too real."

For a long moment, the only sound was Robin's uneven breathing. Sophia leaned forward, grounding the air between them. "Robin, what you're describing is exactly how trauma resurfaces—flashes, sensations, fragments. It doesn't always return in full sentences. And Danny's discoveries may validate what your body already knows. But validation is not the same as re-traumatization. You're safe here. One step at a time."

Robin nodded shakily, tears streaking her cheeks. "One step at a time."

Sophia let that settle, then turned her gaze on Danny. "And you. You speak as though everything was your failure. That you should have stopped it all. That it's your fault Rick went down that path, your fault Robin suffered."

Danny stiffened. "Well, isn't it? I was there. I saw enough to know something was wrong. And then—then he died, right in front of me. And Robin—" His voice broke. "I left her. I left everything."

"Danny," Sophia said gently but firmly, "you were seventeen. You lost your brother in the most traumatic way imaginable. You lost Robin—your friend, your dream, the one place you felt whole. That day shattered you too."

He shook his head. "I wasn't the victim. She was."

Sophia's voice softened, but didn't waver. "Robin was hurt, yes. But Danny, you were harmed too. Rick's choices, Pyle's corruption, the silence of the adults who should have protected both of you—it rewrote your life. You left town carrying survivor's guilt, grief, and shame that wasn't yours to hold. You've never been allowed to name your own trauma. Have you ever even tried?"

Danny's jaw tightened. He looked down, hands trembling. "I thought if I saved others—if I fought trafficking, exposed it, stopped it somewhere else—maybe it would make up for not saving him. Or her."

Robin's hand, tentative, reached across the couch cushion until her fingers brushed his. "Danny . . . you were my safe place. Even then. You tried. And maybe we both need to stop punishing ourselves for not being able to save each other."

Sophia let the silence linger, sacred and heavy. "What if healing doesn't come from saving? What if it comes from grieving— together—what was stolen from both of you? And then, from choosing what to build next?"

Danny swallowed hard, his eyes damp. Robin squeezed his hand once, then pulled back, wiping her face quickly as though embarrassed. But for the first time, neither of them looked alone.

Sophia leaned back, her voice low and steady. "This is where the work begins. Robin, your memories are surfacing now because you're ready. Danny, your guilt is heavy because you've never faced your own wound. Together, with care, we can hold both truths. And we'll go step-by-step. No rushing. No running. Through."

Robin nodded, whispering, "Through." Danny echoed it under his breath, as though trying the word on for the first time.

And in that quiet agreement, something shifted—the first fragile thread of a new beginning.

Coffee to Go

The late afternoon sun was fading when they stepped out of Sophia's office. For a moment, neither spoke. Robin tugged her coat tighter, Danny shoved his hands in his pockets. The air between them felt thinner now, fragile but strangely steadier than before.

Robin cleared her throat. "I could use some coffee."

Danny gave a half-smile. "So could I. But maybe not The Bean?"

She almost laughed—he'd read her mind. "Definitely not The Bean. Too many eyes. Let's just grab something to go."

A few minutes later they emerged from a corner café with steaming paper cups. No pastries, no chatter, no lingering. Just the comfort of warmth in their hands.

They walked side by side down a quiet street, the crunch of fallen leaves beneath their steps. Robin sipped slowly, the bitter edge grounding her. "It feels strange," she murmured, "having pieces of my life show up like broken glass. Sharp. Dangerous. But at least now I know I'm not crazy."

Danny's jaw flexed. "You were never crazy, Robin. You were hurt. Used. And nobody protected you—not me, not my parents, not the people who should have known better." He paused, staring at the cup in his hands. "Sophia's right. I've been carrying this weight like it was mine alone to fix. But maybe healing isn't about fixing. Maybe it's about . . . walking through it. Together."

Robin glanced at him, the faintest relief flickering in her eyes. "One step at a time," she echoed softly.

They stopped at the corner where their streets divided. Danny shifted, reluctant to let the moment end. "I'll keep looking through Rick's things. If there's more, I'll find it."

Robin nodded, but her voice was firm. "And I'll keep working with Sophia. If I can face what's inside me . . . maybe we can face what's outside together."

For a heartbeat, they stood in silence, the paper cups cooling between their palms, their gazes locked. Then Robin drew in a breath and whispered, "Be careful."

Danny managed a smile, small but real. "You too."

They parted then, each carrying not just their coffee but the fragile hope that the next step—wherever it led—would not be taken alone.

Chapter 30

Early the next morning, when Sophia saw Ingrid waiting at the stop sign, she almost cried. Brushing away the tears pricking at her eyes, she quickened her pace and wrapped Ingrid in a longer-than-usual hug.

"Thank you, Ingrid," she murmured. "For being so steady . . . so loving. For being such a constant part of my life."

Ingrid caught on right away that something was stirring deep inside her friend, but she didn't press. Instead, the two fell into step together, walking in silence.

Overhead, an eagle traced wide circles in the pale November sky—majestic, steady, almost protective. The familiar cows stared as they chewed and chewed, their gaze following the women down the lane. Even that was comforting in its predictability.

The cold sun was just rising, laying a faint gold across the frost-silvered fields, whispering its promise of renewal. Gravel crunched beneath their sneakers, grounding them in rhythm. Both women knew from experience that movement itself could be medicine, washing stress from the body, clearing the mind.

After some time, Sophia exhaled deeply, the sound half sigh, half surrender.

"Carrying some heavy loads, my friend?" Ingrid asked gently.

Sophia wanted to blurt it all out—the late-night phone call, the panic in Robin's voice, the fragile courage she'd seen in her eyes just the day before. But instead she kept faith with her trust. "Yeah," she said slowly. "A bit more than usual. Sometimes I feel . . . woefully inadequate."

Above them, crows lifted in a black flutter, calling sharply as they gathered in the trees. The sight snagged against Sophia's mood, a dark chorus against the pale morning.

Ingrid touched her arm. "You don't have to tell me details. But don't forget—you don't carry it alone. Not ever."

Sophia gave a small nod, grateful for the permission to remain silent, yet comforted by the reminder.

"Remember the Fall Festival?" Ingrid added after a while, her tone lightening. "That laughter, the cider, the fiddles?"

Sophia laughed softly, surprising herself. "Yes. That was . . . good."

"Maybe that's the prescription. More moments like that. More joy. We both tend to put fun too far down the list."

"Deal," Sophia said, the word carrying more weight than she expected.

They walked on, the sun climbing higher, warming the tips of the trees.

"How's the Mastermind group?" Sophia asked, glad for the shift.

"It's engaging, rewarding—and somehow gathering an energy that feels like it's leading us somewhere. I'm just not sure where yet," Ingrid said, her eyes shining with quiet conviction.

Sophia smiled. "So awesome, my friend. So awesome."

At the corner they paused, exchanging another hug before parting ways. Ingrid's warmth lingered even as they separated, her steady presence a balm.

But as Sophia turned back toward home, gratitude pressed against her chest alongside something else. A quieter truth, one she hadn't spoken aloud: this town was holding secrets that would not stay buried much longer. And when they surfaced, she prayed the bonds between them would be strong enough to hold.

Chapter 31

The same morning, Robin sat at her kitchen table, her coffee had gone cold. She had promised herself she'd start the day strong, but her eyes kept drifting toward the mirror above the sideboard. Its frame was chipped at the corner, gilt flaking from years of polish. In its glass she caught flickers—not her forty-one-year-old reflection, but a girl too thin, too painted, too afraid. Every time the image vanished, leaving only her present self staring back, she whispered under her breath: *You're safe now. You're safe . . . right?*

She pushed back from the table, dumped the cold coffee in the sink, and poured a fresh cup. *Damn, I've got to wake up if I'm going to make that nine o'clock listing.* Work was her anchor. The creativity, the energy, the way her confidence wrapped around nervous buyers like a warm coat. She was the best in the county—maybe even the state—and she knew it. In that world she was decisive, admired, unstoppable. The fractured pieces of her private life never showed through when she wore the polished mask of "Robin Wellworth, Realtor of the Year."

In the shower, steam rose thick enough to fog the mirror. She let the hot water pound against her shoulders until her skin tingled. *Wash away the doubt, wash away the fear.* She pressed her forehead against the tile and let the warmth soak into her bones. *I am safe. I am strong. Sophia is steady. Danny is home. Danny . . .* Her heart squeezed at his name. His return was a comfort, yes—but also a risk. Was she letting him in too quickly? Was she setting herself up for another shattering loss? She shut off the water before she could answer herself, toweled briskly, and forced her thoughts back to the day ahead.

By lunchtime, she was herself again—the bright, assured professional. Guiding her clients through tough negotiations gave *her* confidence, too. Decisiveness was contagious. Houses became her stage, her scripts. She could read people, coax clarity, close deals. That rhythm, that authority, was her drug. It left her buzzing.

But when she stopped—when she sat too long at her desk—the silence opened doors she'd kept bolted for decades. That was when the memories crept back. Today, unbidden, she saw it: Rick's Mustang. Shiny black, the kind of car that turned heads in the school parking lot. The kind of car no eighteen-year-old Domino's driver should ever have been able to afford. She could still hear the rumble of its engine, feel the way every kid's eyes followed it. Back then, sliding into the passenger seat felt like being chosen. Special. Powerful. Loved.

Only now, with hindsight, she saw the shift. The Mustang had been the marker. After it appeared, Rick was different. Edgier. Angrier. Possessive. She remembered the first time his hand gripped her arm too tightly, bruises blooming where no makeup could quite cover. That was when the sweetness had started to sour, when the ride that had once felt like freedom became a trap.

Her phone rang, snapping her back. She straightened in her chair, pushed the shadows deep down where they belonged, and let the practiced brightness fill her voice.

"Robin Wellworth," she chirped. "How can I help you make your day amazing?"

Chapter 32

Danny stood in Rick's room, the morning sun cutting harsh stripes across the clutter. He hadn't touched the pile of papers he'd uncovered the day before—couldn't. But now, with his parents still asleep and the house heavy with silence, he forced himself to sit at the desk again. The air smelled of dust and old grief. Each drawer, each envelope, felt like it might hold a fuse waiting for him to strike a match.

He started systematically, searching under the drawers, sliding his hands along the rails, even moving the desk out from the wall. That's when his fingers caught on something rough beneath the second drawer on the right. Tape. His chest tightened. With shaking hands, he pried free a manila envelope, brittle with age but still sealed tight.

Slow motion overtook him as he worked the metal clasp open. Inside was a stack of documents, the kind of evidence that made his mouth go dry. He spread them across the desk like puzzle pieces.

The first sheet: lined notebook paper, Rick's handwriting scrawled in the margins. *Car payments – DP.* A long list of cash installments, each checked off. Next to one entry, written in red ink: *$200 interest payment.* Below it, Rick's furious scrawl: *Fuck this. I will NEVER be free.*

Danny gripped the page until his knuckles whitened. He remembered the day Rick rolled up in that black Mustang, the envy of every kid in town. Danny had wondered back then how his brother could afford such a car on a Domino's salary. Now he knew. The "interest payments" had nothing to do with banks.

He reached into the envelope again. A smaller packet slipped out—a bank envelope stuffed with cash, brittle bills that reeked of mildew. His stomach churned.

Beneath it, more papers. A note scrawled in an unfamiliar, blocky hand: *Interest payment $200 due today. Remember: paying on time = freedom. Silence means safety.*

And under that—photos. Danny's gut heaved as he fanned through them: Rick, barely seventeen, in compromising poses, some with older men. Others more damning still—grainy shots of Robin, not with Rick, but alone. In her yard. Walking down Main Street. At the grocery store. Surveillance. A warning: *We are watching her.*

The bile rose in Danny's throat. He barely made it to the bathroom before he retched, gripping the porcelain like a lifeline. When he stumbled back into the room, the photos still waited on the desk, evidence staring at him with cold, unblinking eyes.

Then his phone buzzed. A text.

Morning, buddy. Just checking in. How's everything going? Call me if you need me. —Marcus.

Danny wiped his face with both hands, heart hammering. The timing was uncanny. He looked again at the cash, the notes, the photos. The truth was undeniable now.

Things were moving faster than he'd expected. Too fast. He couldn't afford to make a mistake.

Taking a long, shaky breath, he dialed Marcus.

Chapter 33

Danny pinched the bridge of his nose. "Marcus, for God's sake—I keep puking my guts up like a rookie. I've been working toward this moment my entire adult life, and now that it's here, I'm lost."

"Okay, buddy," Marcus said, voice even. "Slow down. Breathe. Tell me what's going on."

Danny dragged in air, let it out hard. "Rick's room . . . it's a treasure trove. Documents, proof, clarity—everything at once. Your timing on that text was impeccable. You always did have a sixth sense for trouble. And we've got trouble brewing here."

"Tell me what you found, Daniel."

"Oh, Marcus . . . " Danny pressed his hand against the desk to steady himself. "Since I last talked to you, we've had a joint session—Robin, her therapist, and me. She's starting to get flashes, memories surfacing after decades. At the same time, I'm finding puzzle pieces. Clues. And they're starting to fit together fast."

"Robin's the one you're protecting?" Marcus asked quietly.

"Yeah," Danny said. "Her first. Always. And the evidence, too." He hesitated. "I've been tossing it into boxes, but I know that's not good enough."

"Not even close. What have you got so far?"

Danny's voice dropped. "Financial trails. Lists of meetings and payments Rick kept. This morning, I found an envelope full of cash, a payment ledger for a car—a Mustang. Rick couldn't afford that car on Domino's wages, and now I know why. The list showed random 'interest' payments, added without reason. One note in red ink—Rick's hand—'Fuck this! I will never be free.'"

Danny's throat tightened. "You can feel the terror in his handwriting. Like he finally realized he'd stepped into a trap he'd never escape."

"And?" Marcus's tone sharpened.

"And there were photos." Danny swallowed. "Compromising ones. Rick at seventeen. Humiliating. Blackmail. And Robin too—pictures of her at her house, around town, the kind meant to remind her she was always being watched. There were notes—threats—tied to the photos. All roads point to Denver Pyle, the principal. He's out on parole, walking around town right now. And Robin's memories? They're starting to line up with what I'm holding in my hands."

For a moment, only the static on the line. Then Marcus said, low and deliberate, "Okay. First priority: protect Robin. Second: secure the evidence. Third: get your parents out of that house. They're collateral risk right now, whether they know it or not."

Danny raked his fingers through his hair. "They're here, yeah. House full of junk and grief. But the whole plan was to clean it out and get it on the market anyway."

"Perfect cover," Marcus replied. "Use it. Get them into a retirement place, a vacation, whatever. Just not in that house. You're not going to be able to sort through all this with them breathing down your neck. Meanwhile, I'll make some calls on my end."

Danny felt the tremor in his hands begin to steady. "Marcus, are you saying—?"

"Yeah," Marcus cut in. "I'm coming to Westridge. We're overdue for a visit, and you're going to need backup. Get ready."

Danny closed his eyes, the faintest thread of relief weaving through his exhaustion. He whispered into the quiet room, "Thank God."

Danny dropped the phone onto the bedspread and sat back, his pulse still thrumming from the conversation. For years, he'd pictured this moment in fragments—dreams where he charged in like some crusader, or nightmares where he was too late and Robin slipped away forever. But now, reality was messier. Marcus was right: Robin first. Always Robin. Then the evidence. Then the town.

He rubbed his eyes, grit from another sleepless night scraping at the edges. The ledger pages, the notes in red ink, the humiliating photos—they weren't just artifacts. They were chains. Proof that Rick had been trapped. Proof that Robin had been watched. Proof that Danny himself had been blind until it was too late.

Victim, Sophia's voice echoed in his mind. She'd said it plainly in their session: *You, too, were a victim.* The words stung because they were true. Rick had stolen Robin from him, warped their childhood friendship into a battlefield. And then, in one brutal afternoon on a cliffside trail, Danny lost both his brother and the girl he couldn't admit he loved. He'd been seventeen and thought himself grown. In truth, he was just another casualty.

His parents . . . God, how would they survive the truth if it surfaced? They'd already spent twenty-five years embalmed in grief. Asking them to leave their house—Rick's shrine—would rip open wounds they'd barely managed to cover. But Marcus was right. If Pyle or his associates were still moving pieces in town, his parents were sitting ducks. He'd have to find a gentle way out. A "retirement option." Maybe even a vacation. A cover story that kept them safe without feeding them the horrors of what he was discovering.

He leaned forward, resting his elbows on his knees, and let his head fall into his hands. The clock on the wall ticked steadily, like Robin's voice in his memory—*ticking, ticking, ticking.*

There was no more running. No more postponing.

Marcus was on his way. Sophia would make room. Robin was remembering. And Danny? He finally had his marching orders.

He whispered it aloud, steady this time, as if carving it into the silence:

"I will not fail her again."

Chapter 34

The late-afternoon sun in Sophia's office was a wash of honey-colored light that warmed the rug and caught in the rim of Robin's coffee mug. From next door, the yeasty-sweet scent of cinnamon rolls still drifted in from the bakery next door. When Robin and Danny stepped through the door, the hum of traffic outside fell away, replaced by the hush of carpet and the faint tick of Sophia's clock.

"Thank you for clearing your schedule," Danny said, his voice roughened by something that was not quite fatigue, not quite fear. He glanced at Robin, who nodded, her fingers tightening on her bag strap.

Sophia smiled, her eyes steady, her tone gentle but firm. "You're safe here. Both of you. Let's start by breathing—feel the chair beneath you, the air in your lungs, the ground steady under your feet. Here, we are anchored. Here, we can be open."

They obeyed, and the silence that followed was heavy, but not unbearable. Robin drew a breath, then another, and let it spill out in a long sigh. "I need to say this before I lose my nerve. These flashbacks—these memories—they're not easy. But every time I talk with Danny about what he's finding, it feels . . . real. Not something my mind made up. I still see her—me—the too-thin, too-painted girl in the mirror. I see men, too. Hotels. Their faces—hungry, oblivious that I was a child. And then the Mustang . . . " Her voice faltered, then steadied. "Back then, it felt like power. Like being chosen. But now I see it was the start of the trap."

Her hands twisted in her lap, knuckles white. A muscle jumped in Danny's jaw. Sophia leaned forward slightly. "You're not alone in this remembering. Let's stay in the now—feet on the ground, eyes open. You're safe here, Robin. Go on when you're ready."

Robin nodded, though her lip trembled. "And my parents—they never saw. Or they didn't want to. I was so alone." She pressed her palms flat against her thighs, grounding herself.

Danny cleared his throat, the sound raw. "So many things we didn't know then. Messages we didn't read. And I . . . " He looked at Sophia. "I've kept searching Rick's room. And what I've found . . . " He hesitated, glanced at Robin. "I think you need to see it. But only if you're sure."

Robin lifted her chin, though her eyes glistened. "Yes. I need to see."

He spread the papers on the coffee table—ledgers, receipts, lists of payments scrawled in Rick's handwriting. The ink wavered under Danny's trembling fingers. "Car payments," he explained, voice tight. "A hot-rod Mustang that Rick could never have afforded. Payments to 'DP.' And these."

He slid a smaller envelope forward. Photos spilled out—grainy, invasive, cruel. Notes in red ink: *Interest payment due. Silence keeps you safe.* One photo of Robin, snapped from a distance on a street corner. Another of Rick, hollow-eyed, standing beside Dr. Pyle.

Robin picked them up one by one, rocking slightly in her chair, as if the movement could cradle the child she'd been. Her breath came shallow, then quicker.

"Notice your feet," Sophia's voice cut gently through the spiral. "Notice your breath. You are here, Robin. Here in this office. Smell the cinnamon. The lavender. You are safe."

Robin blinked hard, swallowing. She set the photos down, and her hand shook as she reached for the bottle of water Danny passed her. She drank, deeply, then whispered, "I see it now. I wasn't imagining. They watched me. Always."

Danny's voice cracked. "And it trapped Rick, too. He wrote—'I will never be free.' He knew." His eyes burned, guilt flooding his features.

Sophia turned to him. "Danny, you need to hear this: you were a victim, too. Your brother's choices, his entrapment, stole your life as well. Have you ever allowed yourself to grieve that? To name your own trauma?"

Danny went still, as if Sophia's words had struck him in the sternum. His hands curled into fists against his thighs, nails biting his palms. For years he'd carried the story like armor—he was the strong one, the protector who failed. Victim? No. He'd never allowed himself that word. Not once. And now it sat in the air between them like a match held to tinder.

In a flash he saw it again—Robin climbing into the black Mustang, her smile nervous but dazzled, while he stood helpless on the curb. The engine's roar had drowned out his warning. That was the moment the fault line cracked beneath all of them, though he hadn't had words for it then. He'd lost her, lost Rick, lost himself—all in one shuddering heartbeat.

His voice came rough, like gravel. "I never let myself think of it that way. Victim. But I lost everything that day. Rick. Robin. Any chance at a normal life. And I've been punishing myself ever since."

Sophia let the silence settle before speaking again. "You are both carrying unbearable weight. But you're not carrying it alone now." Robin reached over and gently touched his hand.

Danny nodded slowly, then found his voice. "I've been in touch with Marcus—an old colleague. He says we need to move quickly. First priority: keeping Robin safe. And my parents—we need to get them out of this house, into a retirement place, or send them on a trip. Robin, I'll need your help with that—you know this area better than I do."

Robin's voice was steadier now. "I'll help. Yes, of course."

Sophia folded her hands, her tone wrapping them both in steadiness. "Then we have our next steps. Evidence protected. Safety ensured. And for you, Robin—regular sessions here, just you and me. To keep grounding you as these memories surface. For you, Danny—permission to stop carrying this as penance and start carrying it as purpose."

She guided them into one last breath—imagining the room filling with light, fear draining down through the floorboards. When they finally rose, the sunlight had dipped low, throwing long shadows across the coffee table where papers and photographs lay scattered. Shadows and light crossed together.

Robin's hand brushed Danny's as they reached for their coats. Neither pulled away.

Chapter 35

The road curved gently out of Westridge, fields unrolling gold and brown in the dimming autumn light. Robin drove, her hands steady on the wheel though her chest still buzzed from Sophia's words. Danny sat beside her, quiet, watching the blur of trees like he was trying to find answers between their trunks.

Finally, Robin broke the silence. "So—what are you thinking? About your parents?"

Danny rubbed the back of his neck. "I keep circling the same conclusion. They can't stay in that house much longer. Not with what I'm finding. Not with Pyle out there."

Robin gave a quick glance at him before returning her eyes to the road. "A retirement community? Or something short-term first?"

"Vacation," he said immediately. "Feels softer. A gift. I don't want to spook them with talk of permanence before they're ready. Once they're out of the house, I can sort through the rest without them in the middle of it."

Robin nodded, pressing her lips together in thought. "That makes sense. But we'll need to make it appealing. Somewhere they can't refuse." A corner of her mouth lifted. "That's where you lean on me. I sell dreams for a living, remember?"

Danny's chest loosened a fraction at her confidence. "I'll take all the help I can get."

They pulled up to The Inn at Twin Peaks just as the sky flushed pink. The old timber building sat tucked against a grove of pines, its windows glowing warmly. It wasn't crowded—just a handful of cars in the gravel lot. Robin liked it instantly. Privacy without isolation.

Inside, the inn's dining room smelled of cedar smoke and rosemary. Lanterns glowed low on each table, and the hum of soft conversation left plenty of room for privacy. They were led to a booth tucked near a window, the glass misted with the cold.

As the server left them with water and menus, Danny, ordered them each a glass of wine.

Robin leaned forward, lowering her voice.

"Here's how I see it. You pick two or three options. A retirement community they can grow into, and a vacation they'll jump at. Then—when you take them to dinner—you offer the vacation first, framed as a gift. That buys us time. When they come back, the community feels like the next natural step."

Danny's eyes softened. "You make it sound simple."

"It's not simple. But it's clear. And clarity gives people courage."

The words landed in him like an anchor, steadying what had been spinning since the ledger first surfaced. He took a sip of water, then asked quietly, "And if they refuse?"

Robin tilted her head. "Then we try again. With more compassion. With firmer reasons. You're not alone in this, Danny. We'll figure it out."

His throat tightened at the "we." He let the silence stretch, the weight of it not uncomfortable, but binding. Finally, he said, "You balance me out, you know that?"

Robin smiled faintly, her fingers brushing the edge of her glass. "Good. Because God knows I need balancing too."

The waiter returned with the wine and took their order.

Robin added a thought. "You know," she said, "they really have to agree that the housecleaning and packing up is a huge job and that having them on vacation would be easier for you to pack things up."

"Maybe you could get them to agree that they would be helping you out by taking a vacation," she added with a conspiratorial wink.

When the server returned with their food, the moment folded back into warmth: plates of roast chicken and vegetables, bread warm from the oven. They ate, planned, even laughed when Danny admitted he had no idea how to "sell" a vacation to his stubborn mother. Robin teased, "Leave it to me. I'll make it irresistible."

The fire in the stone hearth crackled as they lingered over coffee, its steady rhythm echoing the sense of fragile resolve settling between them. Outside, a hush of wind rattled the shutters, as if the Inn itself was keeping their secret. The server quietly cleared their plates, leaving only the low hum of other diners and the muted glow of the Inn's chandeliers. By the time they stepped into the cool night, their pact was unspoken but clear: this was bigger than either of them alone.

In the car, as Robin turned the key, Danny said, "We can't keep this locked between us and Sophia. At some point, we're going to need more than therapy. We'll need . . . protection."

Robin's grip tightened on the steering wheel. "I know. Which means the law. I actually know someone in town—Rebecca Wright. She's sharp, and she's discreet. I'll call her first thing in the morning."

Danny glanced at her, his jaw easing just a fraction. "Good. The sooner those documents are in safe hands, the better we all sleep."

They didn't talk much the rest of the ride, but the silence between them felt less like distance and more like resolve.

By the time she dropped Danny at his house, the plan felt tangible, as though the Inn itself had given them its quiet blessing.

"Does Saturday work for dinner with your parents?" she asked, her tone steady. "I'll make a reservation at the Inn."

Danny studied her profile in the glow of the dash. The sharpness in her voice was new, stronger. It stirred a flicker of relief—and something like admiration.

"Perfect," he said. "Let me know how your meeting with Rebecca goes."

Finally, the ground began to feel steady beneath their feet.

Chapter 36

Robin sat cross-legged on her couch, phone in her hand, staring at Rebecca Wright's name on the screen. It felt different, heavier than all the other times they'd shared laughs and insights at the Mastermind table. This wasn't sisterhood. This was survival.

She drew in a breath and pressed the button.

"Robin!" Rebecca's warm voice came through, bright and familiar. "What a nice surprise."

"Hi, Rebecca." Robin's throat tightened. She forced herself to keep her tone steady. "I wish it were just a friendly call. But . . . it's not. I need to ask a favor. A professional one."

There was a pause, Rebecca's sharp intuition picking up the shift immediately. "Go on."

"You know I trust our circle, the Mastermind. But this—this is separate. I need your help as an attorney. It's urgent, and it's personal. And I can't risk anyone else knowing, not yet."

Rebecca's voice lowered, the warmth still there but edged with gravity. "All right. Then from this moment, consider this attorney-client. You tell me what you're ready to share, and I'll protect the rest."

Relief and dread collided in Robin's chest. "Thank you. I . . . I'll bring someone with me, soon. Danny Kessler. He has documents—evidence, really. I can't explain over the phone, but we need a safe place to put it. And we need your advice on what comes next. But first I want to come alone."

Rebecca didn't hesitate. "Come by my office tomorrow morning. Early, before my first hearing. We'll lock it down tight."

Robin's eyes stung, but her voice held steady. "Thank you, Rebecca. Truly. You don't know what this means."

"Actually, Robin," Rebecca said softly, "I think I do. And I've got you. Both of you."

When the call ended, Robin sat still for a long moment, the quiet hum of her phone in her hand like a lifeline. For the first time in days, she felt as though they had something solid to stand on.

Robin's Visit with Rebecca

Robin adjusted the cuff of her jacket as she stood outside the heavy glass door of Rebecca Wright's office. She'd sold a hundred homes without flinching, argued down buyers twice her size, but today her knees felt unsteady. This wasn't business. This was her life.

The receptionist gave her a kind smile and gestured her through. Rebecca's office was spacious yet warm, sunlight spilling across bookshelves and a mahogany desk scattered with neat stacks of files. A soft jazz station played low in the background. Rebecca herself rose as Robin entered, elegant in a slate-blue suit, her presence equal parts power and reassurance.

"Robin," she said, her voice rich and steady. "It's good to see you outside the Mastermind circle. Come, sit."

Robin managed a tight smile as she settled into the chair opposite. "I'm . . . grateful you could see me on short notice."

Rebecca's eyes softened. "For a friend, always. Now, tell me what's going on. And before you hesitate—remember, everything you say here is protected."

Robin swallowed, her throat dry. She twisted her ring nervously, then finally let the words tumble out. "I've started remembering things. From when I was a teenager. Things I buried so deep I thought maybe they weren't real. But now they're surfacing, and they're . . . horrifying."

Rebecca leaned forward, her hands clasped loosely. "Memories coming back after trauma is common, Robin. But you wouldn't be here unless something had triggered them. What changed?"

Robin's gaze flicked to the window, then back. "Danny. He's back in town. He's been . . . finding things. Old papers, photos. And every time he shows me something, it matches what I'm remembering. That's what scares me—it means I'm not imagining it. It happened. All of it."

For a long moment, Rebecca said nothing. Her silence wasn't cold; it was listening, weighing, making space. Finally, she asked gently, "Do you feel in danger now?"

Robin hesitated. "Yes. The man at the center of it—Denver Pyle—he's out. Free. Walking these streets again. And if Danny has what I think he has, then we're holding evidence someone might want back badly."

Rebecca's expression sharpened, but her tone remained calm. "Then here's the first thing: I want you to know you came to the right place. What you tell me is confidential. And if Danny brings me those documents, they're protected too. No one can touch them once they're in my custody."

Robin exhaled shakily, relief mingling with fear.

Rebecca leaned in, her voice steady as bedrock. "Second: your healing comes first. We move at your pace. The law can wait a beat if it needs to. But what we can't wait on is keeping you safe."

Robin blinked back tears, whispering, "That's all I want. To feel safe."

Rebecca smiled, not softly, but fiercely. "Then let's start there. Call Danny. Tell him to come see me with you. We'll put everything under protection. And then—together—we'll decide the next step."

Robin nodded, her pulse beginning to slow for the first time in days. When she rose to leave, Rebecca stood with her, resting a steady hand on her shoulder. "You're not that girl anymore, Robin. And you're not alone this time."

Robin Calls Danny

Robin sat in her car outside Rebecca Wright's office, the engine off, her hands still resting on the wheel. For a long moment she just breathed, trying to absorb the steadiness Rebecca had given her. It was the first time in days she didn't feel like she was unraveling.

She picked up her phone, scrolling until she landed on Danny's name. Her thumb hovered for a beat, then she pressed "call."

He answered on the first ring. "Robin?" His voice was taut, as though he'd been waiting.

"It went well," she said, and surprised herself at how much she meant it. "I just came from Rebecca Wright's office. She . . . she's good, Danny. Strong. The kind of person we need in this."

Danny exhaled audibly, relief cutting through the line. "So you trust her?"

"Yes." Robin nodded, though he couldn't see it. "She said she'll take everything under legal protection once you bring the documents. Confidentiality, safety, the whole thing. She even reminded me—we don't have to carry this alone anymore."

For a moment there was silence, then Danny said quietly, "That sounds like exactly what we need."

"I told her you'd come with me," Robin continued. "With the files. We'll do it together. She said to set it up soon, before anything else stirs."

Danny's voice steadied. "Good. Name the time, and I'll be there. I've kept the papers close, but I'll sleep better once they're locked down."

Robin felt her shoulders ease against the seat. "I'll call first thing tomorrow to set the appointment. Then we'll go in together."

"All right," he said, his tone firm now. "Together."

When she hung up, Robin let her head fall back against the seat, closing her eyes. For the first time, the word didn't feel fragile or dangerous. Together.

The Meeting with Rebecca

Rebecca Wright's office smelled faintly of lemon polish. The walls were lined with dark wood shelves, thick with legal tomes, but softened by family photos and a potted fern that looked suspiciously well cared-for. Robin had been here before, in friendlier circumstances—a quick stop to drop something off, a wave after Mastermind—but today, stepping inside with Danny at her side, the air felt heavier.

Rebecca rose from behind her desk, tall and poised, her pearl earrings catching the morning light. "Robin," she said warmly, then turned her gaze to Danny. "And you must be Mr. Kessler. Please, sit. We've got ground to cover."

Danny felt awkward shaking her hand, suddenly aware that his palms were damp. He set the worn leather satchel on his lap like it might anchor him. Robin slipped into the chair beside him, grateful for the firm steadiness of Rebecca's voice.

Rebecca folded her hands, eyes moving between them. "From this moment, everything you say here is protected. That means you can be completely honest with me, and I'll advise you not just as a friend—but as your attorney."

Danny cleared his throat, opened the satchel, and spread a stack of papers onto her desk: the ledger, notes in Rick's cramped handwriting, photographs in yellowing envelopes. His hands trembled, but his voice was steady. "This is what I've found so far. Receipts, payments, threats. Photos of Rick. Photos of Robin. Even some involving . . . men in town. It's darker than I thought, and I've only scratched the surface."

Rebecca leaned forward, her expression sharpening as she sifted through the evidence. She paused at the red-ink scrawl—*Fuck this. I will never be free.* A shadow crossed her face. "This," she said quietly, "isn't just teenage rebellion or poor judgment. This is coercion. This is control. And it's criminal."

Robin hugged her arms to her chest, rocking slightly in the chair. "I keep remembering flashes—bits of what was done to me. And every time Danny shows me something new, it lines up. It terrifies me, but at least I know I'm not . . . imagining."

Rebecca reached across the desk, her hand hovering close enough for Robin to take if she wished. "You're not imagining. And you're not alone anymore."

Danny swallowed hard. "The problem is . . . the man behind it all—Denver Pyle—is out. He's already in town. And I don't trust that he doesn't know we're digging."

Rebecca's eyes narrowed, the lawyer's fire lighting in her chest. "Then we make two priorities: safety, and strategy. First, these documents. I'll have them locked in my firm's safe by the end of the day. No one but me will have access. If anything happens, they can't vanish."

Robin let out a breath she hadn't realized she was holding.

"Second," Rebecca continued, "we'll work on protection. Danny, your parents' safety is part of this too, isn't it?"

Danny nodded grimly. "Yeah. They need to be moved, and soon. We've been talking about Florida. If we can get them down there, it buys us space."

Rebecca's lips pressed into a firm line. "Do it. While they're gone, you finish cleaning out the house, but keep me looped in. If we need a restraining order, or if you find more evidence, I want it in my hands."

Robin looked between them, her voice barely above a whisper. "So this . . . this is really happening."

Rebecca held her gaze, steady as stone. "Yes. But you're not facing it the way you did before. You've got people now. And we're not going to let him—or anyone—erase your truth again."

The room fell into silence, thick but strangely steady. Robin felt the balance tilt—not toward fear, but toward resolve.

Chapter 37

Robin's phone buzzed in her back pocket, the bluegrass ringtone making her smile before she even answered.

"Danny? Well, this is a surprise."

"I know it's last minute," he said, his voice warm and eager. "But I just saw a sign—there's a concert in the square tonight. Country and bluegrass. Starts at seven. I think we need a night of fun. Can I pick you up?"

Robin glanced at the clock. "Seven? That's in thirty minutes."

"I'll swing by. We'll make it."

She hesitated only a second before grinning. "You know what? That's exactly what the doctor ordered. I'll be ready."

Upstairs she moved quickly, showering and slipping into jeans, a thick sweater, and her favorite toe-tapping boots. By the time Danny pulled into the driveway, she was waiting on the porch, cheeks flushed from the rush.

He leaned over as she climbed in. "Well now, aren't we spontaneous?"

"Spontaneous and in need of popcorn," she quipped, already feeling lighter.

The square was alive with autumn smells—popcorn, woodsmoke, hot dogs sizzling on a nearby grill. They found a spot near the band-stand, set up folding chairs from Danny's trunk, and laughed over their "dinner" of hot dogs and popcorn.

Rebecca and Pete were already there, close to the stage. Danny nudged Robin. "That your Mastermind friend?"

"Yes," Robin smiled, lowering her voice. "Her husband plays banjo. They tour bluegrass festivals when he's not lawyering. Looks like we picked the right night."

The music rolled out—fiddles sharp and bright, banjos quick as laughter. Couples clapped along, children twirled in front of the stage, and even Robin found herself singing snatches of old songs she hadn't heard in years.

She leaned closer, her head brushing Danny's shoulder. "You were right. This really was what the doctor ordered."

Danny turned his face just enough to catch her profile in the glow of the stage lights. "I felt it too. We need this—fun, normalcy. And," his voice dropped, softer, "I just feel good being with you."

Her breath caught, but she let herself rest against him, just for a moment. "Me too. It fits, doesn't it?"

"It sure does," he murmured.

When the last song ended, they folded their chairs, tossed away their empty cups, and strolled toward the lot with the rest of the crowd. The night air was crisp, threaded with the lingering hum of fiddles and laughter.

And then Robin froze.

Her hand clutched Danny's arm, her breath slicing into one broken syllable: "Oh . . . God."

Danny followed her gaze. Leaning against a lamppost just beyond the square's edge, half-hidden in shadow, was Denver Pyle. His posture was casual, almost lazy—but his eyes were locked on them, a thin smile curled on his lips.

Danny's arm tightened protectively around Robin's shoulders. He bent his head close and whispered, steady and firm, "Don't look at him. Just keep walking."

Robin swallowed hard, forcing her steps forward. Each one felt like walking through wet cement. Behind her, the lamplight flickered, and she could still feel his gaze burning against her back.

The Ride Home

The car was quiet as Danny pulled out of the lot, the hum of the tires the only sound between them. Robin sat stiffly, arms folded across her chest, as though even now she could still feel Pyle's eyes boring into her back.

Danny kept his gaze fixed on the dark road ahead. His knuckles were white on the steering wheel. "He was too close," he muttered. "Too damn close."

Robin swallowed hard, her voice breaking. "I thought I was imagining it at first. But it was him. I could feel it. Just standing there—watching."

Danny's jaw tightened. "That wasn't chance, Robin. He wanted us to see him. That's his game—control through fear. But we're not giving him that."

Robin turned toward him, searching his profile in the passing glow of headlights. "You sound so certain. But Danny . . . what if he already knows what you've found? What if he's warning us?"

Danny hesitated, then reached over, his hand finding hers on the seat between them. "Then let him. Because we're not kids anymore. And we're not alone. We've got Sophia. Rebecca. Each other. This time, he doesn't get to win."

For a moment, Robin let herself squeeze his hand, drawing strength from the firmness of his grip. Her voice softened. "You really believe that?"

He finally looked at her, his eyes shadowed but steady. "I have to. For you. For Rick. For all of it."

The silence that followed wasn't empty—it carried the weight of all they hadn't said yet. Robin leaned her head back against the seat, her heartbeat slowing. The square's music still echoed faintly in her ears, but beneath it now was a steadier rhythm—the sense that she and Danny were stepping onto the same path.

As the car rolled into her driveway, Danny cut the engine but didn't move. He turned toward her, voice low. "We'll tell Rebecca what happened tonight. Every detail. No more chances. Agreed?"

Robin nodded, her throat tight but her eyes clear. "Agreed."

They sat in the quiet car for another beat, both knowing the night had shifted something between them. Then, with a shared glance that carried more than words could, they each stepped out into the cool air—resolved, together, to face what was coming.

Danny walked Robin up the path to her porch, the quiet of the neighborhood pressing close around them. The porch light cast a soft glow across her face, and for a moment he wished he could stay right there, guard her through the night.

Instead, he set his jaw. "Robin . . . do you have a gun in the house?"

Her brows lifted slightly. "Yes. It's in my safe."

"Then get it out," he said, his voice low but steady. "Load it. Keep it on your nightstand. I hate to even suggest it, but I need to know you can protect yourself if—" he hesitated, the word bitter in his mouth, "if he comes around."

Robin's throat bobbed with the weight of his words, but she nodded. "All right. I'll do it."

Danny exhaled, relief mingling with unease. "Good. I hate to leave you tonight, but I can't leave my parents in that house blind. At least you know what's going on. They don't. I need to be there."

She reached for his hand, squeezing once before letting go. "Go. Take care of them."

He managed a faint smile. "We'll talk tomorrow."

"Deal," she said softly.

He lingered for a beat longer, as though memorizing her face in the glow of the porch light, then finally stepped back toward his car. "Lock the doors. Keep that gun close. I'll see you tomorrow."

Robin watched him go, her heart both steadied and unsettled at once, the sound of his engine fading into the night as she whispered to herself: *Safe. I am safe.*

Chapter 38

Danny's sneakers slapped against the pavement, breath steady but sharp in the cool morning air. Running always cleared his head—at least, it used to. Lately, the pounding rhythm only echoed the urgency in his chest. He veered off his usual loop, letting his feet carry him past Robin's street.

As he rounded the corner, there she was—sitting on her porch with a mug between her hands, as though she'd been waiting for something. Or someone. The sight tugged at him in a way he wasn't ready to name.

He slowed to a jog, then stopped at the bottom of her steps. "Morning," he said, catching his breath. "Tell me that's real coffee you're drinking. I can't stomach another cup of my parents' instant."

Robin smiled faintly, lifting the mug. "French roast. Hot. You want some?"

Danny wiped his forehead with the back of his hand and grinned. "God, yes."

A minute later, he was sitting on the porch rail, cradling a steaming cup while Robin rocked slowly in her chair. The quiet between them felt companionable, not strained.

"You okay?" he asked gently, studying her face.

Robin nodded, though her eyes flickered. "I will be. One day at a time, right?"

"One day at a time," he echoed. He took a long sip, savoring the warmth. "About tonight—are we still good for dinner with my folks? Seven at the Inn?"

"Yes," she said, with more steadiness than she felt. "I'll be ready."

"Good." He tipped his head, relief flashing across his features. "It matters, Robin. Them hearing it from both of us."

Her smile was small but real. "Then we'll make it count."

They lingered for another few minutes, sipping in silence while the neighborhood stirred awake around them.

Danny set down his empty cup, stretched, and jogged down the steps again.

"Thanks for the coffee," he called over his shoulder. Then he hesitated, glanced back, and added, "One thing I feel good about is that the documents are safe for now."

Robin met his gaze, her hand tightening around her own mug. "Agreed."

She watched as he disappeared down the street, his steady stride fading into the quiet of the morning. She let herself exhale fully, as though his words had pressed a lid onto the chaos swirling inside her.

Chapter 39

Danny stepped into the garage, the chill of concrete rising through his sneakers. He flicked on the single bulb overhead, its yellow cone of light swinging across cobwebs and old boxes. The space felt too wide, too hollow. Something was missing.

The Mustang.

For twenty-five years he'd expected to find it here, under a tarp or at least rusting in the corner, a relic of everything that had gone wrong. Instead, the spot was bare, the floor showing only oil stains and the faint outline of tires long gone. His chest tightened.

He stalked back into the house, finding his parents in their usual spots—his father staring at the muted TV, his mother folded into the corner of the couch with a shawl pulled tight.

"What happened to Rick's car?" His voice came out harsher than intended.

His father grunted, not taking his eyes off the screen. "Repo men took it. Sat out there three months before they came. I knew it was only a matter of time. Kid couldn't have been anywhere close to paying it off."

Danny blinked. "Did you get their names? A receipt? Anything?"

His father shrugged. "Didn't care who they were. Not my business. Car wasn't ours to keep."

The words landed like stones, flat and heavy.

Then his mother, quiet until now, turned her gaze on him. Her voice wasn't sharp, but it was edged with something colder. "Rick was dead. And you—" she swallowed hard, her eyes glistening—"you just left. You didn't care then. Why care now?"

Danny's jaw tightened. The anger rose fast, hot, and dangerous. He turned on his heel without answering, retreating down the hall to Rick's room before he said something he couldn't take back.

The Reckoning

Rick's room seemed like it was sealed in like a time capsule. Danny sat heavily on the bed, elbows on his knees, hands raking through his hair. The old photo of him and Rick still leaned against the desk, their boyhood smiles frozen in another lifetime.

His mother's words rang in his ears. *You didn't care then.*

The rage pulsed through him—rage at Rick for dragging Robin into darkness, at Pyle for orchestrating it, at himself for running. His stomach knotted, and for a moment he thought he might be sick again.

He pulled out his phone almost without thinking, thumb landing on Robin's name. She answered on the first ring.

"Danny?" Her voice was warm, steadying.

He let out a shaky breath. "I—I'm drowning, Robin. They told me the Mustang was repossessed, and Mom . . . " He trailed off, the anger burning holes in his throat. "She said I didn't care back then, so why do I care now? God, it's like I can't get out from under it. All of it."

Robin was quiet a moment, then spoke softly. "Danny, listen to me. You can't move forward if you're chained to blame. Not theirs, not Rick's—and not your own. Channeling Ingrid, she continued, "Forgiveness isn't just for them. It's for you. If you don't forgive yourself, you'll never be free enough to fight for what matters now."

Her words landed like cool water on a fever. He sat back, eyes stinging, chest loosening just enough to breathe.

"You think I can do that?" he whispered.

"I know you can," she said firmly. "Because you already started. You came back. You're here. You're choosing to stay."

Danny closed his eyes. *Forgive myself. Forgive them. Move forward.* For the first time, it sounded possible.

The Conversation

That afternoon, Danny found his parents where he'd left them. The TV still flickered, but now the sound was on, the volume low. His father barely glanced up as Danny entered, but his mother's hands tightened on her shawl, wary.

Danny sat down opposite them, leaning forward, his voice low but steady. "I need to say something. To both of you."

His father muted the TV. A small shift, but enough.

Danny swallowed hard. "I'm sorry. I'm sorry I left when Rick died. Sorry I didn't come back, didn't grieve with you, didn't stay to help carry it. I told myself I couldn't breathe here, but the truth is—I was angry, and I ran. And you deserved better."

Silence stretched. His father's jaw worked, eyes fixed on the carpet. His mother blinked fast, tears threatening.

Danny's voice cracked. "I need your forgiveness. I don't expect it right away, but I need you to hear me say the words. I want us to have peace again. I want us to move forward."

For the first time in years, his father turned fully toward him, his gaze direct and searching. "All right then," he said slowly. "Let's start with tonight. We'll go to dinner. No ghosts at the table. Just us."

His mother reached for Danny's hand, tentative but real. "We've all lost too much already. Maybe it's time to stop losing each other."

Danny clasped her hand, holding it tight. For the first time since he'd come home, he felt the possibility of something new taking root—fragile, but alive.

Chapter 40

"Robin!" Mrs. Kessler said warmly as they met in the lobby. "We haven't seen you in so long. I see your ads in the grocery carts, and those awards—'Best Realtor' everywhere. Seems like you're winning all the time." She gave her a brief, affectionate hug.

"Hi, Mr. Kessler." Robin smiled, offering her hand. He nodded in return, polite but reserved, as the quiet clink of silverware and low hum of conversation filled the background.

Once seated and drinks ordered, Danny leaned in. "Thanks for coming with us, Mom, Dad. Robin and I were here for dinner the other night—it was quiet, delicious. We thought we'd share it with you."

His parents exchanged a glance, then shrugged. "Oh, Danny," Margaret said, "it's been a long time since we've been out here."

When the server set their drinks down, Danny lifted his glass. "It's good to be home again." He met each of their eyes in turn. "It's been way too long. Here's to new beginnings."

Glasses clinked. For a few minutes they lingered over menus, making small talk—the recent concert on the square, the Fall Festival. Robin asked if they had gone.

"No," Margaret said, almost apologetically. "We don't get out much anymore."

The food arrived—Pot roast and vegetables, warm bread, steaming bowls of soup—and conversation drifted back to the surface. Danny waited until plates were settled before speaking again.

"You know," he said carefully, "cleaning out the house . . . it's a big job. Just Rick's room alone took me more than a week. And there's still so much more. You deserve a break. You deserve to get away for a bit."

Richard set down his fork. "Danny, we wouldn't even know where to begin planning. We haven't gone on a trip in years. Honestly, we just . . . stay home."

"That's exactly why," Danny pressed gently. "If I'm going to really make progress with the house, I need free rein. And in the meantime, you two could have something to look forward to. I mentioned a couple of places in Florida the other day—friends tell me that one of them is like an amusement park for grown-ups. "Lifetime Vacations" has music every night, even on Christmas. Restaurants everywhere. Dad, they've got woodworking shops that are state of the art. You haven't touched your tools in years."

His father's eyes flickered, just for a second.

"And Mrs. Kessler," Robin added, stepping in with an easy smile, "they've got mah-jongg and bridge groups, pickleball courts, walking clubs. You'd have friends waiting for you the minute you unpacked."

Margaret laughed, lifting her hands. "Whoa, whoa, first, call me Margaret, second—getting a little carried away, aren't you?"

Danny grinned. "Maybe. But maybe it's the kind of 'carried away' you deserve."

Robin leaned forward. "The neat thing is, they offer trial stays. A week in a villa, golf cart included, so you can try it out. Of course winter is their busy season, but even so—you'd get to see the neighborhoods, hear the music, taste the restaurants. And if you like it, you can stay longer."

Richard frowned thoughtfully. "What's so special about this particular place?"

Danny glanced at Robin, then back at his father. "What's special is . . . it's life again. Safe, easy to get around, and filled with people your age. Right now, you two hardly see anyone. I'd like to give you this as a gift—a chance to breathe, to try something new. Stay a month. That gives me time to clean out the house, top to bottom. Then we'll talk about next steps."

Margaret hesitated, her eyes flicking to Richard. "A month is a long time."

"I know," Danny said softly. "But it's about to snow here. Why not trade that for warm nights and music under the stars? Just try it. One step at a time."

Margaret's voice caught a little. "We don't talk much these days. About anything."

Richard looked at her, then back at Danny. His jaw shifted, then softened. "Might not be a bad idea. Maybe it's time we start talking again. Start living again . . . before we run out of time."

Robin brightened. "I actually have former clients who live there now. They rave about it. I could invite them over for coffee, or we could all meet at my office so you could ask them about it yourselves."

For a moment, the four of them sat in the warm glow of the Inn, the air lighter than it had been in years. Danny caught Robin's eyes over their wine glasses, a silent exchange of hope.

Richard cleared his throat. "All right, Margaret. Let's talk about it."

She nodded, just once.

When they stepped into the night, a gust of wind swept down the street. Margaret pulled her coat tighter around her shoulders. "Oh yes," she murmured, almost to herself. "Maybe getting away from this cold wouldn't be such a bad thing."

Robin smiled warmly. "It was wonderful to see you again, Margaret. Richard."

Richard corrected her gently, with the faintest of smiles. "Yes. Richard and Margaret. Good to see you too, Robin."

They parted ways in the parking lot, each heading to their own cars. And as Danny slid behind the wheel, he felt something shift inside. For the first time in years, a window had cracked open.

After Dinner

By the time Danny got home, the house was quiet again, his parents already settled into their familiar routines. He dropped his keys on the counter, loosened his collar, and exhaled. Tonight had gone better than he'd dared hope.

His phone buzzed. Robin.

He answered quickly. "Made it home?"

"Just now," she said. He could hear the soft smile in her voice. "I think it went well, don't you?"

Danny sank into a chair, rubbing the back of his neck. "Better than I expected. I was braced for a fight. Instead . . . I saw a spark. Especially in Dad. Like maybe he actually wants to live again."

"I noticed that too," Robin said gently. "It's the first time I've seen them look at each other with possibility instead of just . . . resignation."

There was a pause, warm and quiet.

"Thank you," Danny said finally. "For being there. For helping me sell the idea without making it feel like we were pushing them out."

"You didn't need me," she teased softly. "But I was glad to be there. And Danny?"

"Yeah?"

"One step at a time," she reminded him. "Forgiveness, freedom, forward. You're doing it."

Danny let her words settle into him like balm. "Thanks, Robin. Sleep well."

"You too."

They hung up, but the line seemed to hum a moment longer in the silence, like neither one of them had quite wanted to let go.

Chapter 41

Robin's phone buzzed just as she was settling at her kitchen table with a cup of tea. Danny's name lit the screen. She smiled, answering quickly.

"Hey, you," she said, her voice lighter than it had been in days.

"Hey yourself," Danny replied, sounding less strained than usual. "I just wanted to give you an update. Mom and Dad actually brought up Florida again this morning. They asked if I'd set up a coffee with those clients of yours who know that retirement community in Florida. They're curious. Can you believe that?"

Robin's eyebrows lifted. "That's huge. It means they're warming to the idea."

"You know, I think my clients are actually planning to leave soon to spend the first half of the year there, so I better get on that right away."

"Great. And it would be nice if Mom and Dad had people they knew down there to show them around a bit." Robin felt a flicker of relief. "I'll reach out to my clients and see when they're free. They'll love sharing their experience."

There was a pause on the line, a different kind of weight shifting into Danny's voice. "By the way . . . we still need to loop Rebecca in about the Mustang repo. I need to finish typing up what Mom and Dad told me, but once I've got it written out, should I go ahead and call her tomorrow morning? She'll be back in the office."

"Yes," Robin said firmly. "Let's keep her in the loop. Email her the written account, then follow up with the call so it's documented and clear."

Danny exhaled, and Robin could almost see his shoulders easing. "All right. That's the plan then. Parents in Florida. And Rebecca in the morning."

Robin smiled to herself. "Sounds like progress."

"Yeah," Danny murmured. "For once, it does."

They said their goodbyes, but when Robin hung up, she stayed at the table a moment longer, tracing the rim of her teacup. So for now, the path ahead looked—if not easy—at least possible.

Monday Morning

Danny sat at the kitchen table, his laptop open to the email he'd sent Rebecca an hour earlier. He'd typed out everything his parents told him about the Mustang—how it sat in the garage for months before being hauled away, no payments ever made, no repo papers left behind. Now the phone was warm in his hand as he listened to the line click alive.

"Rebecca Wright," came her brisk, steady voice.

"Rebecca, it's Danny. I just sent you the account about the Mustang repossession. Did you get it?"

"Yes," she said, and he could hear papers shifting. "I've read it twice already. It's exactly the kind of detail we need. It shows this wasn't a legitimate loan being repaid—it was leverage. Whoever controlled that car, controlled Rick."

Danny rubbed at the back of his neck. "So it adds to the pattern?"

"It does more than that," Rebecca replied, her tone sharpening with purpose. "It reinforces what you've already found: this was a system of coercion. Not just intimidation, but entrapment. It fits with the ledgers, with the photos, with everything Robin is remembering."

Danny let out a long breath. "I wasn't sure it mattered. It just seemed like another dead end."

Rebecca's voice softened. "Danny, every scrap matters. And every time you write something down and put it in my hands, you make it impossible for someone to erase. That's how we protect Robin. That's how we protect you."

He sat in silence for a moment, the weight of her words grounding him.

Rebecca continued, "Keep digging, but keep yourself steady. And if anything else surfaces, no matter how small, send it. I'll piece it together on my end."

"Thanks, Rebecca," Danny said, his voice low.

"You're not alone in this anymore," she reminded him. "Remember that. Both of you."

When the call ended, Danny stared at the phone in his hand, his pulse finally slowing. And now, it felt like the ground beneath them wasn't just steady—it was being reinforced. Brick by brick.

Chapter 42

The fire snapped softly in the hearth, its glow spreading across the long table already set with mugs, plates, and a tray where Rebecca had left her new dessert—something dusted in sugar that looked both mysterious and inviting. The upper room held that peculiar mixture of warmth and crispness, the fire's heat blending with the sharp bite of air drifting through the cracked windows. It felt alive, almost sacred, as though the room itself knew it was about to hold secrets, laughter, and the steady rhythm of shared lives.

Robin arrived first, cheeks flushed from the cold, her shoulders visibly easing as she stepped inside. "Ingrid," she said, her voice carrying both fatigue and relief. "I am so happy to see your face."

Ingrid crossed the room in that graceful way that was hers alone and folded Robin in a brief, grounding hug. "Likewise, my friend. Welcome."

The others followed one by one, beads strung onto a thread of fellowship: Tanya in a flowing African print, radiant and sun-kissed; Rebecca, eyes bright, balancing a dish with the proud secrecy of a cook awaiting judgment; Sandra with her easy laugh; Patsy with a sparkle that hadn't been there weeks ago. By the time Melody breezed in, still carrying the scent of foreign air and faraway markets, the room was filled. Coffee was poured, plates were passed, and the circle settled into its familiar shape.

They began as always—with breath. Ingrid guided them gently: "Gratitude in, heaviness out." The women's shoulders dropped; the fire's glow steadied.

Patsy spoke first, voice tinged with both surprise and joy. "I'm grateful for something simple—dinner with our kids at the club. It's been routine for years, almost stale. But this time . . . something shifted. They actually listened. Asked about my volunteer work. My husband even joined the conversation instead of drifting off. For once, I felt we were truly together."

Sandra leaned forward, eyes alight. "That's beautiful. Mine's simple, too. I kept my one-year-old granddaughter overnight for the first time. Just me and Penny. Her little giggles, the way she looked straight into my eyes—it was healing. Pure joy. I swear, she brought more wisdom in a night than I've found in weeks."

Laughter circled the room, warm as the fire.

Melody chimed in next, her energy brimming after weeks abroad. "I'm grateful to have seen the world again—Cambodia, Kenya, Malawi—all in one stretch. It was exhausting and exhilarating. But more than that, I feel . . . purposeful. Like what I'm doing has weight."

Rebecca nodded vigorously. "I feel that, too. For months I've been wondering if my work is just fueling an endless cycle of entitlement and lawsuits. Then, out of the blue, a client walked into my office with a case that . . . matters. I can't say more here—confidentiality—but it's different. Deep. And for the first time in a while, I feel like maybe this is exactly where I'm supposed to be."

The women murmured encouragement, and Ingrid's eyes glimmered, taking it in.

Robin, cheeks pink now, added quietly but firmly, "This may be hard to imagine, but I feel buoyant. An old friend came back into my life—after twenty-five years. And though I'm still working through hard things with Sophia, this new connection . . . it's breathing life into me. I feel grateful. Stronger than I thought I could."

A ripple of delight spread through the group. Tanya leaned in, eyes wide. "This wouldn't happen to be Danny Kessler, would it? The man I met in Cambodia?"

Robin caught her breath before steadying herself. "It is."

Tanya grinned. "Well, good for you. I can't wait to hear more."

Melody nearly bounced in her chair. "You're kidding me. Danny Kessler? After visiting his center in Phnom Penh, hearing his work firsthand—I've been hoping to interview him for a documentary. Robin, you *must* introduce us."

Robin stilled for a heartbeat, Sophia's voice whispering through her mind—*this is what healing feels like.* She managed a smile. "I'll make the introduction."

The group fell into a brief, thoughtful silence before Ingrid lifted them forward again. "And Tanya—what's making you sparkle this week?"

Tanya chuckled. "I've just come back from a conference in Hawaii. Took a few extra days on Maui, and—miracle of miracles—Rico flew in and joined me. Sun, sand, and time together. I'm grateful for that. But honestly? I'm grateful to be back here, too."

The circle hummed with affirmation.

When the gratitude had circled the room, Ingrid's eyes sparkled in the firelight as she leaned forward. "Thank you, each of you, for what you've shared tonight. It lifts us all. Now," she added, her gaze landing warmly on Rebecca, "you're in the hot seat. And it sounds like you've had some interesting shifts lately."

Rebecca straightened slightly, though her expression softened as she exhaled. "Yes. Thank you for the opportunity, Ingrid. You all know I've been wrestling with my work. Not the volume of it—my practice is full, my staff is strong, and the bills are paid. But sometimes . . . " She paused, searching for words. "Sometimes it feels like I'm just oiling the gears of a system that feeds on conflict. Our society can be so litigious, so entitled. Everyone clawing for their piece of the pie. And I've wondered more than once if by being a lawyer, I'm simply adding to the problem."

The room stilled, each woman listening closely. Rebecca's voice grew quieter, more personal. "But then, out of nowhere, I got a phone call from a client with a case that felt . . . different. It matters. It's not about money, or greed, or one-upmanship. It's about lives. About truth. I can't say more—not here, not yet—but it reminded me that my training, my skills, they don't just have to keep the machine running. They can help shift the balance. They can help heal."

Robin felt her throat tighten, though she kept her gaze fixed politely on her folded hands. Rebecca didn't look at her, but the undercurrent was there, vibrating quietly between them.

Rebecca went on, a steadiness settling in her tone. "That case gave me a jolt of purpose I didn't realize I'd been craving. Maybe I'm not in the wrong business after all. Maybe what needs to change is my focus. To choose, as much as I can, the kind of work that makes a difference. And to trust that those cases will come."

Patsy leaned forward eagerly. "That's exactly what I was saying earlier, about finding purpose again. When the right kind of conversations come, they feed you. They light a way forward."

"Exactly," Rebecca agreed, her eyes flicking around the circle. "It's like I can see a path now that was hidden before. And I'm grateful—for this group, for this space, for the reminder that meaning isn't just for other people. It's for us, too."

Silence lingered for a beat, rich and full, before Ingrid spoke. Her voice was quiet but resonant, the kind that seemed to reach into the marrow. "And this," she said, "is why we gather. To remind each other that the infinite is not far off. It lives within us. We each carry a piece of it, and together we sharpen it, shape it, and hold it steady. Without judgment. Without fear. And always, with love."

The women nodded, some blinking back tears, others smiling softly. The fire crackled, and in that moment, the upper room felt less like a meeting and more like a sanctuary.

Ingrid let the conversation settle, her eyes moving around the circle, resting on each face. The fire reflected in her gaze, glimmering like a blessing.

"Thank you, Rebecca," she said softly. "And thank you all. You've each reminded us tonight what this gathering is truly about—finding meaning, finding courage, finding light in unexpected places."

She raised her palms slightly, inviting them to join. "So let's close as we always do. Breathe in deeply—draw in love, draw in strength, draw in the wisdom of the Infinite within you. Hold it. And then let it go . . . let it wash out the fear, the heaviness, the doubt."

Around the circle, shoulders lifted and fell. Robin drew in the air, rich with coffee and woodsmoke, and tried to let it settle inside her.

"Now," Ingrid continued, her voice a steady current, "picture the step before you—the next right step. It doesn't have to be grand. Just true. See yourself taking it. See yourself supported as you do."

Eyes closed, the women leaned into the silence. Patsy smiled faintly. Sandra exhaled. Rebecca's jaw softened, the faintest curve of peace playing at her lips.

Robin sat very still. In her mind, faces flickered—the hungry eyes of men, the sharp scrawl of red ink, the Mustang's gleam. She wanted to recoil. But into that darkness, Sophia's voice whispered back from memory: *This is what healing feels like.*

She inhaled again, steadier this time. *Safe. Strong. Not alone.*

And she allowed herself to believe it.

Ingrid's eyes opened, sweeping the circle once more. "You are each exactly where you need to be. And as you walk back into the world, remember—you do not walk alone."

The women lifted their heads, some with smiles, some with damp eyes, but all with a sense of belonging.

Robin joined the chorus of voices murmuring thanks as chairs scraped back and plates were gathered. But inside, she held tightly to that single fragile truth: for now, at least, she was not walking alone.

Chapter 43

On the way out to Robin's office, Danny's phone buzzed. A text lit up the screen:

Marcus:

"Hey Buddy, I'm in town. Staying at the Pine Tree Lodge, about 30 minutes outside of town. Can you meet me for a beer?"

Danny thumbed a quick reply. *Yep. How's 4 pm?*

A thumbs-up icon came back almost immediately.

Danny slid his phone into his pocket, then walked back through the house, double-checking each door and window. "All set," he said as he joined his parents at the car. He glanced at the quiet neighborhood—just a sedan parked crookedly across the street, a child's bike on a lawn—and shook off the twinge in his gut. *Paranoid,* he told himself. *But better paranoid than careless.*

Robin's office was just ten minutes away, housed in a crisp brick building near the small mall. Danny slowed as they pulled up. "Yikes. When did they build this?" The newness felt like another slap, a reminder of just how long he'd been gone.

Inside, the glass doors gleamed, the air smelling faintly of citrus. *Wellworth Properties, Ltd.—Robin A. Wellworth, Real Estate Broker* was etched neatly across the second set of doors. Danny's chest tightened. She'd built something impressive here.

A poised receptionist ushered them into the conference room, offering tea, coffee, or sparkling water. His parents exchanged a surprised glance at the professionalism. Danny hid a small smile— Robin had always been determined, but this? This was next level.

Robin rose as they entered, warm and polished. "Mr. and Mrs. Kessler, I'm so glad you could come. Let me introduce you to Sharon and Randy Jones."

The couple stood, friendly smiles wide, handshakes firm. Sharon's scarf was as bright as her eyes; Randy's laugh rumbled as though it had been waiting in his chest all morning.

"So Robin tells us you're considering checking out "Lifetime Vacations," Randy said once everyone settled with coffee.

Margaret smoothed the sleeve of her cardigan, her voice cautious but curious. "Well, both Robin and Danny spoke so highly of it. It . . . sounds interesting. How long have you lived there?"

"Two years," Sharon said, her voice bubbling with enthusiasm. "We spend about six months there every year. Best neighbors, best street, best decision we ever made."

Randy jumped in. "Live music every night of the year—Easter, Christmas, doesn't matter. Golf carts everywhere, outdoor bars, restaurants with patios. We've met more people in two years than we did in the twenty before."

Richard, who'd been quiet until then, leaned forward, surprising Danny. "Lots of golf courses, right? I read that somewhere."

Randy's grin widened. "You bet. And you can get to a lot of them by golf cart."

Sharon laughed. "We nearly gave up our car. And when we want water? There's a boat club nearby. Better than owning your own."

She paused, eyes twinkling. "Oh—and I got to hold an alligator."

Margaret burst out laughing, dabbing her eyes with a napkin. "Richard, maybe you should stick to golf carts, not gators." For the first time in years, Danny saw her shoulders shake with genuine mirth.

Robin leaned in gently, her voice steady. "I've had clients who bought there and said the same thing—it gave them back a rhythm, a sense of community. And there's no pressure. You can go for a month, see if it fits."

Margaret glanced at Richard. "A month?"

He shrugged. "Might not be the worst idea. Better than sitting in front of the TV all winter."

Sharon and Randy traded a knowing look. "That's what we said," Sharon admitted. "We went for the sampler visit, and by the end of the week, we'd bought."

The conversation flowed—airboat rides through the marsh, wildlife sightings, laughter about bears versus gators. And all the while, Danny watched his parents' eyes brighten, their voices rise with animation he hadn't seen in years.

Two hours later, numbers had been exchanged, promises made. As they left, Robin caught Danny's eye over the rim of her coffee cup. *Is this really happening?* her look seemed to say. He answered with a small shrug and a flicker of hope.

On the drive home, Margaret and Richard chatted more than Danny had heard in months. He gripped the wheel tighter, unease flickering beneath the relief. *God, let me keep them safe long enough for this to happen.*

Back in her office, Robin sat alone for a moment, the citrus scent lingering in the air, the sound of laughter still echoing in her ears. She leaned back in her chair, exhaled, and whispered to herself:

"So this is what healing feels like."

Chapter 44

Driving up the driveway, Margaret broke off mid-sentence. "Oh Richard, you left the garage door open again."

Richard blinked, startled, his expression caught somewhere between guilt and confusion. "Did I?"

She sighed, turning to Danny. "He forgets things all the time these days."

Danny forced a nod. He didn't trust himself to speak. He *knew* the door had been shut—he'd checked it himself before they left. The sight of it standing wide open sent a heavy thud through his chest.

"I'll just run in first," he said evenly, masking the urgency in his voice. "Make sure everything's okay. Then I'll come back for you."

His parents, distracted and still buzzing from their animated talk about Florida, barely noticed. Their chatter picked up again, giving Danny cover as he stepped through the yawning mouth of the garage.

Inside, the air was still, but his heart wasn't. He forced a long breath, trying to steady the pounding, but the weight of dread clung tight. The kitchen was undisturbed. The hallway quiet. For a fleeting second, he almost believed he was overreacting—until he reached Rick's room.

The sight knocked the air from his lungs.

The neat stacks of boxes he had carefully taped and labeled were torn open, their contents spilled in jagged heaps across the floor. Papers fanned out like discarded playing cards, photo envelopes ripped and left gaping. Someone had been here. Someone had been searching.

Danny gripped the doorframe until his knuckles went white. *Too real. This is getting too real.*

Forcing his face back into calm, he gathered himself. His parents hadn't stepped foot in this room in twenty-five years, and they weren't about to now. He could shield them from this—for tonight, at least.

Back in the living room, he pushed open the door with a practiced smile. "Come on in. Nothing's been touched. Everything's fine." The lie slipped out easier than it should have.

He poured them each a glass of iced tea, setting it gently in front of them as if nothing at all was amiss. "Why don't you two sit and relax a while. Talk about the Florida. I'll check in with you later—I'm meeting a friend who just came into town for a beer."

They were in good spirits, oblivious, their laughter carrying down the hall. A lucky break.

But Danny knew better. The stakes had just been raised.

He slipped out onto the porch, thumb flying across his phone.

Text to Marcus: *On my way. Someone's raised the stakes.*

Marcus's Reaction

Marcus leaned back in the creaky chair of his Pine Tree Lodge room, boots propped against the edge of the desk. The smell of pine cleaner and fried fish from the attached diner clung faintly in the air. He'd just finished scribbling notes from a phone call with a colleague when his phone buzzed.

Text from Danny: *On my way. Someone's raised the stakes.*

Marcus froze.

The words tightened his gut in the way no tactical drill or courtroom testimony ever had. He read them again, slower this time. He'd been in the game too long to mistake that kind of tone—short, stripped down, urgent. Danny wasn't one to exaggerate. If he said the stakes had shifted, it meant the ground was moving beneath their feet.

He set the phone on the desk, stared at it for a beat, then muttered to the empty room, "So it begins."

His hand moved automatically, sliding open the small duffel he always traveled with. Out came his leather notebook—names, numbers, dead leads and live ones—and a folder of resources he'd kept in case Westridge proved as messy as his instincts had warned. He flipped through a few pages, pulled out a business card, then shoved it back. Too early. Too soon.

Still, his pulse quickened with the familiar edge of a case heating up. He hadn't felt it in years, not like this.

He texted back: *Beer's waiting. But bring everything you've got— details, documents, all of it. We're not treating this like a hypothetical anymore.*

Sliding the notebook into his jacket pocket, Marcus glanced at the window. The late-afternoon sun was bleeding toward the tree-tops, throwing long shadows across the parking lot below. A lone pickup pulled in, idling too long before the driver finally cut the engine. His instincts prickled.

"Time to get to work," he murmured.

He zipped up the duffel, locked the door behind him, and headed down to the lodge bar. Whatever Danny was walking in with tonight, Marcus knew it was going to demand more than advice.

Pine Tree Lodge Bar Scene

The Pine Tree Lodge bar smelled of cedar and fried onion rings, the kind of place where the locals still called each other "buddy" and the booths were cracked but clean. Marcus sat at a corner table, a bottle of beer sweating in front of him, when Danny pushed through the door.

Danny scanned the room quickly—an old habit that had returned full force since the garage incident—then spotted Marcus waving him over.

"Danny Kessler," Marcus said, standing to clasp him in a bear hug. His voice carried the warmth of old times, but his eyes stayed sharp, already reading the tension in Danny's face.

Danny dropped into the chair across from him, setting his leather satchel on the seat beside him like a guard dog, empty now of the evidence he'd given to Rebecca, it still felt like a weight he couldn't quite set down. He exhaled slowly, reached for the beer Marcus slid across the table, and finally said, "It's real. All of it. The ledger, the payments, the threats. And somebody was in the house today."

Marcus didn't flinch. He just took a slow drink, wiped his mouth with the back of his hand, and said, "Then we're past theory. This is live."

Danny nodded, his jaw tight. "Parents think Richard left the garage open. But I checked—it was closed when we left. They tore through Rick's boxes. Papers all over the floor. They're looking for something."

Marcus leaned in, voice low. "And you've still got the key pieces?"

Danny tapped the satchel. "Safe with Rebecca now. Locked down in her firm's vault."

"Good," Marcus said simply. His gaze softened a little. "That was smart. Buying you time."

Danny rubbed a hand across his face. "I'm trying to keep it together, Marcus. For Robin. For my folks. But it's like every hour, the ground shifts again."

Marcus was about to reply when Danny's phone buzzed. He glanced at the screen—Robin.

"Excuse me," he muttered, and swiped to answer. "Hey."

Robin's voice spilled through, bright and warm. "Danny! I just had to call. Today was . . . amazing. Your parents were glowing after that Florida meeting. Margaret said she hasn't felt that energized in years. I think this is really happening!"

Danny's chest eased at the sound of her excitement. He smiled despite himself, the tension in his shoulders loosening a fraction. "That's good to hear. They needed it."

Her laughter trickled through, soft and hopeful. "It feels like things are finally moving in the right direction."

Danny hesitated, glancing at Marcus across the table. Then he said, voice firm but gentle, "Robin . . . I'm glad you called. There's something you should know. When we got home, the garage door was up. Someone went through Rick's boxes. They were looking for something."

Silence. Then Robin's breath caught. "Danny . . . "

"I've got Marcus here with me," Danny cut in. "He's the friend I told you about—the one from the task force. He's in town now, and I trust him. I think . . . it's time you met him. Tonight, if you're up for it."

On the other end, Robin's voice steadied. "Yes. Tonight. Just tell me where."

Danny met Marcus's eyes, and Marcus gave a single nod. "We'll come to you," Danny said into the phone. "We'll explain everything. And this time, we won't be carrying it alone."

Robin's House

The porch light was already on when Danny and Marcus pulled into the drive. Robin sat on the swing, her legs tucked under her, a blanket draped across her lap. She stood quickly when she saw them, relief flashing in her eyes—followed by worry when she registered the set of Danny's jaw.

"Robin," Danny said gently as he came up the steps. "This is Marcus. Marcus, Robin."

Marcus extended his hand, steady, respectful. "Ma'am. It's good to meet you. I wish it were under easier circumstances."

Robin's handshake was firm, though her fingers trembled. "Call me Robin. And thank you for coming."

"C'mon inside," she gestured.

"Make yourselves at home," Robin said, her voice steadier than she felt. She disappeared into the kitchen, returning with three mugs and a plate of shortbread she'd pulled from the cupboard. A small gesture, but it gave her something to do with her hands.

Marcus set his jacket aside, his posture casual but his eyes sharp, taking in the room, the corners, the quiet. Danny noticed it—the old habits of a cop, still intact.

They settled into their seats, the coffee table between them bare except for mugs and cookies. No papers. No photos. Everything dangerous was safe behind Rebecca's legal walls, but the weight of it still hung in the air.

Danny leaned forward, elbows on his knees. "Thanks for making time tonight, Marcus. I didn't want to waste a second. Things are moving fast."

Marcus gave him a half-smile. "Fast is fine. Sloppy isn't. Let's start with what's locked down already. You left everything with Rebecca, right?"

"Every page," Danny said. He glanced at Robin. She nodded too. "She has it under lock and privilege. Nobody touches it without her."

"Good," Marcus said, leaning back. "That's the strongest card you've got. Now the question is—what's next?"

Robin drew in a breath, her fingers tightening around the handle of her mug. "Sophia keeps me grounded. Rebecca makes me feel protected. But this—this doesn't stop in offices. He's out there. Pyle. I saw him."

Danny's jaw clenched, but Marcus lifted a hand, keeping the rhythm calm. "And you've both felt eyes on you since then, yeah? The break-in at the house confirmed it."

Robin swallowed hard. Danny caught the flicker of fear in her eyes before she straightened. "So what do we do? Hide? Wait?"

"No," Marcus said. "You stay steady. That's the first thing. Robin— you keep working with Sophia. Don't underestimate how much that matters. Danny—you keep playing it normal with your folks until they're down in Florida. If they're safe, you're freer to move."

"And you?" Danny asked.

"I start digging," Marcus replied simply. "Parole conditions, old case files, anyone Pyle still talks to. I've got a few strings I can pull— quietly. We don't want to spook him until we know what we're dealing with."

Robin exhaled, some of the tension in her shoulders easing. "It feels strange, sitting here talking about strategy in my own living room. Like . . . I'm hosting a book club, but the book is my life."

Danny reached over, brushing his hand lightly against hers. "You're not carrying it alone anymore. That's the difference."

Marcus studied them both, then said in his steady baritone, "You've got something rare. Most survivors don't get support like this. Use it. Don't push it away."

The silence that followed wasn't heavy this time—it was rooted, like soil settling around a new plant.

Marcus drained the last of his coffee and set the mug down with a quiet clink. "Here's the deal: Rebecca keeps the evidence, Sophia keeps the healing steady, and I'll keep eyes on the ground. You two—stay smart, stay together when you can, and don't let him see you flinch."

Robin managed a small smile. "Sounds almost simple when you say it."

"Nothing simple about it," Marcus replied. "But it's doable. And you've got more on your side than you think."

Danny looked around Robin's living room—warm light, the faint crackle of the fire, Robin sitting straighter now than she had a week ago—and felt, for the first time in years, that maybe Marcus was right.

Chapter 45

Sunday Dinner at the Kesslers'

The kitchen smelled of baked noodles and rosemary when Robin set her casserole dish on the counter. Margaret Kessler raised her eyebrows in surprise.

"Well, isn't this something? We don't get company bringing supper very often," she said, patting Robin's arm. "What a lovely treat."

Robin smiled, brushing off her hands. "Just a little thank you. Danny's told me how much you've let him take over the house these past couple of weeks. I thought you deserved an easy night."

Richard grumbled his usual greeting from the recliner, but he came to the table when Margaret called. Danny watched his parents shuffle into their chairs, noticing how unusual it felt—this simple act of sitting together around a full table. He poured iced tea into their glasses, then raised his own.

"To family," he said, looking at each of them. "And to new beginnings."

They clinked glasses, the sound brittle but promising.

Halfway through the meal, after Margaret had praised Robin's casserole twice, Danny cleared his throat.

"Mom, Dad—Robin and I made a couple of calls this morning. Just checking on details for "Lifetime Vacations," the place we talked about."

Richard paused mid-bite. "Oh? Already?"

Danny nodded, forcing a smile. "Good timing, actually. They had a cancellation. A villa just opened up for a sample week. This is really lucky because with winter approaching, the villas move quicker. So it only works if we grab it now."

Margaret blinked, fork hovering. "This week?"

"Actually Wednesday, and that gives us plenty of time to buy open-ended airline tickets so there's no pressure on when you return: a week, a month or whenever!"

Robin leaned forward, her tone warm, persuasive. "I know it sounds sudden. But it's exactly what you deserve—a real break. You've both been cooped up here so long. This way, you'd get sunshine, live music every night, restaurants, new friends . . . and you don't even have to cook if you don't want to."

Richard chuckled under his breath. "Live music, huh? Every night?"

"Every night," Danny confirmed. "And Dad, they've got wood-working shops, even clubs you can join. Mom—mah-jongg, bridge, pickleball. You name it, they've got it."

Margaret laughed, holding up her hands. "Oh, listen to you. You're making it sound like paradise."

Robin seized the moment. "Why not see for yourselves? Just a week to start. If you like it, maybe stay longer. And meanwhile, Danny can really dig in on the house without worrying about you tripping over boxes."

For a long moment, Margaret and Richard exchanged one of their wordless glances. Then Richard surprised them all. "You know, Margaret . . . might not be the worst idea. Snow's coming. And frankly, this house has been closing in on us."

Margaret sighed, a flicker of wistfulness in her eyes. "I don't know. It feels so sudden."

"That's what makes it fun," Robin said gently. "Spontaneous. An adventure."

Danny reached across the table, his voice softer. "You've carried enough heaviness here. Let me give you this gift. Just try it."

Margaret finally smiled, shaking her head but not saying no. "Well, if it's really all set up . . . "

Richard lifted his tea glass. "Then maybe it's time we started living again."

By the time they'd cleared the table, laughter had replaced hesitation. Margaret fussed over sending Robin home with her casserole dish, Richard even offered Danny a rare clap on the back.

As Robin slipped on her coat, she caught Danny's eye. The relief there mirrored her own. Outside, the cold air carried the faint scent of woodsmoke, and for the first time in weeks, Danny let himself imagine the house—quiet, empty, and safe enough to breathe.

Chapter 46

Danny's Whirlwind Days

The next few days passed in a whirl of motion. Danny barely had time to think, let alone brood, as he shepherded his parents through the practicalities of getting ready for Florida. There were packing lists to organize—what they'd take along, what they wanted boxed and stored, what he should sort later. Finances to settle—bills scheduled in advance in case they decided to extend their stay (*Please, God,* he thought more than once). And endless rounds of reassurance for his mother, who seemed to cycle between excitement and worry.

"What if something happens while we're gone?" she fretted more than once.

"We'll figure it out, Mom," Danny told her, steady and patient. "Robin and I can fly down if you need us. If we put the house on the market while you're away, we'll keep you looped in by phone. Your only job is to have fun—and give us daily reports on the music you're hearing, the people you're meeting. You'll be the ones too busy for us."

She waved him off, but the ghost of a smile always followed.

They shopped together for clothes they hadn't thought about in years—light jackets, shorts, even swimsuits. His parents looked awkward in the dressing-room mirrors, then laughed like school kids when they realized how long it had been. Lunches and dinners out turned into little celebrations, filling in decades of quiet resentment with new conversation, real laughter. For once, it wasn't about what they'd lost. It was about what lay ahead.

The busyness didn't erase the years of abandonment or fear—but it softened them, stitched over with practical tasks and shared anticipation. By the end of the third day, their suitcases stood half-full in the hallway, and the house felt strangely lighter. Danny caught himself thinking: *It's working. We're moving forward.*

Robin in Sophia's Office

Robin stepped into Sophia's office with her usual Tuesday mix of dread and determination. The calm scent of lavender greeted her, the quiet a stark contrast to the chaos in her head. She slipped into the chair across from Sophia and exhaled.

"You've been steady," Robin said, her voice a little shaky. "Helping me hold the pieces together. But there's something I can't quite reach. A memory that brushes up against me like a shadow I can't turn toward. I think I need your help to face it."

Sophia's gaze was gentle, steady. "You're ready," she said softly. "And we'll do this together. Remember—you have control here. We can stop anytime."

Robin nodded. "I know."

They began with grounding: the rhythm of her breath, the pressure of her feet against the floor, the imagined strength of light filling her chest. Sophia's voice guided her lower, down the staircase in her mind, until Robin's heart quickened.

"I see it," she whispered. "The motel sign . . . old, faded. The Pines, maybe? Rick's Mustang in the lot. He told me—" her throat tightened—"he told me he needed me. Begged me. Said it was just this once. And when I resisted . . . " Her body flinched. "He turned cold. He said I had no choice."

Sophia's voice anchored her: "You are safe now. You are here with me. Just tell me what you see, not what you fear."

Robin swallowed hard. "He told me to knock on the pink door—number twelve. Three knocks. My legs were shaking." Her eyes brimmed. "And when the door opened—it was him. Denver Pyle." Her breath hitched as the name left her lips.

The room was silent except for the ticking clock.

Sophia leaned in, her tone calm and sure. "You've named it. That was the shadow. And now it has less power. You are not that girl anymore, Robin. You are here, grounded, safe. Breathe. What do you smell?"

Robin blinked, disoriented but returning. She drew in a shaky breath. "Chamomile tea. Lavender. The wood polish on your desk."

"Good," Sophia said warmly. "That's the present. Let the light fill you. Let it wash away what was forced on you. You're not trapped anymore."

Robin wiped her cheeks with the back of her hand, a shaky laugh slipping out. "Sophia . . . I think I've known this deep down. Seeing him at the concert—that's why I felt it in my gut. I wasn't wrong. It was him."

Sophia handed her a cup of tea. "And you faced it today. You named it, in safety. That's strength, Robin. That's healing."

Robin held the cup in both hands, her fingers trembling. "Then maybe, after all this time," she whispered, "I can believe that healing is possible."

Sophia leaned forward, her voice steady but soft. "Robin, you don't have to stop the memories from coming. But you *can* remind yourself that they belong to another time. A time when you were too young, too unprotected. That isn't now. That girl isn't you anymore."

Robin's fingers twisted at the edge of her sleeve. "But when the faces come, it feels like I'm still her. Like I'm still trapped in that room."

"Then let's give you something to hold onto," Sophia said. "A phrase. Something simple. Something you can say whenever the shadows creep back."

Robin closed her eyes, breathing slowly. For a moment her lips moved silently, testing different words, until finally she whispered, "That was then . . . this is now." She opened her eyes, met Sophia's gaze, and added with more certainty: "I am safe."

Sophia nodded, smiling gently. "Good. Try it again. Out loud."

Robin repeated the words, stronger this time. And as she did, she noticed the tension in her shoulders easing, like the weight was sliding off, just a little.

"That was then. This is now. I am safe."

She sat back, almost surprised at the steadiness in her own voice. Sophia let the silence hold for a beat, then said, "Keep those words close. They'll be a doorway out of the memory and back into the present whenever you need them."

Robin tucked the phrase away like a talisman. For the first time in weeks, she felt like she had a weapon—not against the past, but for her future.

Robin at Home, That Evening

The house was quiet, the kind of quiet that could turn heavy if she let it. Robin set her purse on the hall table and passed the mirror above it. For a split second, the glass betrayed her—thin shoulders, painted lips, eyes too hollow to belong to the woman she was now.

Her breath caught, panic flaring. But then, almost automatically, she pressed her palm to the cool wood of the table and whispered the words Sophia had anchored in her:

That was then. This is now. I am safe.

The reflection steadied. It was only her—forty-one, tired, but steady. A woman who had walked out of Sophia's office lighter, armed not just with memories but with the strength to hold them.

She switched on the lamp, the room flooding with warm light. The heaviness pulled back like a tide. She almost smiled. Maybe this was what freedom felt like—not forgetting, but remembering without drowning.

Robin lifted her chin, squared her shoulders, and walked toward the kitchen to make tea.

She lingered at the kitchen counter, tea steaming in her hands. The memory of the pink motel door still pressed against her chest like a bruise, but now it didn't own her.

Softly, aloud, she tried the words on her tongue: "I am no longer the girl at the pink door. I am the woman who walked out."

The phrase settled into her like an anchor. Every time the shadows stirred, every time her reflection shifted, she would say it. That was then. This is now. She was safe. She was strong. And she was free.

Marcus's Three Days

Marcus had always believed in starting quiet. When he rolled his duffel into the Pine Tree Lodge, thirty minutes outside Westridge, he asked for a corner room with a view of the parking lot. Old habits. You needed to know who came and went. You needed exits.

He'd never set foot in Westridge before, but he wasn't blind to it either. Over the years Danny had told him enough stories—the brother, the girl, the suffocating small-town polish—that Marcus already carried a sketch in his mind. Now, driving its streets for real, he saw the town was exactly as described: pretty storefronts, church spires, banners left up too long after the Fall Festival. And underneath it, the silence of a place that didn't like questions.

Day One (Monday): He drove the town. Not sightseeing—mapping. Every alley, every choke point, the rhythm of the traffic lights. Westridge had grown—new mall, bright banners, a bustle that looked almost wholesome—but Marcus knew better. Shadows never really moved, they just shifted corners. That night he checked in with Danny again, caught the strain in his voice, and knew the kid was balancing more than he let on.

Day Two (Tuesday): The real digging began. Marcus carried a burner phone and spent half the morning on calls to old contacts: Pyle's parole officer, a retired detective who still owed him favors, a clerk who whispered more than she should. In the afternoon, he planted himself at the courthouse. Westridge wasn't fully digital yet—the older records were still in drawers and dusty scanners. No more microfilm reels, but the effect was the same: Marcus hunched over glowing screens, tracing property filings and vehicle registrations until his eyes ached. The Mustang's trail—or rather the hole where its trail should have been—gnawed at him. The paper record stopped in a way that reeked of hands pulling strings. That evening he walked the square, blending into the thinning crowd after the farmers market, watching faces. One man watched him back for too long. Marcus didn't break stride, didn't flinch, but logged the detail.

Day Three (Wednesday): The threads started to tighten. His notebook filled with names, numbers, arrows looping into half-finished patterns. The Mustang looked like it had passed through a shell buyer. A sealed court record hinted at Pyle's first victim—still anonymous, still protected. The air itself felt heavier, as though the town knew something was shifting.

That afternoon, in his lodge room with the curtains half-drawn, Marcus wrote one line across the top of a fresh page:

The stakes are higher than they know.

He underlined it twice. Then he closed the notebook, slid it under his pillow, and leaned back against the headboard, waiting for Danny to let him know that the parents were safely away. Tonight, he'd sit down with Danny and Robin and begin untangling this mess together. But for now, he stayed watchful, steady, a sentinel on the edge of enemy ground.

Chapter 47

The morning was a blur of zippers tugged shut, suitcases weighed and reweighed, and Margaret's anxious refrains of, *Did we pack the checkbook? What about the pills?* Danny moved through it all like a field marshal, steadying his parents with practical reassurance.

Robin arrived right on time in her gleaming black Range Rover. "Chariot service is here!" she teased, helping Richard heave a suitcase into the back. Margaret fussed with her scarf until Robin gently looped it into place for her. "See? Perfect," Robin said.

At the airport, they valet parked—anything to minimize the stress—and Danny secured non-passenger escort passes so he and Robin could shepherd his parents all the way to the gate. The TSA line rattled Margaret, but Robin slipped an arm through hers. "Just like riding a roller coaster," she said lightly. "Hold your breath for thirty seconds, then it's over."

At the gate, Danny's parents looked small and uncertain in the busy tide of travelers, but when their boarding group was called, Richard straightened with something like pride. The hugs were fierce, Margaret whispering into Danny's ear, "We'll miss you."

"Me, too," he promised.

Robin squeezed her hand. "Send us selfies with palm trees. Lots of them."

They watched from the window as the plane lifted into the clear sky, its silver body glinting in the sun. Both exhaled at the same time, as if releasing weeks of pent-up breath.

"Champagne in the air," Danny said, shaking his head. "Can you believe that?"

Robin laughed, relief in her tone. "Second honeymoon, whether they like it or not."

For the first time in days, it felt like momentum was on their side.

By the time they slid into the Range Rover, both were smiling, tension unclenching.

"Your mom," Robin said as she pulled onto the highway, "looked like she might bolt at security for a second. But then—did you see her? She was holding your dad's hand when they boarded. Like a girl again."

Danny let out a laugh that cracked into something like a sigh. "Yeah. Haven't seen that in years." He glanced at her. "Thanks, Robin. For being there."

She tapped the wheel. "We're in this together, remember?"

The Range Rover rolled off the main highway onto a two-lane back road. Pine Tree Lodge appeared suddenly from behind a cluster of oaks, its faded sign tilted, the paint peeling just enough to suggest years of indifference. The long strip of rooms faced a cracked asphalt lot.

Danny muttered, "Hell of a place to hole up."

Robin's eyes swept the façade, casual at first—until she froze. Her grip on the wheel tightened, knuckles blanching.

Pink doors.

Her breath caught in her throat. It wasn't the Lodge's dated siding or the sagging neon "Vacancy" sign. It was the row of bubble-gum pink doors, each one identical, the color burned into her memory. She whispered before she could stop herself: "Oh my God."

Danny turned, alarmed. "What?"

Robin swallowed hard, her gaze locked on door number twelve. Her voice was barely a thread. "This place . . . I've been here before."

Marcus, waiting by his room at the far corner, raised a hand in greeting, unaware of the storm that had just slammed into Robin's chest.

Danny followed her gaze, realization dawning like a thunderclap. He reached across the console, covering her hand where it gripped the gearshift. "We've got this," he murmured. "Not then. Now. Different game."

Robin forced herself to nod, but her heart was a drum against her ribs. She pulled the Rover into a space, the engine ticking as it cooled, and whispered her mantra under her breath:

"That was then. This is now."

"Right," he said firmly, quietly. "But we don't go in."

Danny cracked the window, gestured him over. Marcus jogged up, sharp-eyed, already reading the situation.

"Change of plan," Danny said low. "This place—it's a trigger for Robin. We need safer ground."

Marcus didn't blink. "Understood. Where?"

"Robin's house," Danny replied without hesitation.

Robin nodded quickly, grateful, still pale but pulling herself back to the present. "Yes. Home. My place."

Marcus gave a tight nod. "Good call. I'll follow."

While Marcus was retrieving his car, Danny and Robin switched places without a word. Danny squeezed her hand once more, then shifted the car into gear. As they pulled away, leaving the row of pink doors receding in the rearview mirror, Robin exhaled slowly.

"That was then," she murmured to herself, repeating it like a mantra. "This is now."

Danny glanced at her, caught the steel returning to her voice, and felt a flicker of relief. They were still on edge, yes—but they were moving forward. Together.

Chapter 48

The Range Rover's headlights cut a soft arc across Robin's driveway. Danny helped her carry in the leftover casserole dish she'd brought to his parents' a couple of nights before, while Marcus followed, his duffel slung casually over his shoulder but his eyes scanning the shadows with a soldier's precision.

Inside, Robin lit a lamp in the living room. The warm glow pushed back the heaviness that had settled on her since the motel parking lot. She busied herself with mugs and the coffee pot, grateful for the simple ritual. Danny noticed her hands weren't quite steady as she poured, and without thinking, he reached over and steadied the carafe. A small gesture, but she flashed him a quick, grateful look.

Marcus dropped into a chair, pulled out his notebook, and flipped it open to a page dense with arrows and names. "All right," he said, his voice low but steady. "Now that the folks are wheels-up, it's time we get serious. You two need to know what I've dug up these last three days."

Danny leaned forward, forearms on his knees. Robin sat back, hugging her mug.

Marcus tapped his pen against one name. *Denver Pyle.*

"I started with his parole. On paper, he's clean—conditions say he can't be within a hundred feet of minors, has to check in weekly. But someone vouched for him, someone with pull. I'm working on confirming who. My gut says we're looking at an old network keeping him shielded."

Robin's stomach tightened, but she forced herself to hold his gaze. "And the Mustang?"

Marcus flipped a page. "That trail is murky. Title records show a shell buyer—never the kid, never Rick. Payments were routed through a proxy. Which means the car was less about wheels and more about leverage. Rick was never meant to own it outright. It was bait, plain and simple."

Danny's jaw clenched. "And when he fell behind, the trap snapped shut."

Marcus nodded once. "Exactly. That random 'interest payment' Rick scrawled about? Classic extortion move. Keep the debtor off-balance so they never feel like they're catching up. He was on a leash, same as Robin."

Robin's knuckles whitened around her mug. She took a shaky breath. "I remembered something, earlier this week. With Sophia's help. The first . . . time. It was at a motel." Her eyes flicked to Marcus, then away. "The Pine Tree Inn. I didn't even realize until today—it's where you're staying."

Marcus stilled, his pen hovering. He exhaled slowly. "That's good to know. Bad history tied to that place, then. I'll move out tomorrow."

Robin shook her head quickly. "No—you don't have to uproot. Just . . . now I understand why it hit me so hard."

Marcus didn't argue, just scribbled a note and underlined it twice.

He turned the page again. "One more piece. I've been digging into sealed cases at the courthouse. There's a record of Pyle's first victim, the one he served time for. Name's blacked out—she was under sixteen. But there are ways around that. Between Rebecca's channels and mine, we'll track her down. If she's willing to talk, it could break this wide open."

The room went quiet. Outside, a breeze rattled the last of the autumn leaves against the window.

Finally, Danny spoke. "So what's our move?"

Marcus shut the notebook with a soft snap. "Step one: keep your parents safe, which you just did. Step two: keep this circle tight. No bragging, no confiding outside these walls. Step three: we start pulling threads—victim, car, parole sponsor—and see who twitches."

Robin whispered, almost to herself, "That was then. This is now."

Danny caught it, and for the first time in days, he smiled faintly. He reached over, brushing his fingers lightly against hers. "Now," he said, "we fight smart."

Marcus leaned back, eyes sharp but approving. "Exactly. And from here on out, we fight together."

The room was quiet after Marcus's firm words, the only sound the tick of Robin's grandfather clock. She sat straighter, the warmth of the coffee mug still in her hands, but something stronger was stirring underneath. For days she had felt cornered, waiting for the next blow. Now, she wanted to step forward.

Robin set her mug down and reached for her phone. "We've been reacting," she said, her voice steady. "But it's time to act. Rebecca needs to meet you, Marcus. Tomorrow, if possible. If not, Friday."

Danny nodded instantly. "That's the right move."

Robin scrolled to Rebecca's name and hit call. Her stomach fluttered, but this time with resolve, not dread.

"Robin?" Rebecca's voice was warm, as always, but carried the undercurrent of someone who'd already been briefed to expect weight.

"Hi, Rebecca. I know it's evening, so I'll be quick. Danny and I would like to bring Marcus to meet with you. He's here now, and he's been digging into details we need your help sorting out—especially around the Mustang and Pyle's parole. Are you available tomorrow morning?"

Rebecca didn't hesitate. "I can clear a slot at ten. Bring Marcus, bring what you've got. We'll start putting this into order."

Robin closed her eyes, relief washing over her. "Thank you, Rebecca."

Danny leaned close enough for her to hear him murmur, "Good call."

When she hung up, she looked at both men. "Ten o'clock tomorrow. Rebecca's office."

Marcus nodded, already scribbling it into his notebook. "Perfect. That gives me tonight to pull my notes into something sharper."

Danny exhaled, tension loosening from his shoulders. "Then it's settled. Tomorrow we stop circling this thing—and we start hitting back."

Robin found herself whispering the words that Sophia had given her, the mantra that steadied her whenever the dark threatened to press in. "That was then. This is now."

The men heard her, and for a moment, all three shared the silence—different from before. This time, it hummed with resolve.

Chapter 49

The sky was a clean autumn blue when Robin's Range Rover pulled up in front of Rebecca Wright's brick office building. Danny climbed out of the passenger seat, tugging at the cuff of his jacket as if to steady himself. Marcus followed behind, his stride unhurried, eyes scanning the block the way men like him always did—checking angles, logging exits.

Rebecca's receptionist led them down the hall to the glass-paneled corner office. Sunlight glowed across polished wood and legal tomes. Rebecca rose as they entered, tall and commanding in a charcoal suit, pearl earrings catching the light.

"Danny, Marcus," she said warmly, shaking their hands in turn. "Come in. Sit. I've been expecting you."

The air in the room shifted once the door closed. Rebecca's presence was steady, but not soft—she radiated the kind of confidence that came from years of fighting in the trenches of the law.

"Before we start," she said, sliding her glasses into place, "everything said here is protected. You're my clients now. So speak freely."

Marcus leaned back in his chair, his notebook already open, pen in hand. "Then let's cut straight to it. We've got two live wires: Denver Pyle, and the Mustang. Both stink of money laundering, coercion, and cover-ups."

Rebecca arched a brow. "Tell me what you've found."

Danny exhaled and described his parents' recollection of the repossession—the car that sat untouched in the garage until strangers collected it. "No paperwork, no questions, just gone," he said. "My father swore he never caught their names."

Rebecca's fingers tapped the desk. "That's unusual. Repossessions leave trails. Paperwork. Court filings. If none exists, it means someone wanted it invisible."

Marcus nodded. "I started digging Monday. Ran through the DMV database, old property records, banking slips that survived in Rick's boxes. The car was registered, yes, but to a shell buyer—name flagged in three other counties. Same shell pops up in deals connected to Pyle's circle."

Rebecca's expression sharpened. "So the car wasn't a gift. It was leverage."

"Exactly," Marcus said. "Bait on a hook Rick could never wriggle off."

Robin shifted uneasily in her chair. "That's when everything changed for him. For us."

Rebecca leaned toward her, voice steady but fierce. "Then we pull the thread until the whole sweater unravels. Shell companies can be pierced if we push hard enough."

"And Pyle?" Danny asked, his jaw tight.

Marcus's eyes darkened. "Still walking free. But I've traced whispers about his first victim. Sealed records. The file's buried, but not gone. I'll keep working it."

Rebecca folded her hands. "Then here's our play. I'll file preservation motions quietly, make sure nothing can be shredded if someone catches wind." Silence held for a moment, the kind that bound them more tightly than words.

Then, Rebecca turned her focus to Robin.

"And you?" she asked gently. "Have you uncovered anything on your end?"

Robin's hands tightened in her lap. For a moment she looked to Danny, then drew in a breath and held Rebecca's gaze. "Yes. With Sophia's help, I confirmed a memory I'd buried. The first time Rick forced me into . . . into one of those 'dates,' it wasn't just some faceless man. It was Denver Pyle. And it happened at the Pine Tree Lodge."

Danny's head jerked up, but Rebecca kept her tone even. "You're certain?"

Robin nodded. "It's burned into me now—the pink doors, the number on the room, the smell of that place. I didn't want it to be true, but it is."

Marcus leaned forward, his expression tight but respectful. "That's a hell of a piece of corroboration. The lodge is still in business, still off the books in all the wrong ways. That gives us location, history, and a name tied directly to the earliest abuse."

Rebecca's pen scratched across her legal pad. "And it explains why he still circles here. Men like that revisit their hunting grounds. This isn't just your memory, Robin—it's evidence. Memory plus documentation is what makes cases."

Robin blinked hard, fighting tears. "For so long I thought I was crazy. But now . . . now I know I'm not."

Danny reached over, resting a hand briefly on hers. "No, you're not."

Rebecca closed her folder with deliberate care. "Then we use this. We fold it into the broader strategy. Every thread strengthens the case—and your truth."

Rebecca asked Robin to stay behind after Danny and Marcus stepped out. In the privacy of her office, she guided Robin through giving a detailed statement, word for word, which she promised to preserve under attorney-client privilege. When Robin finally emerged, pale but steady, Rebecca assured her: "No one can erase what you've said. It's recorded now, safe."

When she reached the car where the men were waiting, Danny could see the toll it had taken, but also the faint trace of relief in her eyes.

Once Robin slid into the car, they drove in silence for several minutes, the hum of the road a buffer between them. Then Danny smacked his forehead.

"Oh my God. I totally forgot to tell Rebecca about the break-in. Things are happening so fast that Saturday feels like it was a month ago."

Marcus looked over from the passenger seat. "Good catch. Call her now—better she hears it from us than from someone else later."

Danny put the phone on speaker. Rebecca answered on the second ring, brisk but warm. "Hey, Danny. What did you forget?"

"You must be psychic," Danny said. "While Robin and I were out with my parents on Saturday afternoon, their house was broken into."

A beat of silence. Then Rebecca's tone dropped an octave. "I take it you didn't report it."

Danny winced. "No. We were so focused on getting my parents out of town, it took a back seat. I didn't want them panicking."

"Your instincts were solid," Rebecca said firmly. "Protecting them first was the right move. But now—even five days later—we need to get this on record. Otherwise it disappears into rumor."

She paused, letting that land. "We have two choices: One, you and Marcus dictate a detailed report here, under my protection, so it's timestamped and documented. Or two, we walk it into the Sheriff's office. But know this—reporting it officially will stir the pot. It puts us on their radar."

Robin leaned forward, her voice tight but steady. "I don't care. It's the right thing to do. We can't keep this in the shadows."

Danny exhaled, long and slow. "I hate to admit it, but I agree with Robin."

Marcus' jaw flexed. He didn't speak at first, but the tension in his posture was enough to make the car feel smaller. Finally, he said, "If you do this, you need to be ready for the blowback. Don't expect them to play fair."

Rebecca's voice returned, crisp. "Then let's not waste time. Can you come back to my office now?"

They filed back into Rebecca's office fifteen minutes later, the citrus-clean air doing little to ease the heaviness pressing on their shoulders. Rebecca gestured for them to sit around the conference table. Her desk phone gleamed under the afternoon light, waiting like a loaded gun.

"All right," Rebecca said, steady but firm. "We'll do this clean. I'll place the call. I'll put it on speaker so we're all aligned, but let me take the lead. Keep it factual, nothing extra. We don't want to hand them more than they ask for."

Danny's throat tightened, but he nodded. Robin clasped her hands in her lap, twisting her ring until Marcus reached over and stilled her fingers with the gentlest touch.

Rebecca dialed. The first ring was crisp, the second a little too long. Finally, a gruff male voice answered, "Sheriff's Office, Deputy Hawkins speaking."

"Deputy," Rebecca said smoothly, "this is Attorney Rebecca Wright. I'm calling on behalf of my clients, Daniel Kessler and Robin Wellworth. We need to report a break-in that occurred last Saturday at the Kessler residence."

There was a pause, followed by the scrape of a chair across a floor. *"Saturday?"* Hawkins repeated, the single word edged with something like disbelief—or annoyance. *"And you're reporting it now?"*

Rebecca didn't flinch. "Yes. Priorities at the time involved ensuring the safety of Mr. Kessler's elderly parents, who have since been relocated. The break-in specifically targeted one room in the house. We'd like an official record on file, and an investigator assigned."

Danny leaned toward the phone, forcing his voice steady. "It was my brother's room. Boxes were torn open, everything rifled through. Nothing else in the house was touched. Whoever it was—they were looking for something."

A silence stretched, long enough for Robin's nails to dig into her palms. Then Hawkins cleared his throat. "All right. We'll open a file.

I'll need you to come down to the station tomorrow, Mr. Kessler, to give a full statement."

Rebecca cut in before Danny could respond. "He'll do that—with me present. We'll coordinate a time."

Another pause. Then, clipped: "Fine. Tomorrow morning. Nine o'clock." The line went dead without a goodbye.

The four of them sat in the quiet hum of the office. Marcus exhaled through his nose, low and sharp. "Well. That didn't sound thrilled."

Rebecca folded her hands on the table. "No, it didn't. But it's on record now, and that matters. Still . . . " she glanced between them, eyes dark with warning, " . . . be ready. They'll be watching us closer after this."

Danny rubbed a hand over his face, the weight of it all pressing heavier. Robin reached under the table, touched his knee lightly, grounding him.

Rebecca's voice steadied the air again: "All right. Tonight, go home. Keep your doors locked, lights on. Tomorrow, we'll face them together."

Chapter 50

The lobby of the Sheriff's Office smelled faintly of burnt coffee and floor wax, the kind of sterile mix that felt both tired and permanent. A mounted buck's head on the far wall stared at them with glassy indifference, and a row of battered plastic chairs sagged under the weight of years.

Rebecca walked a step ahead, crisp in her navy blazer, her presence commanding without being loud. Danny followed, his shoulders squared, the tension in his jaw betraying the restless night he'd had. Robin brought up the rear, clutching her bag a little too tightly, her pulse quickening with each echo of their footsteps across the linoleum.

Deputy Hawkins appeared at the counter, his expression unreadable. "You must be Kessler," he said flatly, eyes flicking to Danny, then sliding past to Robin with the faintest glimmer of recognition. "Sheriff's expecting you."

Rebecca's tone cut like clean glass. "Attorney Wright. I'll be present during the statement."

Without argument, Hawkins buzzed them through the door and led them down a narrow hallway into Sheriff Stone's office.

Stone rose from behind his oversized desk, the leather chair groaning in protest. He was broader now than Danny remembered, his once-sharp jawline lost under years of indulgence, but his eyes still carried the same sharp glint—like a man always calculating the odds.

His expression shifted as Danny stepped in—first surprise, then what looked like a smile. "Danny Kessler," he said, voice carrying a practiced geniality. "Now there's a face I didn't expect to see again. You holding up all right back in Westridge?"

Danny hesitated, caught off guard by the warmth in the sheriff's tone. "I'm managing."

Stone clapped a hand on his shoulder with just a bit too much weight, the kind of gesture meant to feel fatherly. "Good, good. You've been through enough in your life. I always told you back then, sometimes the best thing a man can do is walk away. Spare himself the ghosts." His smile thinned. "Course, you came back anyway. Guess some people can't help chasing shadows."

Rebecca smoothly cut in, guiding them back to the business of the break-in report, but the words stuck in Danny's head like burrs.

Rebecca motioned to the chairs before Stone could control the flow. "There was a break-in at Kessler's Saturday afternoon. We're here to make sure it's properly documented. Mr. Kessler can give a statement. Ms. Wellworth was present during part of the afternoon as well."

Stone leaned back, his smile not quite reaching his eyes. "Funny it took nearly a week to come in."

Rebecca's voice stayed steady. "Safety of the parents was the priority. They've since been relocated."

Stone drummed his fingers on the blotter, then gestured to Hawkins. "All right. Record it."

The next thirty minutes dragged like hours. Danny described the open garage, the untouched rooms, the chaos in Rick's room—the torn boxes, the scattered papers. He kept his voice even, but his fists clenched on his knees when he spoke about the deliberate search. Robin added her piece: the timing, the fact that she'd been with Danny and his parents the whole evening, corroborating his account.

Hawkins' pen scratched across the form, each stroke oddly loud in the quiet office. When Danny finished, Stone leaned forward, steepling his fingers.

"Noted," he said, his tone just a hair too dismissive. "We'll look into it."

Rebecca met his gaze without blinking. "We'll expect follow-up, Sheriff. My clients have every right to protection under the law."

For the briefest moment, something flickered in Stone's expression—annoyance, maybe, or calculation—but it was gone as quickly as it came. He forced a smile. "Of course. We'll be in touch."

Back in the car, Robin let out the breath she'd been holding. Danny rubbed the back of his neck.

"Did you see his face?" Robin whispered. "Like he already knew."

Rebecca buckled her seatbelt, her voice cool and firm. "That man's playing a game. The trick is—we don't let him know which cards we're holding."

Late in the afternoon, as they walked through town, the crisp autumn air cooling their nerves, Danny turned the conversation back.

"You know what's bothering me?" he said, eyes narrowing as though replaying a film. "When Rick died, I always thought leaving town was my choice—my way of protecting myself, protecting my parents. But today, Stone reminded me . . . he's the one who put the idea in my head. Said I should walk away. Start fresh somewhere else."

Robin frowned. "Like he was doing you a favor."

Danny's voice hardened. "Like he was cleaning up a mess. Making sure the questions stopped before they got too loud." He shook his head. "All those years I carried the guilt for bailing . . . but it wasn't even mine. I was a pawn."

Robin suggested they stop at The Bean to collect themselves and grab a cup of coffee.

Inside The Bean, the late afternoon light slanted through tall windows, catching in the steam rising from mugs. Danny and Robin slid into line, grateful for the ordinary bustle of clinking cups, the hiss of the espresso machine, the low hum of conversation. For a few minutes, it felt like the weight of the week lifted—just two people ordering coffee, shoulders brushing as they waited.

Danny muttered, almost with a smile, "God, I've missed decent coffee."

Robin tilted her head at him, smirking. "Admit it—this was my idea of a good decompression."

"Fine," Danny said, giving in. "Best idea you've had all week."

While they placed their order, just outside on the sidewalk, three men huddled close.

Sheriff Stone's voice was a low growl, his jaw tight as he jabbed a finger toward the street. "He's back. Against my advice. And he's stirring shit that was supposed to stay buried."

Deputy Hawkins shifted uneasily, eyes flicking toward the café windows. "It's not just him. That girl—Robin Wellworth—she's seeing that shrink. Talking too much. And now someone saw them both walk into a lawyer's office with another man. We can't let this run any further."

Denver Pyle leaned against the brick wall, arms folded, lips curling into something between a sneer and a smile. "So, we move now. Quick and quiet. The longer they dig, the harder this gets to contain."

Stone's face darkened. "Then it ends. Now. I won't let a couple of ghosts wreck twenty years of peace."

The three men fell into silence, their posture tense, like a wolf pack scenting blood.

Inside, Danny and Robin sipped their drinks, letting the warmth bleed some of the tension from their bodies. Robin tapped her mug with a fingernail. "You realize," she said softly, "this is the first time in days I've actually felt normal."

Danny gave her a sidelong look, the corners of his mouth easing. "Yeah. Almost dangerous, isn't it?"

When they stepped back out into the cool air, the moment shattered. Across the street, just beyond the café's awning, three figures were breaking their huddle. Stone, Hawkins, and Denver Pyle.

Robin stiffened. Danny's gut dropped.

The men didn't see them—or pretended not to—but the image was burned into Danny's mind: the sheriff's flushed face, the deputy's nervous glance, Pyle's smug detachment.

Robin gripped Danny's arm. "Did you see—"

"I saw," he muttered, steering her quickly down the block. His pulse hammered in his throat. "Whatever they were saying, it wasn't good."

As Danny and Robin moved away, the three men dispersed in different directions, their conversation sealed behind them. Danny didn't need to hear the words; the look on Stone's face was enough to knot his stomach. Trouble was circling, and they were closer to it than either wanted to admit.

Chapter 51

Robin chose the corner booth at The Lantern Café, a place quiet enough that whispers wouldn't be overheard, but public enough that she could leave quickly if she needed to. She fiddled with her spoon, stirring sugar into a cup of tea she wasn't sure she'd drink. When Melody walked in, a swirl of scarves and restless energy, Robin felt both relief and hesitation at once.

"Robin!" Melody's smile lit up the space, her voice carrying a warmth that made half the café glance over. "You look good. Stronger."

Robin stood, hugged her briefly, then sat again. She leaned in. "Melody . . . thank you for meeting me. I didn't want to do this over the phone."

Melody tilted her head, reading the seriousness in her tone. "This is about Danny, isn't it? About . . . Westridge?"

Robin hesitated, then nodded. "Yes. And about what you told me—wanting to interview him, film his story, maybe pull Bruce in. I need to be honest with you. This is bigger than a documentary. Bigger than a profile."

Melody leaned forward, her eyes bright, almost hungry. "Tell me."

Robin lowered her voice. "There's danger. Real danger. The kind you can't just walk away from once you've stepped into it. If I let you in, you—and Bruce—become part of it. That means surveillance, threats, maybe worse. I can't promise your safety."

Melody's hands stilled on her coffee cup, but her expression didn't waver. "So you're telling me the stakes are life and death."

"Yes," Robin whispered. "And as much as I trust you, you need to know that if this goes public too soon, everything could collapse. We need careful timing. Legal moves first. Protection. Then maybe, when the time is right, the story."

For a moment, Melody said nothing. Then, a slow grin tugged at her lips. "Robin, you know me. Danger doesn't scare me—it focuses me. And if Bruce gets wind of this? He'll insist we fight. He's not just a face on the news. He's a bulldog when he smells a cover-up."

Robin reached across the table, gripping her hand. "Please— think carefully. Once you step in, there's no way back. I had to give you that choice."

Melody squeezed back, fierce and certain. "Then consider me in. I'd rather be in the fire with people I trust than safe on the sidelines while monsters walk free."

Robin exhaled, a knot loosening in her chest, though fear lingered. She managed a thin smile. "All right. But for now—you tell no one. Not Bruce, not yet. First, I'll bring you to Danny and Marcus. Then Rebecca. We'll decide together how much you hear, and when."

Melody nodded, her eyes glinting with excitement. "Deal. But Robin—when the time comes to shine a light on this? Promise me you won't hold back."

Robin's voice was steady now, her own resolve echoing back. "I won't. Not this time."

Robin's Range Rover pulled up the drive, headlights slicing across the quiet street. Danny and Marcus were already inside, papers spread across Robin's dining table, coffee steaming in mismatched mugs.

When Robin walked in, Melody was right on her heels, eyes sparking with curiosity, her scarf thrown back like a banner.

Danny frowned. "Robin . . . "

Robin lifted a hand. "Hear me out. You both know Melody. She's been circling around this already—Cambodia, the shelters, her work. And she has connections. But I told her before she walked in the door: if she joins us, there's no going back."

Melody slipped into a chair before they could argue. "Let's skip the disclaimers. I know what danger looks like. What I don't know is what's happening here. But I want in."

Marcus leaned back, arms crossed, his eyes narrowing in assessment. "Wanting in and being useful aren't the same thing."

Melody met his stare without blinking. "You're right. But I'm not just a tourist with a camera. My boyfriend is Bruce Meyers—he's the anchor on the Channel 7 evening news. If we need air cover— fast—I can deliver it. If you don't think that's leverage worth having, then by all means keep running in circles."

Danny glanced at Robin, startled. Robin just gave a small shrug. "Told you she wouldn't scare easy."

Marcus let the silence hang for a long beat before finally grunting. "Fine. But you play by our rules. No leaks, no surprises. And if you even *think* about running this to Bruce before we say the word, you'll tank everything we're trying to do."

Melody smirked. "Understood. I may love drama, but I know how to keep a lid on a pot until it's ready to boil."

Danny exhaled, dragging a hand over his face. "This circle keeps growing."

Robin looked at him softly. "And maybe that's what it takes. More voices. More witnesses. More people who won't look away."

Marcus picked up his notebook, snapped it shut. "All right, then. Let's get to work."

Chapter 52

Robin sat curled into the familiar chair in Sophia's office, legs tucked beneath her, fingers wrapped around a mug of chamomile tea. The lavender candle flickered low, and for a moment she just breathed it in, letting the air settle her nerves.

"You look . . . steadier," Sophia observed gently, studying her with calm eyes.

"I *feel* steadier," Robin admitted. "At least sometimes. Danny's parents are safe now—they're in Florida. That feels like a huge weight off my chest. And Marcus—he's here, he's helping, and he's good at it. Almost . . . too good. Like he sees threats before I even notice them." She gave a small laugh, but her hand tightened on the cup.

Sophia tilted her head. "So you're surrounded by support. And yet?"

Robin hesitated. "And yet . . . I keep waiting for the floor to drop out. Every new step forward—getting the parents safe, meeting with Rebecca, even just walking down Main Street—I think: 'This is when it'll all go wrong.'"

Sophia nodded, her voice quiet but firm. "That's the trauma speaking. The part of you that learned early on to scan the room for danger, to never fully rest. But Robin—look around. Right now you're here, safe. You're not that girl anymore."

Robin's throat caught. She pressed her knuckles to her lips, forcing the tears back. "I know. But sometimes I feel like she's clawing at me from the mirror, from the shadows. Especially after remembering that first time . . . with Pyle."

Sophia leaned in slightly. "And yet, you faced it. You named it. That memory doesn't own you anymore. It's a piece of the past, not a chain around your ankle. When it creeps in again, I want you to ground yourself with something simple: *That was then. This is now.* Say it out loud if you have to."

Robin let out a shaky laugh. "Yes, I've been using that . . . almost like a rocking chair."

For a long moment, Robin let the words roll through her. That was then. This is now. She whispered them, testing their weight, and felt something loosen inside her chest.

Finally, she looked up, voice firmer. "Thank you. I think I needed permission to draw that line. To remind myself I'm not still trapped."

Sophia reached across, her hand resting lightly on Robin's. "You don't need my permission. But you do need your own. And today, you gave it."

Robin's eyes burned, but this time the tears didn't feel like weakness. They felt like release.

Robin's voice carried a little more steadiness than the week before, but her shoulders betrayed her. She wrapped her arms around herself and said,

"There are still some things you should know, Sophia. For your own safety."

Sophia's eyes softened but stayed firm. "Go on."

Robin took a deep breath. "Danny's friend Marcus is here now—he's ex-law enforcement, sharp as a blade. He's staying at the Pine Tree Lodge." She swallowed hard. "The same place I remembered last week. The same doors. The same rooms."

Sophia's brow furrowed slightly, but her voice was calm. "That must have been a shock."

"You could say that," Robin whispered. "But it doesn't stop there. Sheriff Stone—the one who called Rick's death a tragic accident—he isn't the friend we thought he was. Danny remembered something. It was *Stone* who 'encouraged' him to leave town twenty-five years ago. To 'protect himself.' But now Danny sees it—Stone wanted him gone so the whole mess would die down. And yesterday . . . " Her voice faltered. "We saw him outside The Bean. With Pyle. And Deputy Hawkins. They were furious, whispering like the walls were closing in on them."

Sophia's hands folded neatly in her lap. She did not flinch. "So, the danger is rising."

Robin nodded. "Exactly. And I need you to understand—*the more you know, the more risk you take on.* If they think you're aware of too much . . . "

She trailed off, but Sophia leaned in, her voice steady as stone. "Robin, I don't scare easily. If part of my role is to hold space for truth, then I'll do it. I've kept records of our sessions from the start. Careful notes. If the day comes when the court needs them, I'll be ready. And if the worst were ever to happen . . . " She placed her hand gently over Robin's. "Then your story will not vanish."

Tears welled in Robin's eyes. Relief, fear, gratitude—too many things to name. She squeezed Sophia's hand. "Then keep writing. Every word. Someday, it may be the difference between freedom and silence."

Sophia nodded, unshaken. "I already am."

Chapter 53

Robin's living room still smelled faintly of cinnamon from the tea she'd brewed earlier, but the mood in the room was nothing like cozy. The four of them sat in a loose circle—Danny in the armchair by the window, Marcus leaning forward on the edge of the couch like a sentinel, Melody perched with her reporter's notebook closed on her lap, and Robin, steady in her own chair, clearly both host and anchor.

For a moment, no one spoke. Outside, the late afternoon sun slanted across the porch rails, long shadows stretching like fingers into the room. It was Robin who broke the silence.

"Before we decide anything else, let me be clear about what I bring to this," she said, her voice measured. "I've lived here my whole life. I know who left suddenly, who dropped out of school, who 'moved away' without warning. At the time it all seemed like ordinary life, but now? Those vanishings line up with Pyle's timeline. I can start pulling threads quietly—yearbooks, church rosters, old dance studio records, even casual conversations with women who were a few years younger than me. Someone will remember. If we can put a name to that sealed victim file, we'll have corroboration Rebecca can use."

She sat back, her jaw tightening.

"I'll do it quietly, carefully. But I'll do it. I won't stay silent anymore."

Danny reached across the small table and gave her hand a squeeze, pride flashing in his eyes.

Marcus rubbed his jaw, then leaned in, his voice gravel-low and steady.

"That's good. That's really good. Local eyes and ears matter more than anything. Meanwhile, I'll keep running the bigger net. Pyle's parole officer owes me a call back—if we can pin down who vouched for him, that tells us where his leverage comes from. I've also got the Mustang to chase. Registration history's muddy, and when a paper trail goes blank, it usually means a shell buyer. That tells us someone higher up wanted Rick tied down without leaving their own fingerprints."

He paused, then tapped the notebook open on his knee, pages covered in his tight block handwriting.

"And let's be blunt. We've got cops in this town who don't smell right. Stone's been carrying water for somebody for a long time, and if Hawkins is in his pocket, we don't have the luxury of assuming protection. Every move we make has to assume they're listening."

Danny exhaled slowly, nodding.

"That tracks. When I came back, I wanted to believe maybe it was different—that the sheriff back then was just . . . paternal, trying to keep me safe. But looking back, it was him who told me to leave town. It wasn't my idea. He made it sound noble—like he was doing me a favor. Now I see it. I was a pawn. Me gone meant the questions died with me. It meant Rick's death could get filed under 'tragic accident' and no one would dig further."

He looked from Marcus to Robin, his eyes dark.

"I'm done being a pawn. And if that means circling the wagons tighter, then fine. But I don't want us charging blind."

Melody leaned forward now, her eyes lit with a kind of restless fire.

"You don't have to convince me of the stakes. I've seen trafficking firsthand—in Phnom Penh, in Malawi. The patterns repeat. People vanish into silence, records go missing, people in power look the other way. Westridge isn't unique—it's just hidden better."

She hesitated only a moment before pressing on.

"I can help. Bruce's platform is dangerous, yes—but also powerful. If we need a spotlight, I can get it. That said—Robin's right. If you let me in, then I'm in. That puts me at risk. It puts Bruce at risk. And I don't make that choice lightly."

Her eyes flicked toward Danny.

"But if exposure is the only way to keep you alive—and keep her safe—then that's a risk I'll take."

For a long moment, no one spoke. The only sound was the old grandfather clock. Finally, Marcus leaned back, his gaze sweeping the group.

"So here's how it looks:

- Robin, you start quietly gathering names and stories—threads only locals know.

- Danny, you keep your folks safe and steady, and as you continue to clean out your parents' house, you never know what might show up. You and I'll track the Mustang's history, dig where the records go blank. And remember, Danny you've been doing this work for twenty-five years, so Robin, if you are wondering what a trafficked girl might do or say, pull him in.

- Melody, you hold your fire. Keep notes, build context, but don't pull the trigger on Bruce's platform until we're ready. Exposure too soon gets us killed.

- And me—I'll be the firewall. I'll run interference, keep my eyes on the streets, and make sure we're not blindsided."

Robin drew a breath, then added softly, but with steel underneath:

"And we all stay close to Rebecca. Every scrap of evidence, every story, every memory goes through her. We don't let Stone, or Hawkins, or anyone else box us in without a fight."

Danny nodded, his shoulders squaring. Melody closed her notebook—not to shut it, but to claim the moment. And Marcus simply said, "Then it's settled. Circle's tight. No leaks. We move together."

The fire in the hearth had burned low, shadows stretching across Robin's walls. But instead of feeling smothered, the room felt charged—like the hush before a storm.

Chapter 54

Danny and Robin agreed to meet in the food court of the new mall near her office. Robin had been running flat-out since the weekend, juggling calls to old classmates, delegating property showings to her team, and still keeping her therapy appointments with Sophia. Lunch with Danny gave her an excuse to breathe—and to dream a little.

It was Tuesday, quiet enough that the food court hummed instead of roared. The scents swirled in the open air: garlic and oregano from the little pizza counter, a sweet tang of orange chicken from the wok stand, and, drifting across it all, the warm spice of panang curry that made Robin's stomach growl in spite of herself.

Danny carried a sandwich and fries to the table; Robin slid into her seat with a steaming carton of curry and rice. They clinked their soda cups together like champagne flutes.

"Here's to catching our breath," Robin said, her eyes crinkling.

"And to remembering who we used to be," Danny added, unwrapping his sandwich.

They traded stories as they ate, filling in blanks about people they hadn't thought of in decades. Robin remembered a girl who swore she'd run off to California to become an actress, and Danny dredged up a story about a boy who'd once climbed the water tower on a dare. They laughed like teenagers themselves, the past spilling between them like an old yearbook cracked open.

"That's what I've been thinking," Robin said, tapping her fork against her carton. "We never had a reunion. Not once. Don't you think it's about time we got the old crew together? Even the ones we didn't know so well back then. Might be a way to see what other stories are still hiding in this town. We could make it an open reunion for all classes that graduated around out time there."

Danny raised an eyebrow. "Dangerous idea. You throw a party and people start talking. Secrets get loose."

"That's the point," she said with a grin.

Just then Danny's phone buzzed against the tabletop, cutting through their laughter. His mother's name lit up the screen. He shot Robin a quick grin before swiping to answer.

"Danny!" Margaret's voice was practically bubbling. "I just had to call and tell you—we love it down here. The Joneses have been showing us around like we're family. We've already seen three neighborhoods—each with its own personality! Can you believe that?"

Danny leaned back in his chair, relief flooding through him. "That's fantastic, Mom. I'm so glad you're enjoying it."

"And listen to this," Margaret barreled on, "the Joneses say the average person down here changes houses three times! Isn't that something? You'd think people would just settle in one place, but no—there's always another house for sale, another golf cart to try, another neighborhood to explore."

Robin, overhearing, mouthed a silent *told you so* and Danny chuckled.

Margaret lowered her voice conspiratorially. "Your father even said he might look at houses. Can you picture that? Richard Kessler, willing to move! He found a woodworking buddy who invited him to visit the woodshop next week. I've found a lovely bridge group."

Danny met Robin's eyes, both of them stunned and amused. "That's . . . that's incredible, Mom."

"Well, don't get your hopes up too high yet," Margaret warned, though her tone was giddy. "We're just extending our stay for now. At least through Christmas. But who knows?"

They exchanged more pleasantries—stories about restaurants, new friends, and the surprising joy of Florida sunshine in December— before hanging up.

Danny hung up a few minutes later and set the phone down slowly.

Robin's curry was forgotten, her eyes bright. "Danny. They're staying. They're safe. Through Christmas."

Danny exhaled, long and deep, like a man who'd just set down a boulder. "Yeah. They're safe." He took another bite of his sandwich, but it tasted lighter now, the grease not weighing him down. For the first time in weeks, he smiled without effort.

As they finished lunch, they hurried over to Robin's office.

Strategy Session at Robin's Office

Robin had chosen her conference room for the meeting—a glass-walled space with enough privacy, sunlight streaming over the sleek table, and the faint scent of citrus from the receptionist's diffuser. It felt neutral, safe, not like anyone's turf. She and Danny chatted while they waited for the others.

Marcus arrived first, scanning the hall like always before sitting with his back to the wall. Rebecca swept in with her case notes tucked under her arm, professional but warm. And then Allison—hesitant at the doorway until Robin crossed the room and hugged her gently.

"Thank you for coming," Robin said, her voice softer than usual, as though aware of the courage it had taken Allison to be here.

Allison settled in beside her, folding her hands tightly in her lap. "I'm not sure what I can add. But if what happened to me helps . . . then I want to help."

Rebecca gave her a steady nod. "Your voice is stronger than you realize. You already proved that when you testified back then. We're just connecting the threads now."

Marcus leaned forward, hands steepled. "Let's talk brass tacks. Robin floated the idea of a long overdue high school reunion. A staged event—classes 2000 to 2007. It's bait, plain and simple. Survivors in one place, predators watching their house of cards start to wobble. But it's risky. Very risky."

Danny countered, calm but firm. "Riskier is silence. Survivors isolated are survivors trapped. A reunion gives cover for people to talk. Even if they only whisper to each other afterward, it's enough to break the spell. I've seen it happen in Cambodia, in Manila, in Nairobi. Isolation is the traffickers' weapon. This could be our way of taking it back."

Allison blinked at him. "You really think . . . there might be more? That we weren't the only ones?"

Robin reached across, touching her hand. "That's exactly what I thought for twenty-five years. That it was just me. That's how they keep us quiet. But now we know better."

Rebecca broke the heavy pause. "Here's what we need:

- **Robin**—you'll handle the alumni outreach. Frame it as a celebration. Nothing heavy, just a chance to reconnect.
- **Danny**—background checks. Cross-reference names on the guest list with what we already suspect. If predators show up, we want to know before they walk in the door.
- **Marcus**—security. Eyes at every entrance. You'll run point with the Inn at Twin Peaks. If we don't have control of the environment, we don't do it.
- **Allison**—only if you're comfortable, you and Robin may close the evening with a short word. Not graphic. Just naming resilience. Strength. That you're not alone. It plants the seed."

Allison straightened, her jaw set. "I can do that."

Robin smiled at her, proud and aching all at once. "Then we'll do it together."

Marcus scribbled in his notebook. "Seventeenth or eighteenth, midweek. Gives us three weeks to set the trap. But make no mistake— once the invite goes out, the wolves will smell it."

Rebecca leaned back, the steel in her gaze undeniable. "Then let them. Because this time, the prey is ready."

Chapter 55

Robin texted Melody and asked if she could meet them at her office downtown, but Melody's reply had pinged back almost immediately:

Can't tonight—in the middle of making dinner for Yuki. But if you don't mind coming here, we can meet in my office. Door closes fine. He's used to me working evenings.

So just after six, Robin, Danny, and Marcus slipped through the front door of Melody's tidy home. The smell of garlic and soy drifted from the kitchen. Melody waved them toward a smaller office tucked off the hallway, laptop open on the desk, walls lined with books and files from her nonprofit projects.

"Sorry for the chaos," she said, ushering them in and closing the door firmly behind them. "Yuki's in the kitchen—you'll probably hear him raiding the fridge." She smiled, but her eyes sharpened. "All right. What's so urgent that you three show up at once?"

Danny explained the outline quickly—the reunion, Allison's involvement, the need for someone with Melody's skills and platform to help shape the story, if and when it was time. But for now, she was just covering a long-anticipated social event in town.

Melody's brow furrowed, but not with hesitation. "You're talking about an entire network, aren't you? Not just one bad actor. My God." She leaned back, crossing her arms. "You're right—this isn't just a survivor story. It's a community reckoning. And if you're asking me in, then yes. I'm in."

Before Robin could answer, there was a knock at the door. The handle turned and Yuki poked his head in, hoodie half-zipped, basketball tucked under his arm.

"Mom? Coach Hawkins is opening the gym tonight for extra practice. Jason said he'd pick me up. Can I go?"

Melody glanced up, distracted. "That's fine, honey, just—"

Marcus sat forward sharply. "Coach Hawkins?"

"Yeah," Yuki said, shrugging. "He's been telling us if we want more playing time, we should show up when he opens the gym. Everyone's going."

The air in the room shifted. Robin froze. Danny's jaw tightened.

Melody frowned, sensing something in their faces. "What? He's just—"

Marcus cut in smoothly but firmly. "Why don't I take him tonight? I need to have a word with Hawkins anyway. Wouldn't hurt to watch a practice. It'll only be an hour or so and we'll be back."

Yuki blinked, surprised, shrugged and walked away. But Melody's maternal instincts kicked in—half relieved someone trusted was offering to drive, half unsettled by Marcus's tone.

"Is something wrong?" she whispered slowly.

Marcus didn't flinch. "That's exactly what I intend to find out. You guys fill her in while I'm gone."

He and Yuki left. Melody tilted her head toward Danny and Robin and squinted, "Fill me in? What's going on?"

As they stepped out into the cool air, Danny and Robin briefed her about Hawkins potentially being part of the network.

"Marcus is really good at 'intuiting' those kinds of things, and it was really wise of you to give Marcus that opportunity to do a little detective work. He'll be honest about what he thinks when they get home," Danny shared. "Don't worry. And you probably don't want to mention any of this to Bruce just yet."

Robin added, "Let's get the reunion planned and promoted and then figure out a strong way forward. We are so glad to have you on the team Melody."

After Practice

The moon was shining bright when Marcus steered the truck back toward Melody's house. Yuki sat in the passenger seat, damp hair curling at his temples, gym bag at his feet, sneakers squeaking faintly against the mat. The boy was still riding the buzz of practice, chattering about drills, a scrimmage win, and how "Coach Hawkins has this way of making you believe you can do more than you thought you could."

Marcus let him talk, filing away every word. He nodded where appropriate, asked a few questions, but his mind kept replaying the way Hawkins had moved among the players—too familiar, too ingratiating, scanning for more than athletic potential.

When they pulled into the drive, Yuki slung the bag over his shoulder and hopped out. "Thanks, Mr. Marcus! That was cool of you."

"No problem, champ," Marcus said, giving a quick half-smile. "Go on in. Your mom's waiting."

Yuki jogged up the walk and disappeared inside. Marcus waited until the door shut before killing the engine and following. Melody met him at the threshold, apron still tied at her waist, the scent of garlic and onions drifting from the kitchen.

"Everything go all right?" she asked lightly, but her eyes searched his face.

Marcus hesitated, then lowered his voice. "Practice was . . . fine. But listen, Melody—keep your radar up with that coach. He's not just pushing basketball. He's . . . watching. Too closely."

Her expression froze, the casual smile falling away. "Hawkins?"

Marcus gave a single, sharp nod. "I've seen this before. Nothing to panic Yuki with, but you should know I'll be passing what I saw today to Rebecca. Better to be ahead of it than caught flat-footed."

Melody leaned against the doorframe, arms crossed, her usual quick wit muted. "You're telling me my son's coach is—"

"I'm telling you to be cautious," Marcus cut in gently but firmly. "No conclusions yet. But I trust my gut, and it hasn't steered me wrong in twenty years. Just . . . keep the door open with Yuki. Don't dismiss anything he says, no matter how small."

She swallowed hard, then nodded. "All right. Thank you for watching him. For watching out."

Marcus tipped his head once, already stepping back toward the truck. "That's what I do. I'll be in touch."

As he pulled away, Melody closed the door slowly, hand still on the knob, her heart pounding. For the first time, the danger that had hovered in the abstract was standing on her doorstep—woven into her son's daily life.

Chapter 56

Robin fumbled for her key in the dark. Moonlight brushed the porch, but the house itself felt heavy with silence after such a long day. Danny stepped forward, gently plucking the key from her hand. He unlocked the door and pushed it open so she could flip on the light.

For a moment they just stood in the entry, close enough to hear each other breathe. Danny reached out almost without thinking, and she came willingly, folding into his chest. The scent of her hair filled his lungs. They held on like that for a long moment—two people propping each other up, neither needing to speak.

"Would you be up for a brandy?" she asked softly, tilting her face up.

"Yeah," he murmured, reluctant to let go.

While she slipped into the kitchen for glasses, he found the nearly untouched bottle of Hennessy in the butler's pantry and carried it to the couch. When she returned, they poured two amber measures and let the first sip burn away some of the day's tension.

"It's been a long one," Robin sighed. "But I feel good about what we've done—your parents, Florida, the meeting . . . even lunch today. It all feels like movement forward."

Danny smiled faintly and touched her temple with his lips. "That's because you're brilliant. You keep pulling us through."

They sat in silence for a while, glasses in hand, leaning against one another. Not just for support, though it was that. It felt right. Grounded.

Robin stirred first. "I'll check in with Melody tomorrow, make sure she's okay."

Danny swirled his glass. "Thanksgiving's coming. What do you think about a gathering—just us, the team? Might be good to sit at a table together before the storm."

Her smile curved slowly. "I like it. I'll make the calls. You bring the wine."

He rose, setting his glass in the sink. "I like being here. Maybe too much."

She stepped close, eyes searching his. "I like it too."

He bent and kissed her forehead, meaning to leave it at that—but something in her expression undid him. He pulled her back into his arms, and this time the kiss was deeper, years of longing folded into one impossible moment.

When he pulled away, a single tear traced her cheek. He brushed it away with his lips. "Sleep tight," he whispered.

At the door he hesitated, then walked out into the night. Robin switched on the porch light and stood watching as his car rolled slowly down the street, her chest tight with something that felt dangerously close to hope.

Chapter 57

Marcus hit Rebecca's office right at opening—no knock, just a brief rap and the door eased in on a waft of lemon polish. He carried a plain manila envelope and a small, clear-lidded evidence box. No flourish.

"Morning," Rebecca said, already on her feet. "What've you got?"

"Observations from Westridge High practice," he said, setting the box on her desk as if it were glass. "Plus stills. I kept the originals write-protected."

Rebecca slipped on nitrile gloves without comment. Marcus did the same. He popped the box: inside, a micro SD card sealed in an antistatic sleeve, a dated index card noting time, place, conditions, and a slim notebook opened to a page of bullet points—times, jersey numbers, who stood where, what was said.

"I didn't record any minors' faces tight," he added. "Medium frames, context shots, coach in focus. No publishing—strictly documentation."

Rebecca nodded once. "Chain of custody: from you to me, 8:12 a.m., my office," she said aloud, writing it on the intake form, then initialing. "I'll clone the card, vault the original, and log a preservation memo."

She glanced over his notes, pen hovering. "Walk me through it."

"Hawkins works the perimeter early, puts his hands on shoulders a hair longer than needed. Eye contact lingers. He isolates two boys after drills—tells the rest to hit free throws, 'I've got them.' Tone's too familiar. One kid—Yuki—kept it breezy. The other stiffened. Hawkins chose the second boy, steering him into the equipment room for five minutes. The door stayed ajar an inch—just enough to look harmless, but enough to shield whatever he meant to do. Can't prove intent yet, but the pattern matches pre-offense grooming I've seen a hundred times."

Rebecca's mouth tightened, but her voice stayed steady. "Legally, we're not there. But the pattern is enough for us to move on two tracks: protect and preserve."

"Agreed," Marcus said. "I told Mom to keep her antenna up, nothing more. I'll keep eyes on practice when I can."

Rebecca slid the envelope closer. "I'm adding this to the broader matter. Hawkins now sits on the same board as Pyle and Stone in my head—no allegation yet, but proximity and behavior put him on our map."

She spun her legal pad and outlined, crisp, practical:

1. **Evidence handling.** "I'll mirror the card, hash both copies, and draft a contemporaneous memo. Your notes go to the vault; you keep a scanned copy for field use."

2. **Quiet reporting tree.** "We *could* file a mandatory report, but without a clear disclosure we risk tipping Hawkins and whatever protection he enjoys. I'd rather first request the district's written policies on coach–student contact and closed-door interactions. I can do that as counsel for a concerned parent—Melody—without naming a student."

3. **Parallel leverage.** "If Hawkins has prior complaints, HR has to log them. I'll file a preservation letter to the district and, separately, a narrow public-records request for any complaints against Hawkins, *and* for correspondence between the superintendent's office and Sheriff Stone over the last five years. Different buckets, same net."

Marcus's eyes flicked up. "Stone."

Rebecca didn't blink. "Your instincts are my roadmap. If the Sheriff is gatekeeping, I want a paper trail he can't control."

"Good," Marcus said. "And Pyle?"

"I've got parole conditions inbound," she said. "If we catch one deviation—proximity to minors, contact with former students—we have a pretext to squeeze him without showing our hand."

Marcus tapped the notebook. "I'll build a pattern log on Hawkins—dates, times, who else was present. No speculation in the entries, just verbs and timestamps. If a kid discloses, we move fast."

"Do," Rebecca said. She slid a fresh intake form across. "And give me a brief sworn declaration on yesterday—two paragraphs, factual, signed. It strengthens any preservation requests I send this afternoon."

He took the pen without complaint and wrote—economy of words, dates precise, times down to the minute. When he finished, Rebecca notarized, stamped, and slipped it into a red-tabbed folder marked *Westridge—Active*.

"One more thing," Marcus said, standing. "Hawkins clocked me. Not sure if he recognized me or just didn't like an adult on his edge."

Rebecca considered. "That accelerates our timeline. I'll place the records requests in the next hour and route copies to my off-site counsel account. If anything goes missing at the district, we'll know where to push."

Marcus's mouth tugged—almost a smile. "I'll brief Danny and Robin. And I'll keep Melody updated—carefully."

Rebecca walked him to the door. "Tell Danny his parents' extension buys us space, not comfort. And Marcus—thank you for bringing this in clean."

"Only way it holds," he said, tapping the evidence box.

He left as he'd come—in quiet—already pulling out his phone to text the group: *Docs logged. Hawkins on radar. Meeting later?*

Chapter 58

Robin's Morning Errands

Robin was up early, her to-do list scribbled in the same neat block letters she used on contracts. At the office, she moved briskly through her staff updates: confirming with her assistant that the list of names Rebecca had provided for the Westridge reunion had been entered, proofing the draft invitations one last time, and reminding everyone to double-check their out-of-office coverage for the holiday weekend. Efficiency kept her balanced, like lining up dominoes before the push.

Confirmed the guest list for tomorrow:

- **Robin (hostess)**
- **Danny**
- **Marcus**
- **Rebecca & Pete** (she confirmed she'd bring him along)
- **Melody & Yuki** (Bruce is working that night)
- **Allison**

Next stop was the market. Thanksgiving was only a day away, and she wanted to bring more than her grandmother's sweet potato casserole. Her cart filled quickly: fresh herbs, cranberries, a good sourdough, a wedge of imported brie she knew Melody would appreciate. For a moment, she let herself enjoy the ordinariness of it—pushing a cart, humming to the tune piped over the store's speakers, thinking about table settings instead of court records and locked file boxes.

When she pushed through the sliding doors with her bags balanced in both arms, the crisp late-November air rushed against her cheeks. She was halfway to her Range Rover before she froze.

Sheriff Stone was leaning against the hood of a county cruiser parked two rows over. Deputy Hawkins stood nearby, talking low, his posture easy but his eyes sharp. And between them—God help her—Denver Pyle, heavier now, but unmistakable.

They weren't posturing for the public. They were close, heads bent, voices tight, the kind of huddle men make when pressure is building. Stone noticed her first. He straightened, gave a smile that didn't reach his eyes, and lifted a hand like they were still old neighbors meeting outside the hardware store.

"Well, if it isn't Robin Wellworth," he called across the lot, voice smooth, carrying. "Heard you've been busy these days."

Robin forced a polite smile, adjusting the grocery bags against her hip. "Just getting ready for the holiday, Sheriff. You too?"

"Always," Stone said, but there was an edge to it. His gaze lingered on her, unreadable. "Westridge hasn't changed much in all these years, has it? Funny how old ghosts seem to stir when people start asking questions."

Robin kept her face smooth, careful. Every instinct was on alert. "Funny how life works out," she replied evenly.

"Mm." His smile was thin, his eyes sliding past her toward her car. "Well. Enjoy your Thanksgiving."

It was friendly enough on the surface. But something in the weight of his words—too measured, too pointed—made her stomach twist. Robin walked quickly to the Rover, fumbling only once with her keys, then slid behind the wheel and locked the doors.

As she pulled out of the lot, her pulse still hammering, she caught a last glimpse in the rearview mirror: Stone's head bent close again with Hawkins and Pyle, their faces tight, the intensity unbroken.

The groceries sat heavy on the seat beside her, but Robin couldn't shake the chill pressing against her skin.

Stone at Danny's House

Danny crouched over an old box in Rick's room, his hands dusted with twenty-five years of neglect. The tape had peeled away easily, and he was sorting what remained into stacks—keep, donate, shred. It was mechanical work, but it steadied him.

The sound of tires crunching gravel outside pulled him up short. He straightened, listening. The hum of an engine cut off, and a car door slammed.

Danny moved to the window. Sheriff Stone leaned against his cruiser like he had all the time in the world, his wide stance blocking the late afternoon sun. Danny felt the old reflex in his gut—respect, deference—but it curdled quickly into suspicion.

Stone didn't knock. He waited.

Danny walked out onto the porch, wiping his palms on his jeans.

"Well," Stone drawled, tipping his hat in a mock-casual way. "Back in town, sorting through old ghosts."

Danny crossed his arms. "Something like that."

Stone's eyes flicked toward the garage, then back to Danny. "That's tough work, going through your brother's things. Brings up more than you bargain for, usually."

Danny's jaw tightened. "It needs doing."

A silence stretched. Then Stone tilted his head, the corners of his mouth not quite forming a smile. "You holding up okay, son? I always wondered how you'd do if you came back."

The words hung between them, deceptively kind—but laced with something heavier.

Danny forced himself to nod. "I'm fine."

Stone shifted, resting his forearms on the roof of the cruiser. He says, "You left us once due to a tragic accident, Danny. It would be awfully sad for us to have to go through that again. You take care of yourself . . . and that girl of yours. She's getting to be quite a community leader.

The echo of twenty-five years ago hit Danny like a gut punch. It was Stone's voice that had planted the seed back then. Leave town. Start fresh. Protect yourself. He'd thought it was wisdom. Now it sounded like manipulation.

He swallowed hard, keeping his tone even. "I came back for my folks."

Stone studied him a beat longer, his eyes unreadable. Then, with a nod that was more final than friendly, he slid back into the cruiser.

The engine rumbled, gravel spitting under the tires as he pulled away.

Danny stood on the porch long after the car disappeared, the words still reverberating in his chest: *It wasn't my idea to leave. It was his. Just like it sounds now.*

Dinner at the Bistro

Danny's message lit up Robin's phone just as she was finishing her notes for the day:

Let me buy you dinner and a drink tonight. A little thanks for all the prep you've done for tomorrow. Plus, we both need to breathe before the storm.

Robin smiled, typing back quickly:

You read my mind. Where?

The Bistro, 7 o'clock. I'll grab us a table.

Danny stood as Robin approached, brushing dust off his hands almost unconsciously, as if the clutter still clung to him. He pulled her chair out, and when she sat, the faint scent of garlic with the spice of her perfume, grounding him.

"You look like you've had a day," she said, studying him with a half-smile.

"You could say that." He took a long sip of his beer before leaning closer. "I finally cleared the front hall. You wouldn't believe it—the boxes, the piles of newspapers, coats stacked like they were holding up the walls. It felt like the house was choking me. But I walked through today without brushing my shoulder on anything. For the first time, it didn't feel like a tomb."

Robin's smile softened, warm and proud. "That's huge, Danny. More than you realize. It's like you're making space for something new."

He nodded, then his jaw tightened. "Not all good news, though. Stone showed up at the house while I was hauling boxes out. Pulled into the driveway like he owned the place."

Her breath caught. "What did he want?"

Danny's eyes hardened. "Asked how I was doing, all friendly on the surface. But underneath? It was the same old message—like I'd made a mistake coming back. He didn't say it outright, but the message was pretty clear. Said how sad it would be if I had to leave town again due to a tragic accident . . . like I was stirring up trouble just by being there, and the worst part is that he mentioned you too. Warning me to take care and you, as well."

Robin reached across the table, her hand brushing his. "He's trying to rattle you. And it's working, isn't it? But just remember, that's what bullies do when they feel the ground shifting."

Their food arrived—two steaming plates, the scents of garlic bread and curry floating between them—but neither moved to eat. The air between them was charged, fragile and electric.

Danny lifted his glass, voice rough. "Here's to clearing hallways. Even the ones you don't see right away."

Robin tapped hers lightly against his. "To clear hallways. And to not being pushed out this time."

"Actually, he showed up randomly for me too . . . outside the grocery store . . . similar message. He was busy today trying to feel in charge."

They both let out a nervous laugh. "We've got him shaken," Danny said.

They sat close, leaning toward each other as though the Bistro's hum faded away. For a long moment, the silence was its own language—relief, fear, and something else simmering beneath.

He bent toward her, kissing her forehead first, a quiet thank-you. Then he pulled back just enough to meet her eyes, saw the flicker of something that mirrored his own, and kissed her again—this time longer, deeper, the taste of wine and promise between them.

When they finally drew apart, she whispered, "Tomorrow we host everyone. Tonight, let's just . . . be here."

Danny smiled, the tension in his shoulders loosening. "Best plan I've heard all week."

Chapter 59

Thanksgiving Morning

Danny's text lit up Robin's phone just after seven:
Morning. What can I do to help? Put me to work.

She smiled at the message, thumbs tapping quickly back.

Coffee's on. Bring yourself. I've got potatoes that need peeling.

Morning at Robin's House

When he arrived, the house already smelled faintly of sage, thyme, and onions, the early stages of stuffing cooling on the counter. She met him at the door in a soft sweater, hair pulled back, looking more at ease than he'd seen her in days.

He held up a small grocery bag. "Backup coffee beans and some pastries, just in case. My contribution to the feast . . . oh, and wine, as requested."

She laughed, taking it from him. "Points for showing up prepared."

Soon they were side by side at the kitchen table, a big bowl of potatoes between them. He peeled, she sliced celery and onions, and the rhythm of the simple chores softened the edge of the last few weeks.

"Feels good, doesn't it?" Robin said. "Just . . . doing something ordinary."

Danny nodded, glancing at her. "I'd almost forgotten what that feels like."

They fell into easy chatter—old classmates, how her staff was pulling together the reunion invites, a funny story about his parents calling again from Florida, marveling at golf carts decorated for Christmas. Every so often, their eyes would meet and linger just a little too long, and the quiet hum of normalcy felt almost romantic in itself.

Looking like a pro, she threw a couple of pumpkin pies together.

At one point, when she brushed a curl from her forehead with her flour-dusted hand, he grinned. "You missed a spot." He reached across with his thumb and gently brushed it away. The touch lingered, soft, unspoken.

She looked at him for a long moment, then exhaled. "This—this is what I want to hold onto. Even when things get dark."

"Let's take a walk," Robin suggested, "I don't need to get the turkey in 'til noon. We've got everything ready, table's set, let's just chill a bit."

Danny grabbed their jackets from the hooks in the foyer, next to her old grandfather clock. It slowly, methodically chimed ten as they were walking out the door. "When is everyone coming?" Danny asked as they started down the porch stairs.

"I invited them to come between 4 and 5, so we could enjoy some drinks and hors d'oeuvres."

"Oh good," he teased her, "because we just might not have enough food."

"Never leave them wanting, is my motto," she winked.

He hugged her from the side, and left his arm around her as they walked.

"Melody is bringing Yuki," Robin added quietly. "We'll need to be mindful of our conversations."

"Hmm, right," he wistfully agreed, but his mind was somewhere else.

The air was crisp and clear and fragrant with the smell of autumn leaves.

"This," Robin said softly, "feels almost like a holiday from everything else. Just the smell of sage and woodsmoke in the air, the leaves underfoot—it's almost enough to trick me into thinking life is simple again."

Danny gave a low chuckle, his breath clouding in the chill. "Almost. But I'll take it. After weeks of boxes, court filings, and shadows, this—" he squeezed her shoulder gently, "feels like breathing again."

Danny looked at her, eyes steady. "That's what I want for you. For us. To get back to that—ordinary, safe."

She tilted her head, studying him. "Funny thing is, ordinary never felt so precious until it was gone."

They walked on in silence for a few beats, the crisp air filling the spaces between them. A pair of kids rode by on bicycles, laughing, the sound carrying high on the cold air. Robin smiled faintly. "You know, Thanksgiving always used to feel like a pause button. No matter how messy life was, for one day you cooked too much food, pulled out the nice dishes, and tried to be grateful. This year . . . it feels heavier. But also, more real."

Danny nodded slowly. "Yeah. Gratitude isn't cheap this time— it's hard-won. Maybe that makes it mean more."

For a moment, their eyes locked, the weight of shared battles and small victories pressing close. Danny slid his hand down her arm until their fingers laced together, a quiet promise in the simple touch.

"Come on," Robin said softly after a moment, blinking back the sudden swell of emotion. "Turkey won't cook itself. And besides, we've got a house full of people coming who need to feel this kind of peace too, even if it's just for one night."

They turned back toward Robin's house. Danny gave her hand a squeeze. "Feels good to walk like this. Feels . . . normal."

Robin smiled, the weight in her chest lighter than it had been in weeks. "Let's hold onto this. Just for today."

They crossed the street, as they turned towards Robin's house, leaves scattering across the pavement. That's when a black SUV slowed at the corner. The window rolled down, and Sheriff Stone leaned across the passenger seat, elbow propped on the frame.

Robin's steps faltered. Danny tightened his hold on her hand before releasing it, squaring his shoulders. "Morning, Sheriff," he said evenly.

"We meet again. Happy Thanksgiving to you both," his smile, not quite reflected in his eyes. "Sorry to hear your parents are out of town, Danny. Funny how they left just after you got back. Makes you wonder what they know that you don't know."

The SUV rolled off, tires crunching on gravel. The silence it left behind felt heavier than the November air.

Robin exhaled, long and shaky. "That was . . . deliberate."

"We were just kids when he had any influence over us. Now he's like an old toothless dog, trying to make us feel scared." Danny added, "All bark, no bite left. We are ahead of him. We just can't get sloppy."

They climbed the porch steps in silence, the warmth of earlier still clinging to them, but thinner now—shot through with the reminder that the storm outside was closer than ever.

Thanksgiving Dinner

The late afternoon light slanted golden across Robin's dining room, catching in the crystal glasses and flickering candles. The table was set to perfection—rich autumn colors, sprigs of rosemary, plates that gleamed under the soft glow. The smell of turkey and sage was already thick in the air when the first knock came.

Rebecca and Pete entered together, Pete balancing a bottle of wine and Rebecca holding a warm smile. Marcus came in just after them, carrying a small stack of bakery bread wrapped in brown paper. Allison followed, a little tentative at first, but Robin hugged her firmly, pulling her into the warmth. Then came Melody with Yuki trailing behind her, lanky and energetic, holding a foil-covered dish.

"Looks like a feast," Pete grinned, as coats piled on the rack and the hum of voices filled the house.

They gathered around the table, hands brushing as plates were passed, laughter bubbling when Danny made a show of carving the turkey like he was on TV. Conversation was light at first—work updates, travel stories, jokes about Marcus's "lodging out in the boonies." Yuki devoured mashed potatoes with teenage abandon, Melody trying and failing to slow him down.

But soon, as the wine flowed and the meal settled in, the talk deepened. Gratitude took its place around the table: Rebecca speaking softly about the meaning of finding clients she could truly help; Allison expressing how thankful she was to feel part of something again; Robin's voice catching as she spoke about second chances. Danny, leaning back for a moment, simply said: "I'm thankful to be home. With the right people this time."

The silence afterward was full, not empty—each person letting the words settle.

After Dinner: The Game

It was Danny who broke the mood, clapping his hands. "All right, I'm too full for pie yet. Who's up for a little basketball? Court's still standing at my parents' place, three houses down."

Yuki's face lit up immediately. "Yes! I'm in."

Marcus grinned, rolling his shoulders. "Me and the kid versus you and Pete. Easy win."

Pete groaned theatrically but followed them out. Robin and the other women lingered behind, gathering plates and pouring Baileys into small glasses. "Boys and their games," Rebecca said with a fond shake of her head.

Out on the cracked driveway, the November air bit at their lungs as the men split teams. The ball thudded against pavement, echoing in the cold night. They played hard but playful, trash talk mixing with laughter. Yuki cut sharp across the lane, surprising Marcus with quick reflexes.

"Kid's got moves," Marcus muttered, impressed.

It was in the lull between plays that Yuki dropped it casually, almost as a brag. "Coach Hawkins says I've got varsity written all over me. He's even giving me extra rides to practice." He shot, missed, chased the rebound without noticing the quick glance Danny and Marcus exchanged.

"Nice," Danny said lightly, keeping his tone even. "Take the help, but don't let him run you too hard."

They finished the game with Yuki crowing about his winning layup, cheeks flushed, eyes bright. The men clapped him on the back, his laughter warming the cold night. But Marcus's jaw was tight when the game ended.

Back Inside

The warmth of the house wrapped around them again, the women chatting softly over glasses of Baileys. Yuki flopped into a chair, glowing with pride, Melody smiling at him like he was the only light in the room.

Robin passed around plates of pumpkin pie, the cinnamon-sweet smell soothing after the sharp bite of the night air. Conversation turned to lighter things again—holiday plans, funny family traditions, Allison recounting a disastrous turkey from years past.

When coats were finally pulled on and goodbyes exchanged, there was a heaviness beneath the warmth. A sense that tonight had been a brief reprieve—but only that.

On the porch, Danny lingered beside Robin as the last car pulled away. "It was good," he said softly. "More than good. But did you hear what Yuki said?"

Robin nodded, her smile slipping. "I did. And we'll handle it. Together."

The porch light flickered against their faces as they stood in the chill, knowing the storm was coming closer—but grateful, for one night, that they'd had a table, a team, and the fragile gift of hope.

Chapter 60

Marcus shut his motel door, double-checked the lock, and sat at the edge of the bed with his burner phone. He scrolled through numbers until he found one he hadn't used in years. A former colleague—now in the state AG's organized crime division. Reliable. Careful.

He drew a steady breath and hit "call."

The line clicked twice before a voice answered, clipped but familiar.

"Reynolds."

"Marcus Hale."

A pause, then a low chuckle of recognition. "Well, I'll be damned. You crawling out of retirement, or just calling to ruin my day?"

Marcus leaned back against the headboard. "Maybe both. Listen, You've got a file on Westridge, right? Small town, old cases that never sat right. It's flaring again. What I'm seeing here has all the signs of a trafficking network—still active, maybe thirty years deep. Local law enforcement is compromised."

The levity dropped from Reynolds' voice. "That's a heavy accusation."

"Not an accusation," Marcus said evenly. "Observation. Sheriff himself is in the wind on this—protecting, maybe even profiting. I've got a sitting deputy grooming kids as we speak. And Denver Pyle— you remember that name? He's out, and I think he's still tied in. The pattern hasn't broken. It's evolved."

Reynolds exhaled slowly. "Jesus. What do you have in hand?"

"Evidence is stacking. Survivor testimony. Financial irregularities tied to a shell company. Photos from practice yesterday—deputy isolating minors. But the real play? We've got a chance to bring survivors together, publicly. A reunion in three weeks. If the old network's still circling wagons, they'll show themselves then."

Another pause. "And you're telling me you can do this without blowing cover?"

"That's why I'm calling you, not the Bureau switchboard," Marcus replied. "I need this handled outside local channels. Quiet. If we can set a net around the reunion, we'll flush them. But I need assurances—backup that won't spook them too soon."

Reynolds' voice softened, weight settling into it. "All right. I'll start the wheels, but we'll tread light. I'll need a packet from you— secure drop, chain of custody. You give me your survivors, your photos, your paper trail, and I'll give you federal eyes in the room."

Marcus allowed himself a small nod, though Reynolds couldn't see it. "That's all I need."

"Marcus," Reynolds added, voice low, "if you're right about this . . . you're about to step back into the fire. You ready for that?"

Marcus glanced at his notebook on the nightstand, the single line written across the page: The stakes are higher than they know.

"Already in it," he said, and cut the call.

Chapter 61

Day After Thanksgiving

The conference table in Robin's office gleamed under the overhead lights, a neat stack of manila folders sitting in front of Rebecca. Robin had brought in fresh coffee, the scent mixing with the citrus cleaner her staff favored. She sat with her hands folded, steady but alert—her mind half on the reunion logistics, half on the storm that was building around them.

"Well," Robin began, sliding a sheet across the table. "The *Westridge Gazette* runs our notice in tomorrow's edition. Invites are out, confirmation list is growing. For the first time in years, it feels like the town's going to gather again."

Danny gave her a nod, proud but thoughtful. "That's the bait," he said softly. "Now we make sure we've got the hook."

Rebecca tapped her folders. "And that's what this is about. Marcus and I pulled together a packet for the Attorney General's office. Enough to engage them—but not enough to compromise anyone here."

Marcus leaned forward, arms folded. "We put in copies of Rick's ledger pages, the payment trails, and the photos. They're clean, organized. Plus, my notes on Hawkins at the basketball practice and Stone and Pyle outside The Bean."

Danny's jaw tightened, but he nodded. "That's strong enough to demand attention."

Rebecca raised a hand. "But we stop short of handing over survivor names—other than Robin and Allison, who've already consented. Sophia's notes aren't in here either, not until we have subpoena protection. Survivors control their own voices. That's non-negotiable."

Robin let out a slow breath. "Good. That matters. This has to stay survivor-led."

Marcus pulled a smaller folder from under the pile. "The Mustang shell company—we've got a name. It's a dead end on paper, but Reynolds' office can dig deeper. That's flagged in here."

Danny leaned back, rubbing a hand across his face. "So this is the line—enough to show a network, but not enough for them to kick the door in tomorrow. Which means we keep the reunion on the calendar. That's where we draw them out."

Rebecca's gaze was sharp but warm. "Exactly. The AG's team will observe quietly. We don't need a circus—we need leverage."

Robin looked around the table, her voice steady but tinged with emotion. "Then we hold the line. We give them just enough, we keep each other safe, and we trust the timing. For once . . . we're not the ones running."

Silence lingered for a moment, the weight of the decision settling between them. Then Marcus reached across and closed the packet firmly. "All right. We deliver this Monday. After that, the game changes."

Next Day Strategy Session

The late afternoon light angled across Robin's office windows, catching on the stack of manila folders Rebecca had just closed. The conference table bore the signs of their labor: coffee mugs gone cold, Marcus's notebook scrawled with arrows, Rebecca's legal pad bristling with sticky notes.

"All right," Rebecca said, exhaling. "The AG's office has our first evidence packet. Reynolds is sharp. He'll know what to do with it."

Robin leaned back, rubbing at her temple. "That's a relief. But it feels like we've just taken a small step into a very large battlefield."

"That's because we have," Marcus replied. His tone was calm, but there was a weight behind it that drew both Robin and Danny's eyes to him. "The AG can help us in-state. But we're not just dealing with a county Sheriff who went bad or one creep who slipped through the cracks. The shell company on the Mustang? Out-of-state registration. The financial trail touches two banks in different jurisdictions. And Hawkins? He's not grooming alone. Networks like this don't stay local."

Rebecca frowned, tapping her pen against the pad. "Meaning what, exactly?"

"Meaning," Marcus said, folding his arms, "if we don't widen the net, these guys will wriggle free again. The only way to box them in is with federal jurisdiction. FBI, maybe HSI. The AG can be our bridge, but I can also make a call to a couple of people I trust. Quietly."

Danny shifted in his chair, jaw tight. "That puts us on a bigger stage. It also paints a target on us."

"It does," Marcus said evenly. "But you've already got Stone rattled, Pyle paranoid, and Hawkins sloppy. That's what they look like when pressure is working. The danger's rising no matter what we do. The difference is—if we bring in the Feds, we'll have the muscle to finish this."

Robin sat forward, palms flat on the table. "So we move ahead on two tracks. Rebecca keeps feeding Reynolds the official packets, and Marcus—" she hesitated, "you reach out through your own channels."

Marcus gave a small nod. "Discreetly. Only to people I'd stake my life on."

For a moment, silence filled the room, the weight of what they were considering settling like a heavy cloak. Then Rebecca leaned in, her lawyer's voice quiet but resolute.

"If we do this, there's no turning back. Once federal eyes are on Westridge, everything hidden will be forced into the light."

Robin met Danny's gaze. His steady nod was all the answer she needed.

"Then we're agreed," Robin said softly. "We circle tighter, and we bring the fight to them."

Chapter 62

Robin set the pumpkin pie carefully in the center of the table, brushing a stray wisp of hair from her face. "Don't get excited," she said with a half-smile, "this is the only dessert I know how to make without causing property damage. But Thanksgiving proved it was edible, so—here we are."

The women laughed, warm and easy, as plates and coffee cups passed around. The fire crackled, the December chill pressing at the windows.

When the gratitude circle ended and Ingrid's calm gaze turned to her, Robin felt her stomach flip. She'd been here before, but never like this. Tonight was different.

"Robin," Ingrid said gently, "you're in the hot seat. Tell us—what's rising for you, and what do you need from us tonight?"

Robin glanced at Rebecca, who gave the smallest of nods. Then she drew a breath. "You've all seen the ad in the Gazette by now. The reunion at Twin Peaks Inn on the seventeenth? That's mine."

Sandra leaned forward, curiosity sparking. "It's bold. But . . . why now? Why hasn't there been one before?"

"That's the thing," Robin said, voice quieter now. "There should have been. Reunions, homecomings, all the normal markers that keep a town's heartbeat steady. But Westridge didn't have them. At least, not for the years around mine. We were silenced. And I don't mean by apathy."

The room went very still.

Tanya frowned slightly. "Silenced how?"

Robin dried her sweaty hands on her jeans, grounding herself. "I haven't shared this fully with you before. It's not easy. But since I came back into touch with old classmates, pieces are coming together.

Back then—when I was in high school—what looked like bad luck, or tragedy, or isolated abuse, wasn't. It was organized. Controlled. There was a trafficking ring operating under our noses. And those of us who got pulled into it were coerced into silence. Some through threats, some through shame, some just by the sheer weight of fear."

Gasps, sharp intakes of breath. Patsy's hand flew to her mouth. "You mean—"

"Yes," Robin said, her eyes steady now. "For years, I thought it was just me. My story. My shame. But I've learned I wasn't the only one. And I wasn't imagining why our classes never celebrated, why so many drifted away and never came back. That silence was enforced."

Tanya's brow furrowed, her colorful scarf shifting as she leaned in. "Robin, this is . . . enormous. And terrifying. Are you saying that this reunion is—what? A chance to break that silence?"

Robin nodded. "Exactly. I don't expect people to stand up and spill their trauma at a microphone. But just being in that room together, after twenty years of silence, will send a message. That we're still here. That we survived. That we're done letting fear run the story."

Sandra's voice was quiet but firm. "And you think more will come forward, once they feel the strength of numbers?"

"I don't know," Robin admitted. "Maybe. Maybe not. But even if no one else says a word, the act itself matters. It's saying: we're not invisible anymore."

The group sat with it for a long moment. The fire popped, the scent of pumpkin spice drifted, and in that small upper room something shifted.

Finally, Patsy reached across the table. "Robin, thank you for trusting us. If you need volunteers—calls, decorations, anything—say the word. I can help."

Rebecca, steady as ever, added, "And I'll make sure you're protected. Legally, logistically. No one will blindside you."

Tanya nodded, eyes sharp with a mix of concern and admiration. "And if anyone does try, you'll have us right here. This isn't just your fight anymore."

Robin swallowed, emotion tightening her throat. She'd expected skepticism, maybe even pity. What she felt instead was belief. A sisterhood, stronger than the shadows.

Ingrid let the silence deepen, then spoke with reverence. "You've turned pain into a plan, Robin. That's courage. And courage multiplies. Tonight, let's circle her—give her clarity, action steps, and the assurance that she does not walk alone."

Robin, tearful, and in deep gratitude, reminded the group, "This must remain between us. I am making a bold, public move in full sight of a circle of wolves; please do not breathe this to anyone yet. God knows that I am not into drama, but this is important: My life and the lives of others, may be in danger."

Sandra reached for her hand. "Robin, you're asking us for silence, but you've already broken your own to protect others. That's not drama. That's bravery."

Robin nodded in thanks and continued, "And if we play our cards right, this whole situation has the potential to bring healing to an entire community. And I invite your involvement and your giftings to help move that forward, when the time is right."

The women leaned closer, not just physically but in spirit, layering their support over her words until Robin felt—for the first time in two decades—that she was not a single voice crying in the dark, but part of a rising chorus.

Chapter 63

Robin pulled into her driveway later than she meant to, headlights sweeping across the porch. Her chest still hummed with the aftershocks of Mastermind—gratitude, relief, and a creeping sense of *did I say too much?* The women had been supportive, but old habits whispered caution. She reached for her phone and typed, *Hey, what are you doing?*

Danny's reply came almost instantly: *Cleared the office, my old bedroom and the den today. Finally. Feels like I can breathe again in that house. Could use a beer.*

A smile tugged at her lips. *You're in luck. I've got beer.*

Minutes later, his knock sounded. He looked tired but lighter somehow, dust still on his jeans, hair mussed. She waved him in and popped two bottles.

They sat on the couch, shoulders angled toward each other, sipping in silence at first. The quiet felt companionable, a soft landing after heavy days.

Robin finally broke it. "I laid it all out tonight. Told them more than I planned. They were kind . . . but now I keep wondering if I overshared. Like maybe I made it too heavy for them."

Danny shook his head. "No. You didn't dump weight—you shared it. That's different. You let people step in beside you, Robin. That's strength."

She studied him, the steady way he said it, like he believed it down to the bone. Her chest eased. "I'm still learning what it feels like not to be alone in it."

He met her eyes. "Then keep learning. Because I'm not letting you carry this by yourself anymore."

The words lingered between them, warm and solid. Robin felt her throat tighten—not with fear, but with something startlingly close to hope.

She gave a shaky laugh. "You know, I never thought peeling potatoes and packing boxes would turn into some kind of healing ritual."

Danny grinned. "Beer, boxes, potatoes. Who knew normal could feel so good?" He clinked his bottle against hers, and the soft brush of his fingers against hers made her breath catch just a little.

They drifted into easier talk—her pie victory at Thanksgiving, his parents' calls from Florida, the way Christmas decorations looked ridiculous on golf carts. Every so often, their eyes met and held a fraction too long.

By the time the bottles were empty, Robin felt steadier. She leaned back, exhaling. "I don't say this lightly, Danny . . . but I'm glad you're here."

He smiled, quiet but sure. "Me too."

For a heartbeat, neither of them moved. Then he stood, taking their bottles to the sink, giving her space but leaving the air charged. At the door, he paused. "Sleep well, Robin. You've earned it."

She nodded, a single tear threatening but not falling, and watched him walk down the path into the night.

Chapter 64

Robin curled into her familiar spot on the couch, pulling the soft gray throw across her lap though she wasn't cold. The ritual mattered—it signaled safety. Across from her, Sophia adjusted her glasses, a quiet readiness in her posture.

"You look tired," Sophia observed gently.

Robin gave a short laugh. "That obvious? Between helping Danny with his parents, planning Thanksgiving, and this reunion idea . . . I feel like I'm running on fumes. But it's not just that. It's . . . him. Danny."

Sophia tilted her head slightly, inviting her to go on.

Robin hesitated, fingers worrying the fringe of the throw. "I've been alone for so long, Sophia. I made that work. I told myself independence was safety. No one could betray me if I never leaned on anyone. But now—every time I hear his voice, every time he walks through the door—I feel like I'm sixteen again. Hungry for closeness. And it scares me."

"Because?"

Robin swallowed. Her voice cracked but she pressed through. "Because what if I can't trust myself to see clearly? I've trusted the wrong men before. Betrayal, manipulation, abandonment—it's a scar I carry in every cell of my body. And now . . . I'm drawn to him like air after drowning. But what if I'm wrong? What if he leaves too?"

Sophia let the silence breathe for a moment, then said softly, "Robin, you've already done something powerful here—you're naming the fear, not letting it stay hidden. That means you're not sixteen. You're not trapped. You are a woman with choices."

Robin blinked hard, her throat tight.

Sophia continued, steady and calm: "You've told me Danny has been respectful. Has he shown you patience?"

"Yes. Always," Robin whispered. "He doesn't push. He doesn't demand. But that almost makes it worse—it makes me want to run toward him faster."

"Ah," Sophia smiled knowingly. "So the fear isn't about him. It's about you. Can you trust yourself to step forward without losing the woman you've fought to become?"

Robin sat with that, feeling its weight. Finally, she nodded. "That's it, isn't it? I don't want to mistake need for love. I don't want to hand him all of me just because I'm lonely."

Sophia's voice softened further. "Then make a promise to yourself. Let trust be tested slowly. Not because you're broken, but because you're wise. And every time the fear comes, remind yourself: That was then. This is now. I have choices."

Robin repeated it under her breath, almost like a mantra. That was then. This is now. I have choices.

For the first time in the session, her shoulders eased. She drew a long, slow breath. "You know," she said quietly, "I've always thought of Thanksgiving as a pause, a day to pretend things were fine. This year it feels like . . . I don't know . . . a chance to really start fresh. Maybe with him. Maybe with all of it."

Sophia smiled. "Then let gratitude be your compass, Robin. Not fear. Gratitude for your strength. Gratitude for the people you're letting into your life. That's where the truth will be."

Robin dabbed at her eyes, but she was smiling. "Okay. I think I can hold onto that."

Chapter 65

The conference room at Robin's office had become their unofficial war room. A bulletin board with maps of Westridge and printouts from the *Gazette* hung on one wall, while Rebecca's legal pad sat open on the polished table, her pen poised.

Robin set a plate of Christmas cookies in the middle— her way of making the meeting feel less like strategy and more like solidarity. "Fuel," she said with a half-smile, though her eyes betrayed the strain of the past few weeks.

Danny pulled out the chair beside her, his presence steady, grounding. Across from them, Marcus leaned forward, arms braced on the table, while Rebecca adjusted her glasses and tapped her pen lightly.

"Alright," Marcus said, voice low and even. "Clock's ticking. Less than two weeks until this reunion. If we're using it as bait, we need to be clear: who's doing what, and how fast the net can close once the fish take it."

Rebecca nodded, sliding a printed list across the table. "First: invitations. Robin's staff got them out—thank you. The ad in the *Westridge Gazette* runs again this weekend. The idea is to keep it broad enough to feel innocent, but precise enough to draw the eyes we want."

Robin added quietly, "And judging from the calls I've gotten, people are curious. Some suspicious, even. We've never had a reunion. The timing is unusual. But that curiosity is exactly what we need."

Marcus tapped the list. "Security. I've already looped in the Attorney General's office—they'll have plainclothes observers stationed in the room and around the property. Next step is the Feds. I've got a call scheduled tomorrow with my old Bureau contact. If Stone or Hawkins even sniff trouble, they'll be walking straight into a net."

Danny's jaw tightened. "Good. But let's remember—we're not just baiting them. Survivors may show up. Some may not even realize what they've survived until the energy in that room cracks it open. We have to be ready to hold them."

Rebecca lifted her chin. "Exactly. That's why I'll have affidavits prepped—simple, non-threatening. If anyone comes forward, they can choose to document their story, confidentially, immediately. It could bolster the case and protect them if they're later threatened."

But here's the other piece—we'd be irresponsible if we didn't plan for the *human* fallout."

Robin's brow furrowed, but she nodded. "You mean if someone stands up and . . . cracks?"

"Or even if they don't stand up," Rebecca said. "Disclosures can hit like lightning, as I'm sure you know," she said gently. "A smell, a name, even the room itself can trigger someone. They'll need more than a signature on paper—they'll need support."

Marcus leaned back, arms crossed. "So, what's the plan? We're not running group therapy in the dining room."

"Exactly," Rebecca agreed. "Which is why it needs to be layered and quiet. Legal in front, support in back." She ticked off with her fingers.

"First layer: affidavits. That's me and my team. If someone wants to go on record, it's ready.

"Second: professional backup. Sophia has agreed to be on site—off to the side, not announced, but available if anyone needs immediate grounding or counseling.

"Third: community anchors. Tanya, Sandra, Patsy. They know how to listen, how to hold space without pressing. They'll circulate, keep an eye open, gently steer anyone who looks shaky toward either Sophia or me."

Robin exhaled, relief and gratitude in her voice. "That's exactly what I was hoping. Quiet safety nets, but visible enough for those who need them."

Danny added, "And no announcements. We don't put anyone on the spot. Just us, quietly knowing who's where."

Rebecca's gaze circled the table. "Exactly. We're building a net: legal, therapeutic, communal. Survivors don't need a microphone shoved at them—they need to know they won't fall if they choose to speak."

For the first time that evening, Robin leaned back, her shoulders loosening. "Then let's do it. With those nets in place, I can walk into that room and know I'm not asking people to stand alone."

Marcus gave a rare approving grunt. "That's how you win—not just catching the bad guys, but protecting the ones who finally dare to speak."

Robin's eyes softened. "And it's why I'll speak. Allison and I both. Not to expose details in front of everyone, but to break the silence. To say—we are survivors, and so are you. We're not alone anymore."

For a moment, silence pooled in the room. The weight of it was not fear, but something close to awe—like they were standing on the edge of history.

Marcus broke it. "Alright. Robin and Allison open the door. Danny, you and I monitor the crowd. If Hawkins shows, he's mine. If Stone or Pyle make a move, the Feds need to know immediately. Rebecca, you're our anchor—legal, supportive, orderly, documenting everything."

Danny leaned back, exhaling. "Feels like we're finally on offense."

Robin looked at each of them in turn. "And this time, we're not doing it alone."

Rebecca lowered her pen with a decisive click. "OK, then, we are locked in. December 17. Twin Peaks Inn. The night Westridge stops being silent."

Chapter 66

Coffee Shop Scene – Stone, Pyle, and Hawkins

The Bean was busy for a Thursday morning—students on laptops, retirees with newspapers, the hiss of the espresso machine filling the gaps between conversations. Sheriff Stone slid into the corner booth, his hat set neatly beside him. Deputy Hawkins was already there, stirring sugar into his coffee like he had all the time in the world.

Denver Pyle came last, shoulders hunched under a worn jacket, eyes darting before he sat down.

Stone didn't bother with pleasantries. "She's planning a reunion," he said flatly.

Hawkins raised a brow. "A high school reunion? After all these years? That's what's got you so worked up?"

Stone leaned in, voice low. "Don't play dumb. You think it's coincidence she starts stirring people up just as Kessler shows his face again? She's fishing."

Pyle's jaw twitched. "Fishing for what? Ain't nothing left to find. That girl was always fragile—now she's seeing that shrink, getting ideas put in her head. She doesn't know anything."

"Maybe she doesn't," Stone allowed, "but her lawyer friend does. I've seen them—Kessler, the realtor, and that out-of-town buddy of his—all huddled up like they're planning a parade. And then they walk into Rebecca Wright's office. You don't hire her unless you're looking to make something stick."

Hawkins set his cup down with a soft clink. "So what's the move?"

Stone's eyes narrowed, flicking between them. "The move is we stop underestimating them. Whatever this reunion is, it's not just beer and old yearbooks. She's got something, and if it surfaces, we're all sunk."

Pyle muttered, "So we shut it down."

Stone shook his head. "Not yet. You shut it down too soon, you draw eyes. We watch. We wait. We remind them who runs this town. And if they slip?" His lips curled into a thin smile. "We'll be there to make sure they regret it."

The three men sat in silence for a moment, the noise of the café swirling around their booth. Hawkins finally leaned back, arms folded. "Then I'll keep an eye on the boy. That kid of Melody's trusts me. If they're trying to loop outsiders in, I'll know first."

Stone grunted approval. "Do it. But careful. The last thing we need is attention before we're ready."

When they rose a few minutes later, the table was spotless, coffee cups stacked neatly. To anyone else, they looked like old friends catching up. Only the tightness in their jaws, the stiffness in their shoulders, betrayed the storm brewing beneath the surface.

Marcus Confronts Hawkins

Marcus pushed through the door of The Bean, the warm scent of roasted coffee rolling over him. He'd meant only to grab a black coffee for the road, but instinct kicked in the moment his eyes swept the room.

Corner booth. Sheriff Stone. Denver Pyle. And Deputy Hawkins.

They leaned close, cups nearly empty, the kind of body language Marcus had learned to clock years ago. Men with something to hide. Men circling the wagons.

He didn't hesitate. He picked up his coffee at the counter, then crossed straight toward the booth like he belonged there. When Hawkins finally noticed him, Marcus let his face light up in recognition.

"Coach!" Marcus said, voice pitched warm, just loud enough for nearby tables to hear. He clapped Hawkins on the shoulder like they were old friends. "Good to see you again—how's practice these days?"

Hawkins stiffened, caught off guard. "Uh . . . fine. Same as ever. You are . . . ?"

"Marcus," he supplied easily, leaning on the back of the booth. "We've crossed paths. Back when I was doing work with youth programs. You always had the boys running harder than anyone." He gave a low chuckle, eyes sharp as a blade despite the casual tone. "Glad to see you're still at it."

Stone's eyes narrowed, reading the subtext. Pyle shifted uncomfortably in his seat, muttering into his cup.

Marcus straightened, still smiling like this was a chance encounter. "Well, I'll let you gentlemen get back to catching up. Just wanted to say hello. Keep those kids working hard, Coach."

Then he walked out, his coffee untouched in his hand, never breaking stride until the cold air hit his lungs.

Behind him, the booth was silent. Hawkins cleared his throat, forcing a laugh. "Don't know him that well," he muttered. But Stone's glare said otherwise.

Outside, Marcus allowed himself the smallest smile. Message delivered: *I see you. I'm not afraid. And I know where you sit.*

Chapter 67

Marcus stood, restless, leaning on the back of a chair instead of sitting. His duffel bag was shoved against the wall like he'd just come from a stakeout. Robin's office was quiet that evening.

Danny broke the silence first. "You said you had something we needed to hear."

Marcus nodded, jaw tight. "Yeah. You know I went to practice with Yuki the evening we went to Melody's, right? Just hung around and watched the practice. Most of it was what you'd expect—drills, kids horsing around, nothing out of the ordinary. But then he pulled two boys aside, while the others shot free throws. Tone was . . . too familiar. One of the boys was Yuki; Hawkins took the other one into the equipment room. Door stayed ajar an inch, but still—five minutes out of sight." He paused, eyes narrowing. "That's classic grooming behavior. Couldn't prove intent, but I've seen the pattern. I reported it to Rebecca."

Robin's stomach clenched. "And Yuki?"

"Yuki breezed through it. Kid's sharp, deflected it with humor. But that doesn't make him safe—it just means Hawkins will keep testing until he finds an opening."

Danny muttered a curse under his breath. "So we were right. It's still happening."

Marcus shifted his weight. "It's worse. I saw Hawkins at The Bean this morning. He was with Stone and Pyle. I walked right up to him, shook his hand like we were old friends. 'Hey coach, good to see you, how's practice?' He blanched. Didn't know how to play it. That's leverage—he knows someone's watching, and he doesn't know what I know."

Robin sat back, processing, her fingers tightening on the edge of the table. "So they're still moving in the open. Still convinced they control this town."

Marcus' voice hardened. "Which is why this reunion matters. They think it's just a nostalgia party. A little class fluff. They can't imagine it's a trap. That arrogance is our edge." He paused, then added, quieter: "But make no mistake—if we miss, if this doesn't land—they'll come harder, and dirtier."

Danny met his gaze. "Then we don't miss."

Marcus finally sat, running a hand over his notebook. "Rebecca's affidavits, survivor testimony, financial records—it's all lining up. The Mustang's shell company. And Robin's memory about Pyle being her first forced 'date.' That puts him dead center. When this goes public, he's not just a creep on parole. He's a repeat offender, tied to a pattern. That's enough to haul him back in irons."

Robin exhaled, a tremor she couldn't quite disguise. "So, after twenty-five years . . . we're finally close."

Danny reached across the table, covering her hand with his. "Closer than ever."

Marcus leaned forward. "Then let's make damn sure we finish it."

Chapter 68

The conference room at Robin's office felt almost too small with everyone gathered: Robin, Danny, Marcus, Rebecca, Melody, Bruce, Allison, Tanya, Patsy, Sandra, and Sophia. The winter evening pressed against the windows, but inside there was warmth, coffee, and an unspoken sense of momentum. This was the circle before the storm.

Robin stood at the head of the table, her notebook open, pen tapping lightly against the page. "Alright. One last time before we go live. We've got just under a week, and every detail matters. So let's walk through it."

Logistics and Hospitality

Robin started with what she could control.

"Twin Peaks Inn has confirmed the dining room for 120 people. We've arranged a cash bar and buffet service. I've built in plenty of vegetarian and allergy-friendly options so no one feels excluded."

She flipped a page. "Invitations went out via mail and email, and the *Gazette* notice ran yesterday. We've already had 80 RSVPs, but realistically, I expect more, and some will just show up. Staff at the Inn says they're used to that; they'll handle it."

She glanced up, half-grinning. "I even confirmed dessert. Pumpkin pie. Because apparently, that's become my trademark." The group laughed softly, easing the tension.

Evidence and Legal

Rebecca took over next, sliding a neat folder into the center of the table.

"Affidavits are prepped. Allison's is notarized; Robin's was added this week. I've also secured copies of the Mustang's shell company filings. That paper trail is thin, but enough to suggest concealment."

She tapped the folder. "These go directly to the AG's liaison Monday. We'll hold originals under lock until then."

Her tone sharpened. "If anyone discloses details of this meeting, even casually, we lose the element of surprise. So I'm reminding you—lips sealed."

Allison nodded tightly, her hands folded in her lap. "I've kept quiet for twenty years. I won't falter now."

Security and Safety

Marcus leaned forward, forearms braced on the table. "My team is in place. I've got two federal contacts flying in that morning, blending as attendees. The Inn will have plainclothes security, and I'll walk the perimeter myself beforehand."

He scanned the room. "If Hawkins, Stone, or Pyle show up, don't engage. Not even eye contact. Let us handle it. They'll be watched from the second they cross the threshold."

Danny added, "And remember—this isn't just about nabbing them. It's about showing survivors that the silence is over. That has to be our anchor."

Survivor Care

Sophia spoke quietly, but her words cut through.

"If even one survivor chooses to speak that night, it will take everything they've got. I'll be there as a licensed clinician, ready to provide immediate support if needed. No pressure, no spotlight—just a quiet place to land."

Tanya, Sandra, and Patsy chimed in together, offering to circulate gently during the event. "Sometimes just a friendly face or a supportive word is enough to keep someone from bolting," Sandra said.

Robin met their eyes. "Thank you. That's exactly what I was hoping you'd say."

Media and Message

Melody set down her fork—she'd brought baklava, half-eaten now—and leaned forward eagerly.

"I'll have my documentary crew there, posing as event videographers. Just coverage of a reunion, nothing suspicious. But if something breaks open—a survivor speaks, or if law enforcement makes a move—the cameras will be rolling. We'll control the narrative before Stone and his cronies can spin it."

Bruce added, his voice calm but firm: "And if it escalates, I can guarantee coverage on the evening news within hours. But that's the nuclear option—we use it only if lives or evidence are at risk."

Closing the Circle

Finally, Robin drew a deep breath. "This is more than a reunion. This is about reclaiming the years stolen from us—me, Allison, Danny, and others we don't even know yet. And if it works, it's about making sure Westridge is never again a place where predators hide in plain sight."

The group fell silent for a moment, the weight of her words settling over them. Marcus broke it with his gravelly certainty: "Then let's make damn sure it works."

Rebecca closed her folder. "We're ready."

Robin looked around at each face in turn, gratitude and resolve mingling in her chest. "Then I'll see you all on the 17th. And God willing, we'll walk out of that night not just survivors, but victors."

"I cannot even tell you how much I appreciate your commitment to this," Robin said. "This is what healing looks like . . . for an entire community."

Chapter 69

The dining room at the Twin Peaks Inn glowed with warm light, strings of white bulbs glimmering against garlands of evergreen. A low buzz of conversation filled the air as former classmates signed in at the welcome table, where two volunteers greeted them with name tags and—smiling conspiratorially—slipped a card onto each guest's back. A famous name. Marilyn Monroe. Elvis Presley. Abraham Lincoln.

The first hour unfolded like a reunion should: tentative hellos melting into laughter, friends reunited over cocktails, the game breaking the ice. "So tell me," one man teased, "Could I fall in love with my character?"—and the group around him howled when someone whispered, "Ha! Not a chance."

Melody's crew moved through the room with practiced ease, their cameras small, unobtrusive, catching snippets of laughter and hugs, chalking it up to "local color" for their documentary.

At the back, Marcus lingered by the bar, eyes scanning exits, noting faces. Danny stayed close to Robin, who floated from group to group, greeting people, introducing Allison when the moment seemed natural. There was tension under her ribs, yes—but also an unexpected thrill. This many people had come. And they were having fun.

An hour in, Robin walked to the podium and tapped the mic. The room stilled, not abruptly, but with the ease of people already warmed by company. She stood near the buffet, Allison just behind her, steady as a shadow.

"OK," Robin began with a smile, "show of hands—how many of you have figured out the name taped to your back?" Laughter rippled as about half the room raised their hands. "Good work. For the rest of you—keep asking, keep talking, you'll get there. And that's really why we're here tonight, isn't it? To finally ask, to finally talk, to remember."

Her tone softened. "It's been too long. For some of us—twenty-five years since we've seen each other. And our classes never had reunions. Tonight isn't about catching up on jobs or kids or moves across the country. Tonight is about remembering who we were, and honoring who we've become. For some of us, the years in Westridge were joyful. For others . . . they were complicated. Painful."

A murmur shifted across the room. Robin let it hang, then gestured to Allison.

"This is Allison," Robin said simply. "Some of you know her. Some of you don't. But she and I share something—we've both carried pieces of the past that we thought we had to keep silent. We don't anymore. And neither do you."

Allison stepped forward, her voice clear though her hands trembled slightly. There was a quiet murmur in the room.

"When I was sixteen, I thought I was the only one. The only one hurt, the only one silenced. But silence was the lie." She shared her story with poise and purpose and concluded, "I see now I was never alone. And neither are you."

The room hushed. No confessions, no forced disclosures. Just that simple truth, dropped like a stone into water, rippling outward.

Rebecca, at the side of the room, saw the first shift. A man excused himself from his table, made his way to her, voice low. "My sister . . . class of 2003. She changed after . . . something. I'll give you her number." He scribbled on a napkin.

Near the bar, a woman pressed a folded scrap of paper into Robin's hand: *She wants to talk. Call her.*

Melody's camera captured faces—some softened with compassion, others tightening with discomfort. Marcus caught the man at the bar again, lingering too long, eyes darting toward Allison. Marcus didn't move, but he logged every detail.

Robin closed with gratitude. "This night isn't the end of anything. It's the start. Of remembering, of healing, of refusing to let silence tell our stories anymore. We are the masters of our fate. We decide who we are and who we become. Thank you for being here, for being brave enough to come."

Applause rose—not thunderous, but sincere, filling the corners of the room. And in that moment, for the first time in decades, Westridge felt like a community pulling itself toward light.

Meanwhile, while classmates laughed and reconnected, the inner circle stayed alert.

Marcus leaned casually against a column near the buffet, posture loose, but his eyes catalogued everything: who came in late, who lingered near exits, who avoided eye contact. He noticed two men— neither with name tags—hovering just outside the dining room. They didn't mingle, didn't drink. They simply watched. Marcus slid his phone from his pocket and typed a quick note for later.

Rebecca, though busy with smiles and handshakes, kept her lawyer's eye sharp. She quietly accepted slips of paper, phone numbers written in hurried script, notes folded into napkins. She thanked people with warmth, never pressing, never making them feel exposed. But each slip she tucked into her portfolio carried weight— potential testimony, corroboration, lives long silenced.

At the bar, Pete played genial host, joking with the guys at the bar, but his ears were open. Twice he overheard the same name murmured—Denver Pyle—followed by sharp changes of subject. The name wasn't forgotten. It still had power, still carried a chill through the room.

Melody's crew kept rolling. The cameras framed hugs and clinking glasses, but every so often the lens caught something more: a tense expression, a furtive glance, someone slipping Rebecca another note. Melody, working her mic pack, whispered to her cameraman, "Keep wide coverage. This is bigger than I thought."

Danny stayed close to Robin, but he was scanning too. He noticed how often the black SUV circled the parking lot. Not obvious. Not stationary. But present. He leaned toward Robin once and murmured, "Don't react, but we've got company outside." Her smile never faltered, but her hand gripped his under the table.

And above it all, Ingrid's words from their last Mastermind echoed in Robin's mind: *courage multiplies.* Here they were—laughter and tension, joy and fear—woven into one night. A night where silence cracked and light pushed its way in.

Chapter 70

Robin's conference room was bathed in the aroma of fresh coffee and a hint of citrus air freshener. Chairs were pulled close, coffee cups steaming, legal pads open. The mood was quieter than the reunion's laughter, but no less intense.

Rebecca set her leather portfolio in the center of the table, the spine heavy with folded slips of paper. "Here's what came in," she said, tapping the stack. "Six different people left me notes. Three are solid leads—names, dates, places. Two are vague suspicions, and one is a direct accusation. That's more than I dared hope for in one night."

Danny leaned forward, arms on his knees. "And the SUV outside? Circled at least three times. Same one I've seen before."

Marcus nodded. "I clocked two men near the entry. No name tags, no effort to blend in. They were watching, not mingling. I got partial plates on the SUV—already sent it to a contact. We'll see what comes back."

Robin exhaled, slow. "I knew there'd be whispers, but I didn't expect so many people ready to talk. Allison told me she had three women approach her privately, asking how she found the courage. She said they were shaking. One of them handed her a number." Robin slid a folded slip across the table.

Rebecca took it gently, added it to the portfolio. "We'll treat every one of these like evidence. But the biggest risk now is exposure. They'll know we're gathering momentum. They'll push back."

Marcus's voice was flat, steady. "They already are. The SUV was a warning. Next move won't be so polite."

A silence settled. Then Robin, lifting her chin, said, "That's why we have to keep moving. We've cracked the silence. We can't back off now."

Rebecca ticked items off with her pen. "Here's our action steps: I'll file affidavits this afternoon with the AG's office. Marcus, follow up on the plates. Anyone else who has an observation, put it in writing and give it to me. Robin, you coordinate with Melody—her footage has to be edited down to community-friendly, no graphic exposure, but strong enough to tell the truth. We need that ready for press if something happens."

Danny added, jaw tight, "And we need to lock down security. Not just for Robin, but for all of us. They can't get to everyone, but they'll try."

Marcus leaned back, arms crossed. "I'll set up rotation. No one moves alone. Not until we've got charges on paper."

The ordinary hum of Robin's office filtered in from outside— phones ringing, printers humming, staff voices low. It felt almost jarring against the tension at the table. But as they rose, gathering coats and portfolios, the weight in the room wasn't despair. It was momentum.

Robin thought of the faces from last night—classmates laughing with drinks in hand, shoulders relaxing after years of silence—and she whispered to herself, *courage multiplies.*

Meanwhile, at The Bean

The Westridge Bean was half-full with the midmorning crowd, the smell of burnt espresso and cinnamon rolls hanging thick in the air. Sheriff Stone sat in the corner booth, his hat pushed low, hands folded over a steaming mug. Across from him, Deputy Hawkins scrolled on his phone, eyes darting to the door every time it opened.

Denver Pyle slid into the booth last, his bulk crowding the space, a scowl carved into his face. "That was a circus last night," he muttered. "Some party they threw."

Stone didn't look up. "A reunion. That's all it was." His voice was clipped, too quick.

"Bull," Hawkins said, leaning forward. "You saw who was there. Rebecca Wright. That lawyer doesn't waste her time on beer and name tags. And Kessler—he's not back just to box up his parents' junk. They're planning something."

Stone's jaw tightened. "Maybe. But think about it. Who's going to believe a handful of washed-up grads dredging up old stories? Twenty-five years gone. Nobody cares." He tried for a smirk, but it didn't reach his eyes.

Pyle snorted. "Allison Chambers was there. She looked too comfortable. If she starts yapping again—"

"Then we shut it down," Stone cut him off sharply. "Like we always have."

For a beat, the only sound was the hiss of the espresso machine and the rattle of dishes behind the counter.

Finally, Hawkins muttered, "Still don't get why they'd bother with a reunion now. Unless it's bait."

Stone's gaze flicked to the window, watching the street. "Doesn't matter what it is. We stay close. We watch. And if they push too far . . . " He let the words trail off, his meaning clear.

Pyle leaned back, lips curling into a humorless grin. "Then we remind them what happens when people forget their place."

The three men sat in silence, the tension between them as bitter as the coffee in their cups—blind to the fact that the ground was shifting beneath their feet.

Chapter 71

Pyle's Spiral

Pyle sat in the cracked vinyl booth at the back of a no-name bar, a half-empty glass of bourbon sweating on the table. His knee bounced, his hand tapping a restless rhythm that didn't match the jukebox's hum.

"They think they've won," he muttered, voice low but sharp. "Danny struts back into town like some savior, that woman"—he spit the word—"Robin, with her speeches and her lawyers, smiling like the past doesn't matter. Like she's not the reason my life went sideways."

The bartender passed by, but Pyle didn't notice. His eyes were fixed on nothing, jaw grinding. "Allison, Robin, whoever else crawls out of the shadows—they're emboldened because of him. Because Stone doesn't clamp down like he used to. Because Hawkins acts like a coach, like some respectable man. Respectable." His laugh was jagged, bitter.

He slammed his hand flat on the table. "Well, let's see how respectable they look when the 'survivor queen' doesn't survive at all. Maybe then they'll remember who they're dealing with."

The bourbon glass tipped, amber liquid running across the table like a stain. He didn't bother wiping it. He was already halfway to the door, muttering, "End it tonight. End it before she destroys us all."

Ambush

She left the office after one more late night at work, exhausted. The moment she turned the key, the gas light turned orange. "Oh crap, I don't want to deal with this in the morning; I'll just stop now . . ."

Robin pulled into the station, headlights sweeping across cracked pavement, the faint neon hum of the convenience store flickering overhead. Marcus had insisted on shadowing her—keeping his car parked discreetly across the street, eyes always scanning.

She stepped out, tugging her coat tighter against the chill, and the smell of gasoline hit her like a wall. She slid her card next to the pump, absently rubbing her temple. A long day. A long week. Her mind was on tomorrow's follow-up with Rebecca, not on the black SUV idling too far back in the lot.

Then the world shrank to one sound.

A voice.

"Thought you could just erase me, huh?"

Her stomach clenched, a cold rush of recognition flooding her. *Pyle.* Even slurred, even drunk, that voice was carved into her bones. She turned just as he stepped from the shadows, gun wavering in his hand. His eyes were wild, pupils fully dilated, and the stink of liquor came off him in waves.

"You ruined everything, girl," he hissed. "And now you think you can play queen of this town? Not on my watch."

Her throat closed. For a split second, she was fifteen again, standing at a pink motel door, knees knocking. The air seemed to thin out. She couldn't breathe.

But then training from Sophia surfaced—slow, grounding breaths. *That was then. This is now.*

She held his gaze, forcing her voice steady. "You're finished, Pyle. Everyone knows."

The shot cracked the air. Pain ripped across her shoulder. She staggered, hit the side of her car, and dropped hard to the pavement.

Marcus was already moving. He'd sprinted across the street the second the gun came up. He tackled Pyle from behind, the gun skidding under a parked pickup. The two men crashed into the asphalt, Marcus pinning him with professional efficiency—knee to back, wrist locked, a move born of years in the field.

"Stay down, you son of a bitch," Marcus growled, yanking a zip tie from his pocket. He always carried them. Always.

Pyle writhed, cursing, drunk, spitting. "She deserves it! They all deserve it—"

Marcus slammed him against the hood of the SUV, securing the restraints. Then he pulled his burner phone, his voice clipped, steady.

"Shooter in custody, victim wounded—Westridge Gas on Main. No Sheriff. Repeat—no Sheriff. Patch me to State Police or AG desk only. Need EMS and state uniforms on scene now."

Next call, "Danny, Robin's been shot. Shoulder. She's alive. Stable for now. Meet us at County ER." Click.

"What? Marcus? Hey!" Danny almost crashed his car turning around in the middle of town. "On my way," he whispered to no one, his eyesight blurred by tears.

Marcus shoved his phone back in his pocket and checked Robin, keeping one hand on Pyle's shoulder. Her breath was ragged, but she was still upright against the car, blood darkening her sleeve.

"No Sheriff . . . genius," Robin whispered.

"It's over," Marcus told her, eyes steady. "Help's on the way. And he's not going anywhere."

Robin, pale and sweating, clutched her arm. Marcus crouched beside her, steady hand pressing gauze to the wound from the first aid kit in his trunk. "Stay with me, Robin. Eyes open. You're not going down tonight."

The wail of sirens grew closer, the air flashing red and blue.

When EMS headed out with Robin, Marcus snagged gas station surveillance, before anyone could tamper with it. On the way out, he shot photos on his phone of casing, angles, distance—all the things a defense attorney might later try to wiggle out of.

Tires squealed as he headed to the ER before anyone could try to change the narrative.

ER Scene – After the Shooting

The ER smelled of antiseptic and fear. Fluorescent lights hummed overhead as Robin was wheeled through double doors, Marcus catching up, his shirt still streaked with Pyle's blood and asphalt grime. He handed her off to the trauma team, then planted himself against the wall, arms folded, a sentinel.

Danny burst in minutes later, hair damp with sweat, eyes wild. Marcus intercepted him with a steady hand on his chest.

"She's alive. Stable. Bullet went clean through the shoulder—messy, but not fatal."

Danny sagged against the wall, relief loosening his knees. Then he shoved past, desperate to see her. He caught a glimpse of her pale face through the curtain as nurses swarmed, IVs threading, monitors beeping.

The waiting room buzzed with low voices and restless footsteps. And then the automatic doors whooshed open again. Sheriff Stone strode in, Deputy Hawkins flanking him. Their presence chilled the room more than the December air outside.

"Well, well," Stone drawled, his voice too loud, too casual. "Holiday weekend's off to a rough start, huh? Gas stations at night—always trouble."

Danny whirled, fists clenched. "Don't you dare spin this like a random robbery. We all know who pulled that trigger."

Stone's smile was thin, but a flicker of unease crossed his eyes before he smothered it. "Careful, son. Throwing accusations without proof . . . not smart."

Marcus pushed off the wall, calm but edged steel in his voice. "Funny thing. Proof's not a problem. Witnesses, surveillance footage, and a suspect zip-tied on the pavement when state uniforms rolled in."

Hawkins stiffened. His gaze cut to Marcus, recognition dawning. He hadn't expected him to be here—hands-on, competent, impossible to intimidate.

Stone's jaw ticked, though his smirk never slipped. "If that's the case, then I'm sure justice will take its course. Until then, you all might want to keep your heads down. Dangerous world out there."

As if on cue, Robin's gurney rolled past, a nurse adjusting the IV line. She was pale, but awake, her lips trembling as she focused on Danny.

Her voice came out hoarse but certain: "It was him. I heard his voice. Pyle."

The corridor froze. The word landed like a gavel.

Danny reached for her hand, his throat tight. Marcus's eyes flicked back to Stone. The message in his stare was deliberate, unflinching: *The game is over.*

And for the first time, Stone looked rattled. His confidence cracked, just a hairline fracture—but enough for Marcus to see it. Enough to know the balance of power had shifted.

Nightwatch

The monitors hummed steady in Robin's room, the beeps almost like a lullaby against the chaos that had brought her here. Danny sat at her bedside, his hand wrapped gently around hers, thumb stroking her knuckles in a rhythm as old as comfort.

"They'll want to keep you overnight," he murmured, more to reassure himself than her. "Observation. Just to be safe."

Robin gave a faint smile. "Feels strange being safe in a hospital. But I'll take it."

The door cracked open. Marcus stepped in, still in his field jacket, eyes scanning everything before he relaxed. He pulled up a chair, straddled it backward, and leaned his arms across the back.

"This isn't over," he said flatly. "Stone and Hawkins were blind-sided tonight. They won't forgive that. Which means they're unpredictable. And you"—he jabbed a finger at Danny—"are not staying alone. You're both targets now."

Danny met his gaze without flinching. "I'm not leaving her."

"Didn't say you should," Marcus replied. "I'm pulling a second shift outside this hospital. Got a rotation set. No one gets near this room unless I know their badge number and their mother's maiden name."

Marcus sat for a second, his eyes scanning the monitors, before fixing his eyes on Danny.

"You need to know something else," he said, voice pitched low. "When Pyle went down, I didn't call Stone. Didn't call Hawkins either. I routed it straight through state dispatch. Neutral line. They patched local uniforms, but Stone's office didn't get the first word."

Danny blinked, the weight of it settling in. "You cut him out."

Marcus nodded once. "On purpose. It bought us time—kept him in the dark long enough that by the time he rolled up at the ER, he was already behind the curve. That's why he looked like he swallowed glass. He's used to holding the strings, Danny. Tonight, he didn't even have the puppet."

Robin shifted on the bed, pale but listening. "So he's cracking."

"Starting to," Marcus confirmed. "Stone runs on control. Take that away, and he makes mistakes. Same with Hawkins. They'll double down, maybe lash out, but every crack in their armor gives us leverage."

Danny leaned forward, jaw tight. "So we keep cutting them out. Keep letting them chase shadows while we tighten the net."

"Exactly," Marcus said, his gaze steady. "But that also means they're desperate. And desperate men? They're the most dangerous kind. This is when people like Stone make their sloppiest moves. You're safe inside these walls tonight. Tomorrow morning, we get you home. Danny drives. I'll follow. No shortcuts."

The silence that followed wasn't heavy—it was resolute. Three people, aligned.

Marcus, stood up, and looked at Danny, "So, you hold the line inside. She needs calm, not panic."

Danny looked back at Robin, pale but awake, listening quietly. "I can do that."

Marcus clapped his shoulder once, firmly. "Then we're covered. For tonight." He left the room, his boots echoing down the hallway, leaving Danny and Robin in a pocket of silence.

Alone at Last

Robin shifted slightly in the bed, wincing at the ache in her shoulder. Danny leaned closer, brushing a stray lock of hair back from her face.

"You scared the hell out of me," he whispered.

Her lips curved faintly. "Guess we're even. You've been scaring me since the day you showed up at The Bean."

He chuckled softly, shaking his head. "Not the same."

"Maybe not," she admitted, her voice thin but steady. "But I'm still here. And so are you. That counts for something."

Danny pressed a kiss to her temple, lingering. "It counts for everything."

Her eyelids grew heavy, her words slipping out in a dreamy murmur. "You know what I wish right now?"

"Hm?" he prompted softly.

"I wish I could curl up close—just so you'd know how much I want to feel safe with you, how much I want to let you protect me."

His chest tightened. He bent nearer, his voice rough. "If I thought I could fit in that cot without hurting you, I'd do it in a heartbeat."

A faint smile touched her lips as she drifted off. "Then save it for when we're home. We'll figure it out."

Chapter 72

By morning, the December light cut through the blinds, pale and cold. Robin was stiff but upright, her arm bandaged, color returning to her cheeks. Danny was waiting with her discharge papers in hand, stubborn as a guard dog.

"You sure you're ready for this?" he asked.

Robin smirked. "Ready as I'll ever be. And if I stay one more hour, they'll start charging me rent."

"Ha. Trust me. They are already charging you rent," Danny answered with a wink.

Marcus was already in the hallway, phone pressed to his ear. When he saw them, he clicked off and pocketed it. "Car's out front. I'll tail you back. Don't stop for gas, don't stop for coffee. Straight home. Once you're settled, we regroup."

Robin squeezed Danny's hand as he wheeled her out. "One step at a time," she whispered. "But today . . . today I'm alive."

Danny glanced at her, his jaw tight but his eyes full. "And I'm not letting you out of my sight again."

The hospital's automatic doors whispered open, spilling them into the cool early morning air. It was barely past ten, but after the chaos of the night, it felt later. Robin leaned into Danny's steady arm as they crossed the lot. Marcus followed a step behind, his stride still taut with vigilance, though the shadows under his eyes betrayed the hours catching up with him.

The drive home was quiet. Robin's head rested lightly against the window, the glow of streetlamps sliding over her face. Danny kept one hand on the wheel, the other occasionally brushing against hers on the console, a silent tether. In the rearview mirror, Marcus's headlights stayed close, never wavering.

"Strange comfort, isn't it?" Robin murmured. "Knowing he's back there."

Danny glanced at her. "Comforting, yes. Strange that we need it? Absolutely. But I'm not complaining."

When they pulled into Robin's driveway, Danny cut the engine and looked back at Marcus's car as it rolled in behind. "He won't admit it, but he's dead on his feet," Danny said softly.

Robin's lips curved faintly. "Then let's not make him keep watch in the cold. He's earned better."

Inside, the house glowed from the morning light streaming in the window, but the house still felt chilly. Robin settled onto the couch with a tired exhale while Danny dropped his keys in the bowl by the door. Let me make a fire and get it cozy in here.

While Danny was crinkling up newspaper and piling logs, Marcus came in, eyes still scanning the street before he shut the door.

He struck a match as he said, "Thanks for sticking Buddy. But you need a break. Sit down before you fall down."

Marcus gave a faint, almost sheepish snort. "I've done worse on less sleep."

"Yeah, and look how well that turned out," Robin teased, her voice soft but steady. She gestured toward the guest room down the hall. "It's yours. No arguments. You'll hear us if anything happens, and we'll wake you if we need you."

Danny was already moving toward the kitchen. "Give me ten minutes and I'll have breakfast going. Real coffee, eggs, maybe even pancakes. You crash after that."

For the first time all night, Marcus's shoulders eased, just a fraction. He dropped into a chair, rubbing a hand over his face.

Two minutes later, the Keurig hissed out his reward. Marcus latched onto the mug like it was a lifeline. "Oh man, I needed that," he said, voice gravelly.

Danny slid coffee to everyone and dropped bacon into the skillet. "It's not breakfast if it doesn't smell like bacon," he said, the sizzle filling the kitchen with a comfort none of them realized they'd been starving for.

In under ten minutes, the table was set. Marcus ate like a soldier— efficient, wordless, three minutes flat. He pushed back his chair, gave Danny a firm nod of thanks. "Don't let me sleep long."

Robin shook her head. "Sleep as long as you need. You've carried enough for one night."

His eyes softened, just for a moment, before he disappeared down the hall.

Robin's gaze lingered on Danny as he clattered pans in the sink, the smell of bacon still clinging to the air. The ordinary sound felt like salvation. The storm outside was still circling, but for this small window, they had warmth, food, and each other.

Danny dried his hands, then ducked into her bedroom. He came back with a pillow, puffed it once, and set it carefully behind her. His hands were steady, gentle.

"You too," he said, lowering his voice like a vow. "I want you strong again. For now, I just want to watch you breathe and thank God for that—for the rest of my life."

Robin's throat tightened. She let him ease her feet into his lap, the weight grounding them both. He leaned back, eyes closing briefly, one hand resting lightly over her ankle. The moment stretched, hushed and fragile, but wrapped in the kind of peace that felt almost like a miracle.

Then Robin's scream cut through the air.

Danny bolted down the hall, heart pounding, and burst into her bedroom. She was upright in bed, drenched in sweat, eyes wide and unfocused.

"Robin, it's me," he said urgently, climbing onto the edge of the bed. He gathered her trembling hands into his. "It's okay. You're safe."

Her breathing hitched, ragged. "He—he was right there. His voice. That laugh—"

Danny held her tighter. "It was just a dream. You're here. With me. He's not going to touch you again."

Marcus appeared in the doorway, instantly alert. He crossed the room and crouched beside the bed, steady but calm. "Listen to me. Pyle's not walking around free. He's locked up. I saw the paperwork myself. He's at the county jail on no bond, waiting arraignment."

Robin blinked at him, grounding. "For sure?"

"For sure," Marcus said, voice like iron. "Tuesday morning he'll stand in front of a judge. Attempted murder charge, plus violations from his old record. He's not slipping out of this."

Danny brushed her damp hair back. "Hear that? You can breathe now."

Robin nodded shakily, finally letting her head rest against his chest. For the first time since the shooting, she allowed herself to believe she might really be safe—for now.

Chapter 73

The courthouse steps gleamed with frost as Marcus guided Robin and Danny through the crowd. Rebecca met them at the entrance, portfolio under her arm, eyes sharp.

Inside, the air smelled of old paper and too much coffee. They slipped into the second row of benches just as deputies brought Pyle in, shackled and glaring. His swagger was gone, his eyes bloodshot, jaw tight.

"All rise," the bailiff called.

The judge scanned the paperwork with clipped efficiency. "Mr. Pyle, you are charged with attempted homicide, aggravated assault with a firearm, and parole violations. Given your prior record, bail is denied. You will remain in custody pending trial."

A ripple moved through the room. Robin gripped Danny's hand, her shoulder still aching but her spine straight. She whispered, almost to herself: "He's not walking back into my nightmares."

Pyle twisted around at that, his gaze locking on her. His lips curled in a snarl, words too low for anyone else, but Robin saw them: *This isn't over.*

Marcus leaned forward, his voice a quiet growl in Robin's ear. "Let him snarl. Every word just digs his hole deeper."

Rebecca gave a firm nod. "The system's moving. Now we keep pressing until the whole rotten structure collapses."

They walked out into the brittle December air together—closer, steadier, ready to face Christmas with something that almost felt like hope.

Chapter 74

Group Message from Ingrid – Sent Evening of December 23

Ingrid: "My dear friends,

Let's begin our New Year together—grounded, grateful, and ready for what's ahead. This month has been heavy in more ways than one, and yet, here we are: stronger, wiser, more knit together. That deserves space.

We'll meet on **New Year's Day**. No hot seat this time. Instead, just cookies, tea, and honest reflection. Bring your favorite holiday cookies (save a few in the freezer if you must!) and bring your **dreams for the year ahead**. Also bring gratitude for the year past, no matter how complicated.

This will be our reset. Our gift to one another. A moment to breathe and begin again.

"We will start this year as we mean to continue: connected, courageous, and free."

Responses from the Women

Patsy: "Well, there goes my first batch of cookies—already ate them! Guess I'll be baking again. But I wouldn't miss this for the world."

Sandra: "Perfect way to start the year. After the whirlwind of December, I'm eager to focus on what really matters."

Tanya: 🔥🔥 "Ready to dream BIG. Let's do this."

Melody: "Count me in. I'll bring Yuki's favorites—though I can't promise they'll make it past him. 🐱"

Rebecca: "Thank you, Ingrid. After everything we've faced, beginning together feels like the strongest step we could take. I'll bring Pete's favorite shortbread—and my full heart."

Robin: (reading the messages silently, her heart swelling) "For too long I thought carrying my story alone was strength. But I'm learning true strength is letting trusted people carry pieces of it with me.

Thank you for being my circle. Because of you, I'm walking into this new year with hope."

Chapter 75

The Call to Rebecca

R obin had just finished making a grocery list she knew she wouldn't have time or energy to fill when her phone buzzed. Rebecca's name lit the screen.

"Robin, it's settled," Rebecca said without preamble. "Pete and I are bringing the whole Christmas Eve dinner. Turkey, sides, dessert—the works. You don't lift a finger except to pour wine."

Robin laughed, the sound bubbling up despite her lingering aches. "Rebecca, I can't let you do all that—"

"You can and you will," Rebecca interrupted firmly, but there was warmth under the steel. "You've been through hell, and you're still healing. Besides, I like feeding people. Let me do this."

Robin pressed the phone closer, touched by her friend's fierce generosity. "All right. But at least let me set the table."

"Deal," Rebecca said. "Oh, and Marcus already volunteered to wrangle Danny into getting a tree. Don't argue. Just enjoy the break."

Robin hung up, leaning back in her chair. For the first time in days, she felt like Christmas might actually happen here, in her home—messy, patched together, but real.

Picking the Tree

The lot smelled of pine and cold earth, strings of colored lights twinkling overhead. Danny walked between rows of firs, brushing frost from branches, while Marcus followed with a tape measure in hand, muttering about ceiling height.

Robin trailed behind them, her coat wrapped tight, cheeks flushed from the cold. "I feel like I've got two twelve-year-olds arguing over who gets the bigger toy," she teased.

Danny shot her a grin. "It's not about bigger. It's about balance. This one—perfect shape." He patted a seven-foot spruce.

Marcus snorted. "Leans left. You'll be trimming branches to keep it upright. This one's better." He pointed to a sturdier pine.

Robin laughed, watching them squabble, the ordinary bickering wrapping around her like a quilt. "You two do realize I get the final vote, right?"

They both stopped, turned to her in mock offense. "What?" they chorused.

Smiling, she walked past both choices and tapped the branch of a smaller but perfectly symmetrical tree. "This one. It'll fit the corner by the window. No arguments."

Danny and Marcus exchanged a look, then shrugged in unison. "She's the boss," Marcus said.

As the attendant tied the tree to the roof of the car, Robin slid her arm through Danny's, the cold air sharp but her heart warm.

Christmas Eve Dinner

By late afternoon, the house glowed with soft lights, the scent of pine and cinnamon in the air. Rebecca arrived first, Pete behind her carrying foil-covered pans that filled the kitchen counter in minutes.

"Dinner is served, or will be in about an hour," Rebecca announced, setting a pie down with a flourish.

Marcus showed up not long after, freshly shaved but still carrying the quiet watchfulness that never left him. He put a bottle of wine on the counter, nodded at Danny, then bent to hug Robin carefully.

They gathered around the table just after dusk, candles flickering, plates heaped high. Conversation flowed—light at first, holiday stories, jokes about the tree-hunting adventure, a memory or two from Christmases past.

But as dessert plates were cleared, the talk grew more reflective. Marcus leaned back, arms folded. "We've all been on edge. Tonight—let's breathe. But don't forget, Stone and Hawkins aren't done. We stay ready."

Rebecca reached for Robin's hand. "Ready—but together this time. That's the difference."

Danny's gaze lingered on Robin, steady and full. "Together is everything."

Robin exhaled slowly, taking in the faces around her table, the warmth of food and fire, the sense that—just for this night—they'd carved out something safe. Something worth fighting for.

As Rebecca and Pete gathered up their things to leave, hugs were given all around (more gently for Robin), Marcus followed them out.

Danny said, "Hey, partner, where are you going?"

"Safety Patrol," Marcus replied.

"I appreciate the thought, but what I appreciate more is that you are warm and fed in here, in the guest room, nothing much comfortable in that old rat trap, right?"

Marcus laughed and said, "No argument there. Thanks."

Chapter 76

The house had settled into stillness after Rebecca and Pete left, their laughter fading down the street. Marcus had retreated to the guest room with a quiet "Merry Christmas," leaving Robin and Danny alone with only the glow of the tree lights and the faint crackle from the fireplace.

Robin moved carefully, mindful of her healing shoulder, and settled onto the couch with a quilt draped over her legs. Danny poured two small glasses of wine and joined her, handing one over before lowering himself beside her.

For a while, they just sat. The air smelled of pine and cinnamon. Outside, the night was hushed, snowflakes whispering against the window.

Robin let out a soft laugh. "You realize this is the first Christmas in a long time that doesn't feel . . . empty. It's strange. I'm exhausted, half-broken, but there's something whole about tonight."

Danny turned toward her, his voice low. "That's what I want for you, Robin. For us. To feel whole again. Not haunted. Not alone."

She studied him in the shifting light, her eyes searching his face. "Then we need to say some things out loud. No more letting shadows fill in the blanks."

Danny straightened a little, nodding. "Okay. Say it."

Robin's voice was steady, but her hands tightened around the stem of her glass. "If you've ever thought—even for a second—that I didn't want you . . . that's wrong. Not back then. Not now. The last twenty-five years didn't change that."

His brow furrowed, softened by something like hope. "I don't ever want to assume. I've seen what pressure does. I'd never put that on you."

"No." She reached for his hand, squeezed hard. "If I hesitate, it's not because I don't want you. It's because I'm still sorting out the lies from the truth. You're not those lies. You never were."

Danny's throat worked, his thumb brushing the back of her hand. "Then hear me. I'll never hurt you. Not with guilt, not with games. You could make me sleep on that couch for the next ten years, and it wouldn't change a thing. I will love you for the rest of my life. Period. No qualifiers."

A tear slipped free down Robin's cheek, but her smile was luminous. "That's what I needed. Not safety nets, not careful silence—just the truth."

They leaned into each other, foreheads touching. Danny pressed a kiss to her temple, lingering there as though anchoring her in place.

Robin whispered, "Tonight, I want you right here. Not on the couch. Just hold me. That's all. That's everything."

He exhaled a shaky laugh, relief flooding his face. "Then that's what I'll do. No pressure. Just love. For as long as we get."

The tree lights flickered, their glow catching in her hair. For the first time in decades, the space between them was clear—no shadows, no lies. Just love spoken plain.

Robin shifted under the quilt, leaning against his chest. "Merry Christmas, Danny."

He tightened his arms around her, his lips brushing her hair. "Merry Christmas, Robin."

Chapter 77

Christmas day was quiet, a light smattering of snow frosted the grass outside. Coffee steamed in the kitchen, and the silence was filled with hope.

Marcus leaned forward in his chair, forearms resting on his knees. "Pyle's arraignment was Tuesday. So, he's locked up tight. No bail. That buys us a solid block of time." He looked from Robin to Danny. "Stone and Hawkins are rattled, but they're not dumb. They'll lay low for a beat, see how the pieces fall. That means right now—" he jabbed a finger lightly on the coffee table, "we actually have a window."

Robin's brow furrowed. "A window for what? To just . . . pretend all of this isn't happening?"

"Exactly," Marcus said, no hesitation. "Pretend. Be normal. Get out of town. Go south, catch your breath. You two have been living in fight-or-flight for weeks. That's not sustainable."

Danny shifted, his jaw tight. "And leave you here? With both houses?"

Marcus smirked. "Don't flatter yourself, Kessler. I wouldn't mind a real bed, a working kitchen, and something besides motel coffee. House-sitting isn't a step down."

Robin gave a soft laugh, but her wheels were turning. "So . . . you're saying go."

"I'm saying *strategic retreat*," Marcus corrected. "You come back clearer, stronger. I stay here, keep an eye on things. If Stone twitches, I'll know it."

Danny's protest faltered, dying under Marcus's steady look. Robin reached for his hand. "It could be good for us, Danny. A reset. Just a few days."

He finally exhaled, the tension loosening from his shoulders. "South, huh? Maybe the beach. Even if it's cold."

Marcus sat back, finally taking a sip of his coffee. "That's the idea. You two get sand. I'll hold the line here. Clean exchange."

And suddenly, the air felt lighter. The decision, once spoken, was already a step toward healing.

Chapter 78

The road unwound southward in long ribbons of gray asphalt, the December sky pale and streaked with lavender. Robin leaned her head against the window, watching the barren fields slide past. For the first time in months, her body wasn't braced for the next crisis. Danny's hand rested lightly on the gearshift between them, his thumb brushing hers every so often, anchoring her.

They reached the coast just before dusk. The inn was small, the kind of place where every room came with a quilt that looked hand-made and windows that framed the restless Atlantic. Waves crashed against the winter-dark beach, a steady heartbeat beneath the howl of the wind.

After a simple dinner at a seaside café, they bundled up and walked along the sand. The cold bit at their cheeks, but Robin felt alive, the salt air filling her lungs with something sharper and freer than she'd known in years. Danny held her hand, their boots crunching over broken shells.

She broke the silence first. "Tell me about Cambodia."

He glanced at her, surprised. "You sure?"

"I don't want just the polished version. I want to know what it cost you—and if it still calls to you."

Danny took a long breath, the wind tearing at his scarf. "The center . . . it saved me as much as it saved those kids. Gave me a reason to get up every day. But it was brutal, Robin. Every win came with three losses. Some nights I lay awake wondering if anything I'd done mattered." His voice roughened. "And yeah, part of me still feels pulled back there. But the other part—the bigger part—feels pulled here. To you. To this town. To what's starting to take root."

Robin stopped, turning to face him. The tide rushed in, cold foam licking at their boots. "So if we build this Healing Center in Westridge . . . you'd be in? Not just in name. Really in?"

He didn't hesitate. "With everything I am. Cambodia taught me the worst of humanity, but also the resilience of people who shouldn't have survived at all. That's what I can bring here—lessons from the fight, and maybe a roadmap for healing."

Her throat tightened. "I've spent so many years thinking I had to carry it all by myself. And now . . . " She shook her head, tears spilling fast in the raw wind. "Now I don't know what to do with the fact that I'm not alone anymore."

Danny cupped her face in his hands, his thumb brushing away the salt—sea spray or tears, he couldn't tell. "You don't have to figure it out tonight. But know this: I'm not leaving. Not this time. Not for Cambodia. Not for anything. You're my home now."

The words struck deeper than the wind ever could. She leaned into him, their kiss soft at first, then fiercer—years of silence and longing collapsing into one electric moment. When they finally broke apart, she laughed through her tears.

"Guess this is what a new beginning feels like," she whispered.

Danny smiled, pulling her close as the waves thundered behind them. "Then let's begin."

The inn was small, almost forgotten, perched just beyond the dunes. Their room smelled faintly of salt and cedar, the kind of clean that only comes from sea air. When Robin cracked the window, the muffled roar of the Atlantic drifted in, constant and grounding.

After their walk, they returned to the room, kicked off their shoes, and settled into the overstuffed chairs by the window. Danny had brought a bottle of red wine from the innkeeper's stash, and the glasses were still half-full on the table between them.

Robin pulled her knees up under her sweater and glanced out at the water. "Tell me something," she said softly. "That center you built in Cambodia—it's still yours, isn't it?"

Danny nodded, eyes steady. "It is. I set it up to be self-sustaining, with local leadership. They don't need me there every day anymore. But sometimes I wonder . . . if going back would be abandoning what's happening here. Or if staying here means turning my back on them."

Robin reached for her glass, then thought better of it, letting her hands rest in her lap. "Do you want to go back?"

A long pause. The sound of waves filled the space between them. "Part of me does," Danny admitted. "Those kids—those families—they taught me how to fight for something bigger than myself. But part of me knows the fight is right here now. Westridge has ghosts of its own. Maybe I was meant to bring what I learned there, here."

Her chest tightened. She'd been bracing for him to say he'd leave. Instead, he was giving her the very thing she'd been longing for: the possibility of staying, of choosing this place, this fight . . . and maybe even her.

"What if you didn't have to choose?" she asked carefully. "What if the Healing Center we've been talking about—what if that's the bridge? Your experience overseas . . . my scars here . . . Rebecca's grit . . . Marcus's backbone . . . everyone's part of it. Maybe this town doesn't just get healed. Maybe it becomes a model."

Danny leaned forward, elbows on his knees, studying her. "You sound like you've already seen it built."

"Maybe I have." She smiled faintly. "In my head, anyway."

He let out a low laugh, running a hand through his hair. "You know, every time I think I'm dragging you into the mess I brought home, you turn it into something bigger. Something worth the fight."

Robin felt her throat tighten, but she didn't look away. "Maybe that's what happens when you finally stop running from the truth. You start dreaming again."

Danny reached across the small table and took her hand, his palm warm and solid around hers. He didn't rush. He just held it, thumb brushing lightly along her knuckles.

"You know what I see when I look at you, Robin?" he said, his voice low, almost reverent. "Strength. Not brokenness. You think you're scarred, but all I see is someone who kept standing when everything in the world tried to knock her down."

Her breath caught. For a moment she thought she might cry, but instead she laughed softly, shaking her head. "You make me believe that maybe I'm . . . enough."

He leaned in then, slow, deliberate, his lips brushing hers once, then again, deepening into a kiss that carried all the unspoken years between them. When he pulled back, his forehead rested gently against hers.

"You're more than enough," he whispered. "You're the reason I'm here."

Outside, the waves rolled on, steady as a heartbeat. For the first time in decades, Robin didn't feel like she was surviving. She felt like she was beginning.

The kiss lingered in her mind long after they'd settled back into their chairs. Robin traced the rim of her glass, eyes on the dark stretch of ocean.

"You know," she said finally, voice soft but steady, "none of this would be happening if you hadn't come back. Not the reunion, not Allison talking, not me finding my voice again. I don't think I would've had the courage."

Danny's brow furrowed. "Robin, you would've found it. Maybe not like this, maybe not now, but you've always had it in you."

She shook her head, a faint smile tugging at her lips. "Maybe. But I needed you to remind me. You . . . coming back—it cracked something open. And now, I can't go back to silence."

Danny reached across the small table again, enclosing her hand in both of his. "Then I'll take it. Every hard moment, every fight ahead—if it means you never feel like you're carrying it alone again."

Her heart tightened at the earnestness in his voice, but she didn't move closer. Not yet. She leaned back in her chair, watching the surf. "I want to hold onto this . . . slowly. Tonight, let's just breathe. Let's just be."

Danny studied her for a long moment, then nodded, respect threading through his expression. "Slow it is. No pressure. Just us."

Later, when they turned in, the room felt hushed, expectant. Robin slipped beneath the quilt, her shoulder still tender but her spirit steadier than it had been in years. Danny stretched out on the other bed across the room, the glow of the moon tracing the lines of his face.

"Good night, Robin," he said softly.

She smiled into the pillow. "Good night, Danny. And . . . thank you. For coming back."

The surf roared on outside, but in the quiet room, peace settled over them both—not the finish line, but the turning point they hadn't dared to hope for.

The Next Night

The day had been slow and sweet. They'd walked the beach, shoes in hand, toes numb in the cold Atlantic surf. They'd wandered through a sleepy seaside town, laughing over tacky souvenirs and sharing a basket of fried shrimp at a corner diner. By the time they got back to the inn, dusk had settled, and the sound of waves filled the quiet room like a heartbeat.

Robin stood by the window, arms wrapped around herself, watching the horizon swallow the last light. Danny came up behind her, close but not touching, waiting.

"Feels like the whole world is holding its breath," she said softly.

Danny's voice was low, steady. "So are we."

She turned then, and the look in her eyes was no longer hesitant but certain. "I told you last night—if you ever think I don't want you, you're wrong. I do, Danny. I've wanted you for longer than I'll admit out loud. What I need is to know we're not stepping back into the old shadows. I need this to be ours. New. Safe."

He closed the small distance between them, cupping her face gently, reverently. "Robin, I swear to you—I'll never push, never manipulate, never hurt you. Whether it's tonight or next year, I'll love you just the same. Always."

Tears shone in her eyes, but her smile was sure. "Then tonight," she whispered. "Because I want to remember this as the night I chose you, freely, with my whole heart."

When he kissed her, it was unhurried, a careful layering of trust and longing. Their hands tangled, then bodies, the years of distance collapsing into the space between heartbeats. Clothes fell away like old walls crumbling, leaving only warmth, breath, and the fragile miracle of starting over.

Later, tangled in sheets with the ocean's rhythm steady outside, Robin pressed her face into his chest. "For the first time, ever" she murmured, "I don't feel like I'm surviving. I feel like I'm living."

Danny kissed her hair, holding her close. "And I'll spend the rest of my life making sure you keep that feeling."

They didn't rush to leave the next morning. Breakfast in bed, long walks, hours of quiet conversation about everything from the Healing Center to childhood memories filled the days.

And each night, the intimacy grew easier, more natural, less like a fragile new step and more like the rhythm they had always been meant to find together.

By the time December 30 rolled around, they were no longer just two people haunted by the past—they were partners, dreaming forward.

Chapter 79

The old highway stretched long and quiet, pine forests on either side blurring past in winter's muted green. Robin leaned back in the passenger seat, one leg tucked under her, a paper cup of coffee warming her hands. Danny drove with one hand on the wheel, the other resting lightly over hers on the console, a simple touch that had become second nature over the past week.

They'd left the inn reluctantly, their bags tossed into the backseat along with half a dozen shells and pebbles Robin had pocketed from the beach. Each one felt like a keepsake of a turning point she still barely dared believe had happened.

"Feels strange heading north," she murmured. "Like we're leaving more than just the ocean behind."

Danny glanced over, his eyes steady. "We're not leaving it. We're carrying it with us. What we built down there—it's not just a getaway, Robin. It's . . . us. Finally."

Her chest tightened, but it wasn't fear anymore. It was recognition. "Do you realize we only have one more day left in this year?" she asked softly. "It's been a long time coming, but, I'm actually ready for the new one. Not scared. Not avoiding it. Ready."

He squeezed her hand. "Then that's how we start. Ready. Together."

Silence fell again, but it was full and warm. Robin turned her gaze to the trees flashing by, her reflection faint in the glass. "You know," she said after a while, "for twenty-five years I thought the best parts of me had been stolen. But this week . . . you gave them back to me."

Danny's jaw worked as he swallowed, eyes fixed on the road. "You gave them back to yourself. I just . . . showed up. Finally."

The road signs ticked down toward Westridge, each mile marker bringing them closer to the work waiting there—the affidavits, the healing center plans, the reckoning still brewing with Stone and Hawkins. But for now, in the quiet of their car, it was just two people who had clawed their way back from loss, choosing to believe in love and life again.

"New Year's Day," Robin whispered, almost to herself. "Cookies, gratitude, dreams. Ingrid was right—it feels like the perfect way to begin."

Danny lifted her hand to his lips, kissed it gently. "And you'll walk into that room knowing who you are. No longer a survivor in hiding, but a healer."

Robin smiled, the glow of the sunrise catching her eyes. "Sounds powerful," she whispered in reverence.

"And I'll be right beside you all the way," he promised.

And as Westridge's outskirts came into view, the two of them carried that word like a shield into whatever waited next.

Keeping Watch

Robin's house was unnervingly quiet without her and Danny. For Marcus, quiet didn't mean peace—it meant opportunity for trouble. He set his duffel in the guest room, checked the locks once, then again, and only then let himself breathe.

For the first time in weeks, he had more than a motel room and a burner phone. A kitchen. A decent bed. And a base of operations that didn't stink of stale coffee.

He spread his notebooks across Robin's dining table, pages of arrows and names overlapping photos from practice, receipts Rebecca had pulled, affidavits Allison had helped gather. The chaos slowly bent to order: one folder for Rebecca, one packet earmarked for the AG, another still too raw to send but too important to ignore.

That afternoon, his phone buzzed. Rebecca.

"Allison connected me with someone who's ready to talk," she said, her tone steady but protective. "A girl from the class of 2009. Not ready to go public, but willing to be heard. Would you . . . ?"

Marcus was already grabbing his jacket. "Where?"

The meeting was quiet—just a library side room, Allison sitting beside the woman as a silent anchor. She spoke in halting pieces, but the story was unmistakable: same pressure tactics, same names in the periphery. She'd buried it, thought she was the only one. "Hearing Allison had survived cracked something open and made me feel—less crazy."

Later that evening, another came forward—through a cousin who had seen the *Gazette* ad. This one didn't want to be in the spotlight, but her story matched the pattern line for line. Marcus took careful notes, promised nothing beyond: "Your voice matters. You've been heard."

Walking back to Robin's afterward, winter wind biting at his face, Marcus knew these weren't just stories anymore. They were strands of a net, pulling tighter around Stone, Hawkins, Pyle—and anyone else who'd hidden in their shadow.

Back at the house, he did his rounds: checked locks, walked the perimeter, left his car in plain view. Once, he spotted Hawkins's truck creep past. He didn't flinch, didn't wave—just stood in the window with his coffee mug until the taillights disappeared. Message sent.

He allowed himself small mercies: a real meal from Robin's pantry, six hours of dreamless sleep, a hot shower that didn't smell like rust. He jotted thoughts in his notebook before bed:

- *Victims corroborating. Net tightening.*
- *Rebecca packet ready / AG brief aligned.*
- *Stone spooked. Hawkins circling.*

By the time Danny and Robin returned from their trip, Marcus had the table cleared, packets neatly stacked. Survivors confirmed, evidence organized, predators rattled.

He would hand them a house that was still standing, a case that was stronger, and—though he'd never admit it—a man a little steadier himself.

For now, he settled deeper into the guest room bed, ears still tuned to every creak, every engine passing by. Sentinel, still. But with a glimmer of something more than survival waiting on the other side.

Just about then, they pulled in the drive, tires crunching the gravel.

Chapter 80

Robin's POV

It was early afternoon when we gathered, sunlight pouring through Ingrid's windows like a benediction. She'd cracked the panes just enough to let in the crisp air, while a fire flickered in the hearth. Fresh air and warmth, side by side—just like us. The Christmas cookies laid out on the table were almost unnecessary, yet somehow perfect. Sweetness on top of something already rich.

I had come to love the coziness of this room—the way the chairs seemed to draw us closer, the familiar faces around me, so different yet woven into the same tapestry. Most of all, I had grown familiar with the feeling of being held here, truly held, by trust and love.

Ingrid shepherded us as always, not with force but with grace, nudging us to be honest, to stretch, to believe bigger. She reminded us that gratitude wasn't cheap—it was hard-won, and that made it more powerful.

As I looked around the circle, I saw more than women. I saw stories reshaping themselves.

Melody, once just the entertainer, now carried herself like a woman holding the microphone for others. Her camera wasn't just for spectacle—it was for truth.

Patsy, with her easy laugh and enviable life, had found that her wealth meant little without purpose. Watching her talk about using her abundance to seed something real—a center, a refuge—reminded me that generosity can fill the hollowness of shallow years.

Sandra's eyes no longer held only pain from betrayal; they held resolve. She spoke about turning her own survival into fuel for helping others through their darkest valleys.

Tanya was as tall and graceful as ever, but now she moved with a certainty that rippled outward. She was becoming a mirror for other women: showing them their strength, their beauty, their possibility.

Rebecca had always been steady, but now I saw fire. She was using the very tools of law that had once seemed cold and unyielding, turning them into shields for the vulnerable and swords against silence. She made order out of chaos, justice out of whispers.

And me . . . I almost laughed, sitting there. Because for years I believed my wings had been broken beyond repair. But in this circle, with these women—and with Danny by my side again—I realized they had been mended. Stronger, even. Wings not just to carry me, but to lift others.

We ended the afternoon not with resolutions, but with a plan. By spring, when cherry blossoms would scatter their fragrance across Westridge, a Healing Center would open its doors. A place for truth, recovery, and community reborn.

Later, as the fire burned low and we hugged goodbye, I carried that vision in my chest like a second heartbeat.

That night, Danny and I sat with Marcus, the television humming. Bruce's voice filled the room, calm but insistent. Melody's documentary flickered across the screen: faces of survivors, voices breaking silence, the caption reading:

Who Knew? A Testament of Healing.

And for the first time in decades, I knew this truth with absolute certainty: we were no longer alone.

Epilogue

Ribbon Cutting, Springtime

The air carried the first breath of spring—crisp but threaded with warmth, the cherry blossoms just starting to open along Westridge's main street. Banners hung from lampposts: *Westridge Healing Center – Opening Day*.

A crowd had gathered, spilling past the sidewalk. Former classmates, town leaders, families, and quiet survivors who had come not for the cameras but for the promise.

Robin stood at the front, hand clasped in Danny's. He gave her a steady squeeze, and she returned it, their glance lingering like a vow. The ribbon stretched in front of them, bright against the morning sun.

Behind her, Ingrid and Sophia stood shoulder to shoulder. Before the ceremony began, Sophia pulled Robin into a fierce hug. "You made it through the fire," she whispered. "Now you get to light the way." Ingrid pressed her hand over theirs, completing the circle.

Rebecca was there too, Pete beside her, her expression a mix of pride and steel—both attorney and friend.

In the front row, Anna and Winsome—Ingrid's steady circle of support—watched with quiet, glowing pride.

Melody moved with her camera crew at the edge of the crowd, headset slightly askew, eyes sharp. And there was Yuki, tall and lanky, holding a reflector board, joking with another tech. His easy laugh carried over the hum, a sound so normal it tugged at Robin's chest.

Robin took a step forward. Her voice carried, not with drama but with clarity.

"Twenty-five years ago, silence nearly broke us. Today, we open a place built on the opposite: truth, safety, and healing. This isn't just a building—it's a promise. That was then. This is now. And we begin again, together."

Applause rippled, then swelled. Danny handed her the scissors, and together they cut the ribbon. The fabric snapped clean, the crowd cheering.

Somewhere in the front row, a few of the survivors who had quietly come forward exchanged looks of relief, even pride. Their stories were no longer secrets—they were threads woven into something stronger.

Robin felt Danny's arm slip around her waist as the cheering rose. *The fight for justice wasn't finished—trials still waited—but for this day, hope was louder.*

And as the doors of the Healing Center opened and people began to stream inside, Robin knew the truth of it in her bones: Westridge was no longer defined by what had been broken, but by what had been rebuilt.

The End

Want to Go Deeper?

Dear Reader,

First, let me say thank you. Thank you for choosing this book, for opening its pages, and for letting these characters live in your imagination. Writing this story has been a journey of hope, healing, and courage—and knowing that it's now in your hands fills me with gratitude.

This isn't just a novel to me. It's an invitation. An invitation to talk about the things we so often keep silent: pain, survival, resilience, and community. My deepest hope is that as you read, you'll recognize pieces of yourself—and find encouragement to step into your own "now."

Book clubs have a special magic. Around tables or couches, with coffee or wine (or cookies!), stories come alive in new ways. You get to laugh, debate, wonder, and sometimes cry together. That's where real transformation begins: in conversation. So I've included the discussion guide that follows as a tool to spark those conversations. Use what serves you, skip what doesn't, and most of all—make it yours. Share your thoughts, your stories, and your questions.

And if you feel moved, I'd love for you to leave a review or share the book with someone you care about. Your voice helps this message reach further than I ever could on my own.

Above all, remember: Think bravely; act boldly. You have strength, courage, and power within you, to change your life and change the world. Your voice matters, now and always.

With love and gratitude,

Marianne

Book Club Discussion Guide

Opening the Conversation

1. What were your first impressions when you finished the book? Did it end the way you expected, or were you surprised?

2. Which character did you connect with most strongly? Why?

Character Journeys

1. Robin carries both deep scars and deep strength. Which moment felt like her biggest turning point?

2. Danny left Westridge as a way of surviving. What do you think about the choices he made then—and the courage it took to come back?

3. Marcus plays both protector and investigator. How does his role change the dynamic of the story, and of Robin's healing?

Themes and Ideas

1. The book explores secrets kept by families and communities. What impact does silence have on individuals? On a town?

2. "That was then, this is now" becomes a kind of mantra in the story. How do you see this theme playing out in the lives of the characters? In your own life?

3. The Mastermind group becomes a place of safety and inspiration. What role do supportive communities play in overcoming hardship?

The Wider Picture

1. The idea of a Healing Center emerges as both a literal and symbolic step forward. What role do you think healing spaces—whether formal or informal—can play in our world today?

2. Melody and Bruce bring media attention to the survivors' voices. How do you think storytelling—through journalism, art, or conversation—contributes to justice and healing?

Personal Reflection

1. Did any part of Robin's story echo something from your own life or from people you know? How did it make you feel?

2. After reading this book, what is one action, big or small, that you feel inspired to take—in your own life, family, or community?

Personal Notes

For more information about Marianne Clyde, visit:

www.isntsheamazing.com

www.ingramcontent.com/pod-product-compliance
Lightning Source LLC
Chambersburg PA
CBHW031052020726
47495CB00007B/1840